W9-CTM-595

GOLD MINERS &
GUTTERSNIPES

GOLD MINERS & GUTTERSNIPES

TALES OF CALIFORNIA BY

MARK TWAIN

SELECTED, WITH AN INTRODUCTION,
BY KEN CHOWDER

CHRONICLE BOOKS • SAN FRANCISCO

Library of Congress Cataloging-in-Publication Data
Twain, Mark, 1835–1910.
   Gold miners and Guttersnipes: tales of California / by Mark
Twain; selected, with an introduction by Ken Chowder.
      p.   cm.
   Includes bibliographical references.
   ISBN 0-87701-881-2
   1. Gold mines and mining--California--Fiction. 2. California--
Fiction.   I. Chowder, Ken.   II. Title.
PS1303.C47   1991
813'.4--dc20   90-24399
                                                        CIP

Special thanks to The Mark Twain Project, The Bancroft Library,
University of California, for their considerable assistance with
this book. This book is dedicated to the memory of James D.
Hart, former Director of The Bancroft Library.

Cover photograph: Courtesy, The Mark Twain Project, The
Bancroft Library. Hand tinting by Kathy Warinner.

For a note on the text, see page 209.

Book and cover design by Kathy Warinner.
Composition by On Line Typography
Printed in the United States of America.

Distributed in Canada by Raincoast Books
112 East Third Avenue, Vancouver, B.C. V5T 1C8

10 9 8 7 6 5 4 3 2 1

Chronicle Books
275 Fifth Street
San Francisco, CA 94103

CONTENTS

INTRODUCTION

Mark Twain was born in the West. Samuel Clemens, of course, was not; his birthplace was Florida, Missouri—"a little hamlet," he wrote, "where nothing ever happened." By the time he came West in July 1861, he was twenty-five: he'd retired from school at the age of twelve to become a printer, and later helped his brother Orion edit the Hannibal (Missouri) *Journal;* he spent four years as a Mississippi river pilot, and finally deserted the Confederate army militia after a single fortnight of "rain and retreat" in 1861.

At the time, Orion had just been appointed secretary to the territorial governor of Nevada, so together they traveled overland by stagecoach to Carson City, Nevada. The Civil War may have chased Twain West, but he came laden with some classic American baggage: the glittering hope of striking it rich. "Smitten with the silver fever," as he put it, he went out prospecting in Humboldt and Esmeralda counties, and in short order he'd accumulated a long string of failures in the pick-and-shovel line. And by September of 1862 he was willing to accept an offer of twenty-five dollars a week to be a reporter for the Virginia City (Nevada) *Territorial Enterprise.*

The next February, the byline Mark Twain appeared in the newspaper for the first time. The pen name itself already had a history, a family tree. Clemens' first pseudonym, which he adopted at the age of sixteen, was "W. Epaminondas Adrastus Perkins." That was followed by the much more concise "W. Epaminondas Adrastus Blab"— then "Rambler," "Grumbler," "Peter Pencilcase's Son, John Snooks,"

"Thomas Jefferson Snodgrass," "Quintus Curtius Snodgrass," and the plain but accurate "Josh." "Mark Twain," of course, was the boatman's call signifying 'safe water'; this final choice was an emblematic one, for most of Twain's great work was to hearken back to the past, particularly his own past on the Mississippi, as if he was always looking for safe haven in the depths of memory.

He stayed in Nevada for nearly three years; he was not, at first, a likely candidate for eventual emigration to California. "Those rotten, lop-eared, whopper-jawed, jack-legged . . . Californians. . . . How I *hate* everything that looks, or tastes, or smells like California!" he wrote. But that was before he'd seen San Francisco. He came once in early 1863; then again that May, and stayed through June; once again in early September, and stayed till October. "My visit to San F is gradually drawing to a close, and it seems like going back to prison . . . after living in this Paradise," he wrote back home. "I have lived like a lord."

Later, in *Roughing It*, he described his final departure from Virginia City as the result of a duel fought with a rival editor: the governor had just declared duelling a serious crime, so Twain hightailed it out of town to escape the law. But this story, though nicely dramatic, seems to be a nearly total fabrication. Elsewhere in *Roughing It*, he comes closer to the probable truth: "I wanted to see San Francisco. I wanted to go somewhere. I wanted—I did not know *what* I wanted."

In May 1864, Twain took the stagecoach over the mountains to San Francisco. His Virginia City newspaper gave him an editorial send-off: "Mark Twain has abdicated the local column of the *Enterprise*, where by the grace of Cheek, he so long reigned. . . ." The piece went on to call him the "Monarch of Mining Items," the "Prince of Platitudes," the "Profaner of Divinity," and the "Detractor of Merit." Twain "will not be likely to shock the sensibilities of San Francisco long. The ordinances against nuisances are stringently enforced in that city."

He did not expect to write in California. He'd invested in several silver mines, and came west hoping to sell his stock at enormous profit. So he spent his first days in San Francisco in idyllic if dissolute "butterfly idleness." His pal Steve Gillis and he changed lodgings five times in four months. One day Gillis' father asked for them at an old address, and their former landlady launched into a tirade. Twain, amused, replicated it in a letter to a friend: She said, "They are gone, thank God!— and I hope I may never see them again. . . . They didn't care a snap for the rules of the house. . . . O, I never saw such creatures. . . . They used to bring loads of beer bottles up at midnight, & get drunk, & shout & fire their pistols in the room." She closed: "They had no respect for God, man, or the devil."

Twain's metropolitan idleness didn't last long. His entire life was to be marked by massive investment mistakes—culminating in his long, almost-addictive support for the Paige mechanical typesetting machine, which finally caused his bankruptcy in 1894—and in 1864 his mining stocks did not take long to crash past bottom. "The wreckage was complete," he wrote. "I was an early beggar and a thorough one."

In June his poverty obliged him to take a job as city reporter on the San Francisco *Morning Call*. The *Call* was "the washerwoman's paper," the most popular and cheapest (subscriptions twelve and a half cents a week) newspaper in California. In Virginia City, Twain had acquired a considerable following and reputation; as he'd written his mother, "I am prone to boast of having the widest reputation as a local editor, of any man on the Pacific Coast." On the *Call* he was forced into an endless, deadening repetition of local items, daily trekking from Police Court to Station House to City Prison, then making the dull nightly round of the all six of the city's theaters. "It was fearful drudgery, soulless drudgery," he wrote in his autobiography. "It was an awful slavery for a lazy man." Soon he'd relegated most of the work to an assistant; editor George Barnes saw no need to pay them both, and fired Twain in October. Later Barnes, with astonishingly acute hindsight, claimed to have told Twain, "You are capable of better things in literature."

For two months after the dismissal, Twain wrote, his "sole occupation was avoiding acquaintances." Finally, in December, he abandoned San Francisco for Jim and Billy Gillis' cabin in Jackass Gulch, near the Stanislaus River in the mountains of Tuolomne County. The Twain-induced legend has it, again, that he beat it out of town because the police were after him; again, there's nothing to substantiate his claim. More likely, he still harbored glimmering hopes of fabulous wealth waiting to be pried from the earthly depths. This time it was gold, and he spent three months pocket-mining in the California hills.

He didn't find gold. He found rain and dieted on dishwater and beans. But in a sense, Twain did strike it rich there: he heard the tall tale he transfigured into "Jim Smiley and His Jumping Frog." He published it in the New York *Saturday Press* in November of 1865, and the story soon began to make his national reputation: "Mark Twain's story ... called 'Jim Smiley and His Jumping Frog,' has set all New York in a roar. ... It is voted the best thing of the day."

By then he'd returned to San Francisco ("Home again — home again at the Occidental Hotel"). His mining bubble was burst forever. Almost by the process of elimination he had found his life's calling: he was going to be Mark Twain, a writer, as he put it, of "literature of a low order, i.e. humorous." His "poor, pitiful business" in life was "to excite the laughter of God's creatures." He began to contribute extensively to a number of California periodicals; for the first time he became part of a literary circle, the Bohemians; Bret Harte became his good friend, and in California, at least, he was famous. Proudly he wrote his mother, "I am generally placed at the head of my breed of scribblers in this part of the country."

He was a writer, but not just a writer: he was already becoming Mark Twain, the comic character, the much-beloved fool/satirist. For his first public lecture, in San Francisco in October 1866, he drew up a typical announcement, which included these mock-advertising lines:

A SPLENDID ORCHESTRA
IS IN TOWN, BUT *HAS NOT* BEEN ENGAGED
ALSO A DEN OF FEROCIOUS BEASTS WILL BE ON EXHIBITION
IN THE NEXT BLOCK
MAGNIFICENT FIREWORKS
WERE IN CONTEMPLATION FOR THIS OCCASION,
BUT THE IDEA HAS BEEN ABANDONED
A GRAND TORCHLIGHT PROCESSION
MAY BE EXPECTED; IN FACT THE PUBLIC ARE PRIVILEGED
TO EXPECT WHATEVER THEY PLEASE ...
DOORS OPEN AT 7 O'CLOCK. THE TROUBLE WILL BEGIN AT 8.

The lecture was sold out, and Twain a great success. He went on a triumphal tour, speaking before packed houses in Sacramento, Marysville, Grass Valley, Nevada City, You Bet, Red Dog, Virginia City, Carson City, Gold Hill, Silver Hill, and Dayton. When a Grass Valley newspaper reported his appearance there, it was in the way of fond teasing: "Crowds are flocking into Hamilton Hall, as we write, to hear Mark Twain's lecture. ... But a moment ago we saw the lecturer preparing himself for a clear voice with a copious dose of gin ... after which he started for the Hall with the irregular movement of a sternwheel boat in a heavy wind. ..."

Not that life was easy for him. It never would be, for Mark Twain. In late 1865, he wrote his sister-in-law: "I am utterly miserable... If I do not get out of debt in 3 months,—pistols or poison for one—exit *me*. (There's a text for a sermon on Self-Murder—Proceed.)" Early the next year, he was put in jail overnight for public drunkenness; Albert Evans, a vicious rival columnist, took public delight in Twain's humiliation. The stench of the city's slaughterhouses, Evans wrote, is "a stench which is only second in horrible density to that which prevails in the Police Court when the Bohemian of the Sage-Brush is in the dock for being drunk over night." One night soon thereafter, he put the barrel of a pistol against his head. "Many times I have been sorry I did not succeed," he later wrote, "but I was never ashamed of having tried." In 1866 he spent four months in Hawaii; when he returned, San Francisco seemed a prison. "All the wild sense of freedom gone," he wrote. "The city seems so cramped, & so dreary with toil & care & business anxiety. God help me, I wish I were at sea again!"

Such restless shifts of mood, and even character, were quintessentially Twain. He was always fascinated with twins, doubles—the twain within us, as it were. "Every one is a moon, and has a dark side which he never shows to anybody," he wrote; but his own writings clearly show both of his sides. His ambivalence, and his paradoxical mixture of parts, has often been compared to his country as a whole. All his life, as Justin Kaplan comments, Twain "had plutocratic ambitions but at the same time believed that money was evil and created evil"; and as Wallace Stegner writes, "A democrat to the bone, he grew to hate the damned human race."

Even the shape of Twain's life seemed to mirror his country's psychic history: he came from the heartland, and then was a part of the westward push, the almost-unconscious nineteenth-century grab for gold; like Huck Finn, he "lit out for the territories." He became fabulously successful and powerful; later, he grew embittered and self-critical. Finally he exiled himself to Europe, where he wrote books about ... life on the Mississippi, among other things.

Much of this history was still ahead of Twain when he left San Francisco in early 1867, sailing for Europe as a correspondent for the *Alta California.* Certainly he intended to return to San Francisco. He considered himself a Californian by then: he was listed in the ship's manifest as "Mark Twain, barkeeper, San Francisco." He even seemed conscious of a connection between his own rising star and that of his chosen state. In his farewell appearance to San Francisco he waxed uncharacteristically grandiloquent about his new home state: "Behold the things that are in store for you," he said. He foresaw California as "an empire" that would "shame the bravest dreams of her visionaries." "This straggling town shall be a vast metropolis ... your waste places shall blossom like the rose, and your deserted hills and valleys shall yield bread and wine for unnumbered thousands...." Like California, Twain's own future seemed almost unimaginably bright; he was embarking for the wide world, with a good headstart on immortality. "Has any other State so brilliant a future?" he asked. "Has any other city a future like San Francisco?"

He returned only once, for three months in 1868. But even beyond that, he would still claim his kinship with California. In a letter to the "California Pioneers," he wrote:

> If I were to tell some of my experience, you would recognize old California blood in me; I fancy the old, old story would sound familiar no doubt. I have the usual stock of reminiscences.... I have been through the California mill, with all its "dips, spurs and angles, variations and sinuosities." I have worked there at all the different trades and professions known to the catalogues. I have been everything, from a newspaper editor down to a cow-catcher on a locomotive, and I am encouraged to believe that if there had been a few more occupations to experiment on, I might have made a dazzling success at last, and found out what mysterious designs Providence had in creating me.

Ken Chowder
San Francisco

IN THE METROPOLIS OF SAN FRANCISCO

**I have always been rather
better treated in San Francisco
than I actually deserved.**

LETTER TO HIS MOTHER AND SISTER

Lick House, S.F. June 1 [1863]

My Dear Mother & Sister

The Unreliable [Twain's friend Clement T. Rice of the Virginia City *Daily Union*] & myself are still here, & still enjoying ourselves. I suppose I know at least a thousand people here—a great many of them citizens of San Francisco, but the majority belonging in Washoe—& when I go down Montgomery street, shaking hands with Tom, Dick, & Harry, it is just like being in Main street in Hannibal & meeting the old familiar faces. I *do hate* to go back to Washoe. We fag ourselves completely out every day, and go to sleep without rocking, every night. We dine out, & we lunch out, and we eat, drink and are happy—as it were. After breakfast, I don't often see the hotel again until midnight—or after. I am going to the Dickens mighty fast. I know a regular village of families here in the house, but I never have time to call on them. Thunder! we'll know a little more about this town, before we leave, than some of the people who live in it. We take trips across the Bay to Oakland, and down to San Leandro, and Alameda, and those places, and we go out to the Willows, and Hayes Park, and Fort Point, and up to Benicia; and yesterday we were invited out on a yachting excursion, & had a sail in the fastest yacht on the Pacific Coast. Rice says: "Oh, no—we are not having any fun, Mark—Oh, no, I reckon not—it's somebody else—it's probably the "gentleman in the wagon!" (popular slang phrase.) When I invite Rice to the Lick House to dinner, the proprietors send us champaign and claret, and then we do put on the most disgusting airs. Rice says our calibre is too light—we can't stand it to be noticed!

I rode down with a gentleman to the Ocean House, the other day, to see the sea-horses, and also to listen to the roar of the surf, and watch the ships drifting about, here, & there, and far away at sea. When I stood on the beach & let the surf wet my feet, I recollected doing the same thing on the shores of the Atlantic—& then I had a proper appreciation of the vastness of this country—for I had traveled from ocean to ocean across it, on land, with the exception of crossing Lake Erie—(and I wish I had gone around it.) *Sam*

from MARK TWAIN IN THE METROPOLIS
[*Golden Era*, June 26, 1864]

To a Christian who has toiled months and months in Washoe; whose hair bristles form a bed of sand, and whose soul is caked with a cement of alkali dust; whose nostrils know no perfume but the rank odor of sage-brush—and whose eyes know no landscape but barren mountains and desolate plains; where the winds blow, and the sun blisters, and the broken spirit of the contrite heart finds joy and peace only in Limburger cheese and lager beer—unto such a Christian, verily the Occidental Hotel [in San Francisco] is Heaven on the half shell. He may even secretly consider it to be Heaven on the entire shell, but his religion teaches a sound Washoe Christian that it would be sacrilege to say it.

Here you are expected to breakfast on salmon, fried oysters and other substantials from 6 till half-past 12; you are required to lunch on cold fowl and so forth, from half-past 12 until 3; you are obliged to skirmish through a dinner comprising such edibles as the world produces, and keep it up, from 3 until half-past 7; you are then compelled to lay siege to the tea-table from half-past 7 until 9 o'clock, at which hour, if you refuse to move upon the supper works and destroy oysters gotten up in all kinds of seductive styles until 12 o'clock, the landlord will certainly be offended, and you might as well move your trunk to some other establishment. (It is a pleasure to me to observe, incidentally, that I am on good terms with the landlord yet.) ...

It has been many a day since San Francisco has seen livelier times in her theatrical department than at present. Large audiences are to be found nightly at the Opera House, the Metropolitan, the Academy of Music, the American, the New Idea, and even the Museum, which is not as good a one as Barnum's. The Circus company, also, played a lucrative engagement, but they are gone on their travels now. The graceful, charming, clipper-built Ella Zoyara was very popular.

Miss Caroline Richings has played during the past fortnight at Maguire's Opera House to large and fashionable audiences, and has delighted them beyond measure with her sweet singing. It sounds improbable, perhaps, but the statement is true, nevertheless. . . .

The birds, and the flowers, and the Chinamen, and the winds, and the sunshine, and all things that go to make life happy, are present in San Francisco to-day, just as they are all days in the year. Therefore, one would expect to hear these things spoken of, and gratefully, and disagreeable matters of little consequence allowed to pass without comment. I say, one would suppose that. But don't you deceive your-self—any one who supposes anything of the kind, supposes an absur-dity. The multitude of pleasant things by which the people of San Francisco are surrounded are not talked of at all. No—they damn the wind, and they damn the dust, and they give all their attention to damning them well, and to all eternity. The blasted winds and the infernal dust—these alone form the eternal topics of conversation, and a mighty absurd topic it seems to one just out of Washoe. There isn't enough wind here to keep breath in my body, or dust enough to keep sand in my craw. But it is human nature to find fault—to over-look that which is pleasant to the eye, and seek after that which is dis-tasteful to it. You take a stranger into the Bank Exchange and show him the magnificent picture of Sampson and Delilah, and what is the first object he notices?—Sampson's fine face and flaming eye? or the noble beauty of his form? or the lovely, half-nude Delilah? or the muscular Philistine behind Sampson, who is furtively admiring her charms? or the perfectly counterfeited folds of the rich drapery below her knees? or the symmetry and truth to nature of Sampson's left foot? No, sir, the first thing that catches his eye is the scissors on the floor at Delilah's feet, and the first thing he says, "Them scissors is too modern—there warn't no scissors like that in them days, by a d——d sight!"
MARK TWAIN

For a few months I enjoyed what to me was an entirely new phase of existence — a butterfly idleness; nothing to do, nobody to be responsible to, and untroubled with financial uneasiness. I fell in love with the most cordial and sociable city in the Union. After the sage-brush and alkali deserts of Washoe, San Francisco was Paradise to me. I lived at the best hotel, exhibited my clothes in the most conspicuous places, infested the opera, and learned to seem enraptured with music which oftener afflicted my ignorant ear than enchanted it, if I had had the vulgar honesty to confess it. However, I suppose I was not greatly worse than the most of my countrymen in that. I had longed to be a butterfly, and I was one at last. I attended private parties in sumptuous evening dress, simpered and aired my graces like a born beau, and polked and schottisched with a step peculiar to myself — and the kangaroo.

from LETTER FROM MARK TWAIN
[*Territorial Enterprise*, May 16, 1863]

This young man ["The Unreliable"] insisted upon taking me to a concert last night, and I refused to go at first, because I am naturally suspicious of him, but he assured me that the Bella Union Melodeon was such a chaste and high-toned establishment that he would not hesitate to take any lady there who would go with him. This remark banished my fears, of course, and we proceeded to the house of amusement. We were the first arrivals there. He purchased two pit-tickets for twenty-five cents apiece; I demurred at this kind of hospitality, and reminded him that orchestra seats were only fifty cents, and private boxes two dollars and a half. He bent on me a look of compassion, and muttered to himself that some people have no more sense than a boiled carrot — that some people's intellects were as dark as the inside of a cow. He walked into the pit, and then climbed over into the orchestra seats as coolly as if he had chartered the theatre. I followed, of course. Then he said, "Now, Mark, keep your eye skinned on that doorkeeper, and do as I do." I did as he did, and I am ashamed to say that he climbed a stanchion and took possession of a private box. In due course several gentlemen performers came on the stage, and with them half a dozen lovely and blooming damsels, with the largest ankles you ever saw. In fact, they were dressed like so many parasols—as it were. Their songs, and jokes, and conundrums were received with rapturous applause. The Unreliable said these things were all copyrighted; it is probably true—I never heard them anywhere else. He was well pleased with the performance, and every time one of the ladies sang, he testified his approbation by knocking some of her teeth out with a bouquet. The Bella Union, I am told, is supported entirely by Washoe patronage. There are forty-two single gentlemen here from Washoe, and twenty-six married ones; they were all at the concert last night except two—both unmarried. But if the Unreliable had not told me it was a moral, high-toned establishment, I would not have observed it.

***

FROM A LETTER TO HIS MOTHER AND SISTER

Lick House, San Francisco
June 4, 1863.

My Dear Mother & Sister

My visit to San F is gradually drawing to a close, and it seems like going back to prison to go back to the snows & the deserts of Washoe, after living in this Paradise. But then I shall soon get used to it—all places are alike to me. I have put in the time here, "you bet." And I have lived like a lord—to make up for two years of privation, you know. . . .

***

FROM ROUGHING IT

San Francisco, a truly fascinating city to live in, is stately and handsome at a fair distance, but close at hand one notes that the architecture is mostly old-fashioned, many streets are made up of decaying, smoke-grimed, wooden houses, and the barren sand-hills toward the outskirts obtrude themselves too prominently. Even the kindly climate is sometimes pleasanter when read about than personally experienced, for a lovely, cloudless sky wears out its welcome by and by, and then when the longed for rain does come it stays. Even the playful earthquake is better contemplated at a dis—

However there are varying opinions about that.

————•+•————

RAIN
[*Morning Call*, Aug. 23, 1864]

One of those singular freaks of Nature which, by reference to the dictionary, we find described as "the water or the descent of water that falls in drops from the clouds—a shower," occurred here yesterday, and kept the community in a state of pleasant astonishment for the space of several hours. They would not have been astonished at an earthquake, though. Thus it will be observed that nothing accustoms one to a thing so readily as getting used to it. You will always notice that, in America.

————•+•————

from ROUGHING IT

The climate of San Francisco is mild and singularly equable. The thermometer stands at about seventy degrees the year round. It hardly changes at all. You sleep under one or two light blankets summer and winter, and never use a mosquito bar. Nobody ever wears summer clothing. You wear black broadcloth—if your have it—in August and January, just the same. It is no colder, and no warmer, in the one month than the other. You do not use overcoats and you do not use fans. It is as pleasant a climate as could well be contrived, take it all around, and is doubtless the most unvarying in the whole world. The wind blows there a good deal in the summer months, but then you can go over to Oakland, if you choose—three or four miles away—it does not blow there. It has only snowed twice in San Francisco in nineteen years, and then it only remained on the ground long enough to astonish the children, and set them to wondering what the feathery stuff was.

During eight months of the year, straight along, the skies are bright and cloudless, and never a drop of rain falls. But when the other four months come along, you will need to go and steal an umbrella. Because you will require it. Not just one day, but one hundred and twenty days in hardly varying succession. When you want to go visiting, or attend church, or the theatre, you never look up at the clouds to see whether it is likely to rain or not—you look at the almanac. If it is winter, it will rain—and if it is summer, it won't rain, and you cannot help it. You never need a lightning-rod, because it never thunders and it never lightens. And after you have listened for six or eight weeks, every night, to the dismal monotony of those quiet rains, you will wish in your heart the thunder would leap and crash and roar along those drowsy skies once, and make everything alive—you will wish the prisoned lightnings would cleave the dull firmament asunder and light it with a blinding glare for one little instant. You would give anything to hear the old familiar thunder again and see the lightning strike somebody. And along in the summer, when you have suffered about four months of lustrous, pitiless sunshine, you are ready to go down on your knees and plead for rain—hail—snow—thunder and lightning—anything to break the monotony—you will take an earthquake, if you cannot do any better. And the chances are that you'll get it, too.

San Francisco is built on sand-hills, but they are prolific sand-hills. They yield a generous vegetation. All the rare flowers which people in "the States" rear with such patient care in parlor flower-pots and greenhouses, flourish luxuriantly in the open air there all the year round. Calla lilies, all sorts of geraniums, passion flowers, moss roses— I do not know the names of a tenth part of them. I only know that while New Yorkers are burdened with banks and drifts of snow, Californians are burdened with banks and drifts of flowers, if they only keep their hands off and let them grow.

A TRIP TO THE CLIFF HOUSE
[*Morning Call*, June 25, 1864]

If one tire of the drudgeries and scenes of the city, and would breathe the fresh air of the sea, let him take the cars and omnibuses, or, better still, a buggy and pleasant steed, and, ere the sea breeze sets in, glide out to the Cliff House. We tried it a day or two since. Out along the railroad track, by the pleasant homes of our citizens, where architecture begins to put off its swaddling clothes, and assume form and style, grace and beauty, by the neat gardens with their green shrubbery and laughing flowers, out where were once sand hills and sand-valleys, now streets and homesteads. If you would doubly enjoy pure air, first pass along by Mission Street Bridge, the Golgotha of Butcherville, and wind along through the alleys where stand the whiskey mills and grunt the piggeries of "Uncle Jim." Breathe and inhale deeply ere you reach this castle of Udolpho, and hold your breath as long as possible, for Arabia is a long way thence, and the balm of a thousand flowers is not for sale in that locality. Then away you go over paved, or planked, or Macadamized roads, out to the cities of the dead, pass between Lone Mountain and Calvary, and make a straight due west course for the ocean. Along the way are many things to please and entertain, especially if an intelligent chaperon accompany you. Your eye will travel over in every direction the vast territory which Swain, Weaver & Co. desire to fence in, the little homesteads by the way, Dr. Rowell's arena castle, and Zeke Wilson's Bleak House in the sand. Splendid road, ocean air that swells the lungs and strengthens the limbs. Then there's the Cliff House, perched on the very brink of the ocean, like a castle by the Rhine, with countless sea-lions rolling their unwieldy bulks on the rocks within rifle-shot, or plunging into and sculling about in the foaming waters. Steamers and sailing craft are passing, wild fowl scream, and sea-lions growl and bark, the waves roll into breakers, foam and spray, for five miles along the beach, beautiful and grand, and one feels as if at sea with no rolling motion nor sea-sickness, and the appetite is whetted by the drive and the breeze, the ocean's presence wins you into a happy frame, and you can eat one of the best dinners with the hungry relish of an ostrich. Go to the Cliff House. Go ere the winds get too fresh, and if you like, you may come back by Mountain Lake and the Presidio, overlook the Fort, and bow to the Stars and Stripes as you pass.

———•———

from CONCERNING THE ANSWER TO THAT CONUNDRUM
[*The Californian*, Oct. 8, 1864]

When we got to the Cliff House we were disappointed. I had always heard there was such a grand view to be seen there of the majestic ocean, with its white billows stretching far away until it met and mingled with the bending sky; with here and there a stately ship upon its surface, ploughing through plains of sunshine and deserts of shadow cast from the clouds above; and, near at hand, piles of picturesque rocks, splashed with angry surf and garrisoned by drunken, sprawling sea-lions and elegant, long-legged pelicans.

It was a bitter disappointment. There was nothing in sight but an ordinary counter, and behind it a long row of bottles with Old Bourbon, and Old Rye, and Old Tom, and the old, old story of man's falter and woman's fall, in them. Nothing in the world to be seen but these things. We staid there an hour and a half, and took observations from different points of view, but the general result was the same—nothing but bottles and a bar. They keep a field-glass there, for the accommodation of those who wish to see the sights, and we looked at the bottles through that, but it did not help the matter any to speak of; we turned it end for end, but instead of increasing the view it diminished it. If it had not been fashionable, I would not have engaged in this trivial amusement; I say trivial, because, notwithstanding they said everybody used the glass, I still consider it trivial amusement, and very undignified, to sit staring at a row of gin-bottles through an opera-glass. Finally, we tried a common glass tumbler, and found that it answered just as well, on account of the close proximity of the scenery, and did not seem quite so stupid. We continued to use it, and the more we got accustomed to it, the better we liked it. Although tame enough at first, the effects eventually became really extraordinary. The single row of bottles doubled, and then trebled itself, and finally became a sort of dissolving view of inconceivable beauty and confusion. When Johnny first looked through the tumbler, he said: "It is rather a splendid display, isn't it?" and an hour afterwards he said: "Thas so—'s a sp-(ic!)-splennid 'splay!" and set his glass down with sufficient decision to break it.

We went out, then, and saw a sign marked "CHICKEN SHOOTING," and we sat down and waited a long time, but finally we got weary and discouraged, and my comrade said that perhaps it was no use—may be the chicken was not going to shoot that day. We did not mind the disappointment so much, but the hiccups were so distressing. I am subject to them when I go abroad.

—•—

THE OLD THING
[*Morning Call*, July 1, 1864]

We conversed yesterday with a stranger, who had suffered from a game familiar to some San Franciscans, but unknown in his section of the country. He was going home late at night, when a sociable young man, standing alone on the sidewalk, bade him good evening in a friendly way, and asked him to take a drink, with a fascination of manner which he could not resist. They went into Johnson's saloon, on Pike street, but instead of paying promptly for the drinks, the sociable young man proposed to throw the dice for them, which was done, and the stranger who was a merchant, from the country, lost. Euchre was then proposed, and two disinterested spectators, entirely unknown to the sociable young man—as he said—were invited to join the game, and did so. Shortly afterwards, good hands were discovered to be plenty around the board, and it was proposed to bet on them, and turn the game into poker. The merchant held four kings, and he called a ten dollar bet; but the luck that sociable young man had was astonishing—he held four aces! This made the merchant suspicious—he says—and it was a pity his sagacity was not still more extraordinary—it was a pity it did not warn him that it was time to quit that crowd. But it had no such effect; the sociable man showed him a check on Wells, Fargo & Co., and he thought it was safe to "stake" him; therefore he staked his friend, and continued to stake him, and his friend played and lost, and continued to play and lose, until one hundred and ninety dollars were gone, and he nothing more left wherewith to stake him. The merchant complained to the Police, yesterday, and officer McCormick hunted up the destroyer of his peace and the buster of his fortune, and arrested him. He gave his name as Wellington, but the Police have known him well heretofore as "Injun Ned;" he told the merchant his name was J. G. Whittaker. Wellington Whittaker deserves to be severely punished, but perhaps the merchant ought to be allowed to go free, as this was his first offence in being so criminally green.

---

from ROUGHING IT

[A] large Chinese population . . . is the case with every town and city on the Pacific coast. They are a harmless race when white men either let them alone or treat them no worse than dogs; in fact they are almost entirely harmless anyhow, for they seldom think of resenting the vilest insults or the cruelest injuries. They are quiet, peaceable, tractable, free from drunkenness, and they are as industrious as the day is long. A disorderly Chinaman is rare, and a lazy one does not exist. So long as a Chinaman has strength to use his hands he needs no support from anybody; white men often complain of want of work, but a Chinaman offers no such complaint; he always manages to find something to do. He is a great convenience to everybody—even to the worst class of white men, for he bears the most of their sins, suffering fines for their petty thefts, imprisonment for their robberies, and death for their murders. Any white man can swear a Chinaman's life away in the courts, but no Chinaman can testify against a white man. Ours is the "land of the free"—nobody denies that—nobody challenges it. (Maybe it is because we won't let other people testify.) As I write, news comes that in broad daylight in San Francisco, some boys have stoned an inoffensive Chinaman to death, and that although a large crowd witnessed the shameful deed, no one interfered. . . .

All Chinamen can read, write and cipher with easy facility—pity but all our petted voters could. In California they rent little patches of ground and do a deal of gardening. They will raise surprising crops of vegetables on a sand pile. They waste nothing. What is rubbish to a Christian, a Chinaman carefully preserves and makes useful in one way or another. He gathers up all the old oyster and sardine cans that white people throw away, and procures marketable tin and solder from them by melting. He gathers up old bones and turns them into manure. In California he gets a living out of old mining claims that white men have abandoned as exhausted and worthless—and then the officers come down on him once a month with an exorbitant swindle to which the legislature has given the broad, general name of "foreign" mining tax, but it is usually inflicted on no foreigners but Chinamen. This swindle has in some cases been repeated once or twice on the same victim in the course of the same month—but the public treasury was not additionally enriched by it, probably.

Chinamen hold their dead in great reverence—they worship their departed ancestors, in fact. Hence, in China, a man's front yard, back yard, or any other part of his premises, is made his family burying ground, in order that he may visit the graves at any and all times. Therefore that huge empire is one mighty cemetery; it is ridged and wrinkled from its centre to its circumference with graves—and inasmuch as every foot of ground must be made to do its utmost, in China, lest the swarming population suffer for food, the very graves are cultivated and yield a harvest, custom holding this to be no dishonor to the dead. Since the departed are held in such worshipful reverence, a Chinaman cannot bear that any indignity be offered the places where they sleep. Mr. Burlingame said that herein lay China's bitter opposition to railroads; a road could not be built anywhere in the empire without disturbing the graves of their ancestors or friends.

A Chinaman hardly believes he could enjoy the hereafter except his body lay in his beloved China; also, he desires to receive, himself, after death, that worship with which he has honored his dead that preceded him. Therefore, if he visits a foreign country, he makes arrangements to have his bones returned to China in case he dies; if he hires to go to a foreign country on a labor contract, there is always a stipulation that his body shall be taken back to China if he dies; if the government sells a gang of Coolies to a foreigner for the usual five-year term, it is specified in the contract that their bodies shall be restored to China in case of death. On the Pacific coast the Chinamen all belong to one or another of several great companies or organizations, and these companies keep track of their members, register their names, and ship their bodies home when they die. The See Yup Company is held to be the largest of these. The Ning Yeong Company is next, and numbers eighteen thousand members on the coast. Its headquarters are at San Francisco, where it has a costly temple, several great officers (one of whom keeps regal state in seclusion and cannot be approached by common humanity), and a numerous priesthood. In it I was shown a register of its members, with the dead and the date of their shipment to China duly marked. Every ship that sails from San Francisco carries away a heavy freight of Chinese corpses — or did, at least, until the legislature, with an ingenious refinement of Christian cruelty, forbade these shipments, as a neat underhanded way of deterring Chinese immigration. The bill was offered, whether it passed or not. It is my impression that it passed. There was another bill — it became a law — compelling every incoming Chinaman to be vaccinated on the wharf and pay a duly appointed quack (no decent doctor would defile himself with such legalized robbery) ten dollars for it. As few importers of Chinese would want to go to an expense like that, the law-makers thought this would be another heavy blow to Chinese immigration.

... [W]hat the Chinese quarter of any Pacific coast town was and is like — may be gathered from this item which I printed in the Enterprise while reporting for that paper:

CHINATOWN.—Accompanied by a fellow reporter, we made a trip through our Chinese quarter the other night. The Chinese have built their portion of the city to suit themselves; and as they keep neither carriage nor wagons, their streets are not wide enough, as a general thing, to admit of the passage of vehicles. At ten o'clock at night the Chinaman may be seen in all his glory. In every little cooped-up, dingy cavern of a hut, faint with the odor of burning Josh-lights and with nothing to see the gloom by save the sickly, guttering tallow candle, were two or three yellow, long-tailed vagabonds, coiled up on a sort of short truckle-bed, smoking opium, motionless and with their lustreless eyes turned inward from excess of satisfaction—or rather the recent smoker looks thus, immediately after having passed the pipe to his neighbor—for opium-smoking is a comfortless operation, and requires constant attention. A lamp sits on the bed, the length of the long pipe-stem from the smoker's mouth; he puts a pellet of opium on the end of a wire, sets it on fire, and plasters it into the pipe much as a Christian would fill a hole with putty; then he applies the bowl to the lamp and proceeds to smoke—and the stewing and frying of the drug and the gurgling of the juices in the stem would wellnigh turn the stomach of a statue. John likes it, though; it soothes him, he takes about two dozen whiffs, and then rolls over to dream, Heaven only knows what, for we could not imagine by looking at the soggy creature. Possibly in his visions he travels far away from the gross world and his regular washing, and feasts on succulent rats and birds'-nests in Paradise.

Mr. Ah Sing keeps a general grocery and provision store at No. 13 Wang street. He lavished his hospitality upon our party in the friendliest way. He had various kinds of colored and colorless wines and brandies, with unpronounceable names, imported from China in little crockery jugs, and which he offered to us in dainty little miniature wash-basins of porcelain. He offered us a mess of birds'-nests; also, small, neat sausages, of which we could have swallowed several yards if we had chosen to try, but we suspected that each link contained the corpse of a mouse, and therefore refrained. Mr. Sing had in his store a thousand articles of merchandise, curious to behold, impossible to imagine the uses of, and beyond our ability to describe.

His ducks, however, and his eggs, we could understand; the former were split open and flattened out like codfish, and came from China in that shape, and the latter were plastered over with some kind of paste which kept them fresh and palatable through the long voyage....

Mr. See Yup keeps a fancy store on Live Fox street. He sold us fans of white feathers, gorgeously ornamented; perfumery that smelled like Limburger cheese, Chinese pens, and watch-charms made of a stone unscratchable with steel instruments, yet polished and tinted like the inner coat of a sea-shell.° As tokens of his esteem, See Yup presented the party with gaudy plumes made of gold tinsel and trimmed with peacocks' feathers.

We ate chow-chow with chop-sticks in the celestial restaurants; our comrade chided the moon-eyed damsels in front of the houses for their want of feminine reserve; we received protecting Josh-lights from our hosts and "dickered" for a pagan God or two. finally, we were impressed with the genius of a Chinese book-keeper; he figured up his accounts on a machine like a gridiron with buttons strung on its bars; the different rows represented units, tens, hundreds and thousands. He fingered them with incredible rapidity— in fact, he pushed them from place to place as fast as a musical professor's fingers travel over the keys of a piano.

They are a kindly disposed, well-meaning race, and are respected and well treated by the upper classes, all over the Pacific coast. No Californian gentleman or lady ever abuses or oppresses a Chinaman, under any circumstances, an explanation that seems to be much needed in the East. Only the scum of the population do it — they and their children; they, and, naturally and consistently, the policemen and politicians, likewise, for these are the dust-licking pimps and slaves of the scum, there as well as elsewhere in America.

———

from FOURTH OF JULY
[*Morning Call*, July 6, 1864]

GRAND PROCESSION, FIREWORKS, ETC.— In point of magnificence, enthusiasm, crowds, noise, wind and dust, the Fourth was the most remarkable day San Francisco has ever seen. The National salute fired at daylight, by the California Guard, awoke the city, and by eight o'clock in the morning the sidewalks of all the principal streets were packed with men, women and children, and remained so until far into the afternoon. All able-bodied citizens were abroad, all cripples with one sound leg and a crutch and all invalids who were not ticketed for eternity on that particular day. The whole city was swathed in a waving drapery of flags — scarcely a house could be found which lacked this kind of decoration. The effect was exceedingly lively and beautiful. Of course Montgomery street excelled in this species of embel-

———

°A peculiar species of the "jade-stone"— to a Chinaman peculiarly precious.

lishment. To the spectator beholding it from any point above Pacific street, it was no longer a street of compactly built houses, but simply a quivering cloud of gaudy red and white stripes, which shut out from view almost everything but itself. Some houses were broken out all over with flags, like small-pox patients. . . .

THE FIREWORKS—The huge framework for the pyrotechnic display was set up at the corner of Fifth and Harrison streets, and by the time the first rocket was discharged, every vacant foot of ground for many a square around was closely crowded with people. There could not have been less than fifteen thousand persons stretching their necks in that vicinity for a glimpse of the show, and certainly not more than thirteen thousand of them failed to see it. The spot was so well chosen, on such nice level ground, that if your stature were six feet one, a trifling dwarf with a plug hat on could step before you and shut you out from the exhibition, as if you were stricken with a sudden blindness. Carriages, which no man might hope to see through, were apt to drive along and stop just ahead of you, at the most interesting moment, and if you changed your position men would obstruct your vision by climbing on each others' shoulders. The grand discharges of rockets, however, and their bursting spray of many-colored sparks, were visible to all, after they had reached a tremendous altitude, and these gave pleasure and brought solace to many a sorrowing heart behind many an untransparent vehicle. Still we know that the fireworks on the night of the Fourth, mottoes, temples, stars, triangles, Catherine wheels, towers, pyramids, and, in fact, every department of the exhibition, formed by far the most magnificent spectacle of the kind ever witnessed on the Pacific coast. The reason why we know it is, that that infamous, endless, Irish giant, at Gilbert's Museum, stood exactly in front of us the whole evening, and he said so.

A number of balls and parties and a terrific cannonade of fire crackers, kept up all night long, finished the festivities of this memorable Fourth of July in San Francisco.

FROM **PLEASURE EXCURSION**
[*Territorial Enterprise*, Nov. 1865]

We lunched, then, and shortly began to drink champagne—by the basket. I saw the tremendous guns frowning from the fort; I saw San

Francisco spread out over the sand-hills like a picture; I saw the huge fortress at Black Point looming hazily in the distance; I saw tall ships sweeping in from the sea through the Golden Gate; I saw that it was time to take another drink, and after that I saw no more. All hands fell to singing "When we were Marching Through Georgia," and the remainder of the trip was fought out on that line. We landed at the steamboat wharf at 5 o'clock, safe and sound. Some of those reporters I spoke of said we had been to Benicia, and the others said we had been to the Cliff House, but, poor devils, they had been drinking, and they did not really know where we had been. I know, but I do not choose to tell.

HOUSE AT LARGE
[*Morning Call*, July 1, 1864]

An old two-story, sheet-iron, pioneer, fire-proof house, got loose from her moorings last night, and drifted down Sutter street, toward Montgomery. We are not informed as to where she came from or where she was going to — she had halted near Montgomery street, and appeared to be studying about it. If one might judge from the expression that hung about her dilapidated front and desolate windows, she was thoroughly demoralized when she stopped there, and sorry she ever started. Is there no law against houses loafing around the public streets at midnight?

---

from TROT HER ALONG
[*Morning Call*, July 30, 1864]

For several days a vagrant two-story frame house has been wandering listlessly about Commercial street, above this office, and she has finally stopped in the middle of the thoroughfare, and is staring dejectedly towards Montgomery street, as if she would like to go down there, but really don't feel equal to the exertion. We wish they would trot her along and leave the street open; she is an impassable obstruction and an intolerable nuisance where she stands now....

DISGUSTED AND GONE
[*Morning Call*, July 31, 1864]

That melancholy old frame house that has been loafing around Commercial street for the past week, got disgusted at the notice we gave her in the last issue of the *Call,* and drifted off into some other part of the city yesterday. It is pleasing to our vanity to imagine that if it had not been for our sagacity in divining her hellish designs, and our fearless exposure of them, she would have been down on Montgomery street today, playing herself for a hotel. As it is, she has folded her tents like the Arabs, and quietly stolen away, behind several yoke of oxen.

FROM MYSTERIOUS
[*Morning Call*, Aug. 9, 1864]

If you have got a house, keep your eye on it, these times, for there is no knowing what moment it will go tramping around town. We meet these dissatisfied shanties every day marching boldly through the public streets on stilts and rollers, or standing thoughtfully in front of gin shops, or halting in quiet alleys and peering round corners, with a human curiosity, out of one eye, or one window if you please, upon the dizzy whirl and roar of commerce in the thoroughfare beyond. The houses have been taking something lately that is moving them a good deal. It is very mysterious, and past accounting for, but it cannot be helped. We have just been informed that an unknown house—two stories, with a kitchen—has stopped before Shark alley, in Merchant street, and seems to be calculating the chances of being able to scrouge through it into Washington street, and thus save the trouble of going around. We hardly think she can, and we had rather she would not try it; we should be sorry to see her get herself fast in that crevice, which is the newspaper reporter's shortest cut to the station-house and the courts....

FROM "MARK TWAIN'S" FAREWELL
[*Alta California*, Dec. 15, 1866]

"My Friends and Fellow-Citizens:
    I have been treated with extreme kindness and cordiality by San Francisco, and I wish to return my sincerest thanks and acknowledg-

ments. I have also been treated with marked and unusual generosity, forbearance and good-fellowship, by my ancient comrades, my brethren of the Press—a thing which has peculiarly touched me, because long experience in the service has taught me that we of the Press are slow to praise but quick to censure each other, as a general thing—wherefore, in thanking them I am anxious to convince them, at the same time, that they have not lavished their kind offices upon one who cannot appreciate or is insensible to them.

"I am now about to bid farewell to San Francisco for a season, and to go back to that common home we all tenderly remember in our waking hours and fondly revisit in dreams of the night—a home which is familiar to my recollection, but will be an unknown land to my unaccustomed eyes. I shall share the fate of many another longing exile who wanders back to his early home to find gray hairs where he expected youth, graves where he looked for firesides, grief where he had pictured joy—everywhere change! remorseless change where he had heedlessly dreamed that desolating Time had stood still!—to find his cherished anticipations a mockery, and to drink the lees of disappointment instead of the beaded wine of a hope that is crowned with its fruition!

"And while I linger here upon the threshold of this, my new home, to say to you, my kindest and my truest friends, a warm good-bye and an honest peace and prosperity attend you, I accept the warning that mighty changes will have come over this home also when my returning feet shall walk these streets again.

"I read the signs of the times, and I, that am no prophet, behold the things that are in store for you. Over slumbering California is stealing the dawn of a radiant future! The great China Mail Line is established, the Pacific Railroad is creeping across the continent, the commerce of the world is about to be revolutionized. California is the Crown Princess of the new dispensation! She stands in the centre of the grand highway of the nations; she stands midway between the Old World and the New, and both shall pay her tribute. From the far East and from Europe, multitudes of stout hearts and willing hands are preparing to flock hither; to throng her hamlets and villages; to till her fruitful soil; to unveil the riches of her countless mines; to build up an empire on these distant shores that shall shame the bravest dreams of her visionaries. From the opulent lands of the Orient, from India, from China, Japan, the Amoor; from tributary regions that stretch from the

Arctic circle to the equator, is about to pour in upon her the princely commerce of a teeming population of four hundred and fifty million souls. Half the world stands ready to lay its contributions at her feet! Has any other State so brilliant a future? Has any other city a future like San Francisco?

"This straggling town shall be a vast metropolis; this sparsely populated land shall become a crowded hive of busy men; your waste places shall blossom like the rose, and your deserted hills and valleys shall yield bread and wine for unnumbered thousands; railroads shall be spread hither and thither and carry the invigorating blood of commerce to regions that are languishing now; mills and workshops, yea, and factories shall spring up everywhere, and mines that have neither name nor place to-day shall dazzle the world with their affluence. The time is drawing on apace when the clouds shall pass away from your firmament, and a splendid prosperity shall descend like a glory upon the whole land!

"I am bidding the old city and my old friends a kind, but not a sad farewell, for I know that when I see this home again, the changes that will have been wrought upon it will suggest no sentiment of sadness; its estate will be brighter, happier and prouder a hundred fold than it is this day. This is its destiny, and in all sincerity I can say, So mote it be!"

HEALTH & DEATH

{ I have made it a rule
never to smoke more than
one cigar at a time. }

EARLY RISING, AS REGARDS EXCURSIONS TO THE CLIFF HOUSE
[*Golden Era*, July 5, 1864]

Early to bed, and early to rise,
Makes a man healthy, wealthy and wise.
Benjamin Franklin

I don't see it.
George Washington

Now both of these are high authorities—very high and respectable authorities—but I am with General Washington first, last, and all the time on this proposition.

Because I don't see it, either.

I have tried getting up early, and I have tried getting up late—and the latter agrees with me best. As for a man's growing any wiser, or any richer, or any healthier, by getting up early, I know it is not so; because I have got up early in the station-house many and many a time, and got poorer and poorer for the next half a day, in consequence, instead of richer and richer. And sometimes, on the same terms, I have seen the sun rise four times a week up there at Virginia, and so far from my growing healthier on account of it, I got to looking blue, and pulpy, and swelled, like a drowned man, and my relations grew alarmed and thought they were going to lose me. They entirely despaired of my recovery, at one time, and began to grieve for me as one whose days were numbered—whose fate was sealed—who was soon to pass away from them forever, and from the glad sunshine, and the birds, and the odorous flowers, and murmuring brooks, and whispering winds, and all the cheerful scenes of life, and go down into the dark and silent tomb—and they went forth sorrowing, and jumped a lot in the grave-yard, and made up their minds to grin and bear it with that fortitude which is the true Christian's brightest ornament.

You observe that I have put a stronger test on the matter than even Benjamin Franklin contemplated, and yet it would not work. There-fore, how is a man to grow healthier, and wealthier, and wiser by going to bed early and getting up early, when he fails to accomplish these things even when he does not go to bed at all? And as far as becom-ing wiser is concerned, you might put all the wisdom I acquired in these experiments in your eye, without obstructing your vision any to speak of.

As I said before, my voice is with George Washington's on this question.

Another philosopher encourages the world to get up at sunrise because "it is the early bird that catches the worm."

It is a seductive proposition, and well calculated to trap the unsus-pecting. But its attractions are all wasted on me, because I have no use for the worm. If I had, I would adopt the Unreliable's plan. He was much interested in this quaint proverb, and directed the powers of his great mind to its consideration for three or four consecutive hours. He was supposing a case. He was supposing, for instance, that he really wanted the worm—that the possession of the worm was actually nec-essary to his happiness—that he yearned for it and hankered after it, therefore, as much as a man could yearn for and hanker after a worm under such circumstances—and he was supposing, further, that he was opposed to getting up early in order to catch it (which was much the more plausible of the two suppositions). Well, at the end of three or four hours' profound meditation upon the subject, the Unreliable rose up and said: "If he were so anxious about the worm, and he couldn't get along without him, and he didn't want to get up early in the morning to catch him—why then, by George, he would just lay for him the night before!" I never would have thought of that. I looked at the youth, and said to myself, he is malicious, and dishonest, and unhandsome, and does not smell good—yet how quickly do these trivial demerits disappear in the shadow when the glare from his great intellect shines out above them!

I have always heard that the only time in the day that a trip to the Cliff House could be thoroughly enjoyed, was early in the morning; (and I suppose it might be as well to withhold an adverse impression while the flow-tide of public opinion continues to set in that direction.)

I tried it the other morning with Harry, the stock-broker, rising at 4 A.M., to delight in the following described things, to wit:

A road unencumbered by carriages, and free from wind and dust; a bracing atmosphere; the gorgeous spectacle of the sun in the dawn of his glory; the fresh perfume of flowers still damp with dew; a solitary drive on the beach while its smoothness was yet unmarred by wheel or hoof, and a vision of white sails glinting in the morning light far out at sea.

These were the considerations, and they seemed worthy a sacrifice of seven or eight hours' sleep.

We sat in the stable, and yawned, and gaped, and stretched, until the horse was hitched up, and then drove out into the bracing atmosphere. (When another early voyage is proposed to me, I want it understood that there is to be no bracing atmosphere in the programme. I can worry along without it.) In half an hour we were so thoroughly braced up with it that it was just a scratch that we were not frozen to death. Then the harness came unshipped, or got broken, or something, and I waxed colder and drowsier while Harry fixed it. I am not fastidious about clothes, but I am not used to wearing fragrant, sweaty horse-blankets, and not partial to them, either; I am not proud, though, when I am freezing, and I added the horse-blanket to my overcoats, and tried to wake up and feel warm and cheerful. It was useless, however—all my senses slumbered, and continued to slumber, save the sense of smell.

When my friend drove past suburban gardens and said the flowers never exhaled so sweet an odor before, in his experience, I dreamily but honestly endeavored to think so too, but in my secret soul I was conscious that they only smelled like horse-blankets. (When another early voyage is proposed to me, I want it understood that there is to be no "fresh perfume of flowers" in the programme, either. I do not enjoy it. My senses are not attuned to the flavor—there is too much horse about it and not enough eau de cologne.)

The wind was cold and benumbing, and blew with such force that we could hardly make headway against it. It came straight from the ocean, and I think there are ice-bergs out there somewhere. True, there was not much dust, because the gale blew it all to Oregon in two minutes; and by good fortune, it blew no gravel-stones, to speak of—only one, of any consequence, I believe—a three-cornered one—it struck me in the eye. I have it there yet. However, it does not matter—for the future I suppose I can manage to see tolerably well out of the other. (Still, when another early voyage is proposed to me, I want it understood that the dust is to be put in, and the gravel left out of the programme. I might want my other eye if I continue to hang on until my time comes; and besides, I shall not mind the dust much hereafter, because I have only got to shut one eye, now, when it is around.)

No, the road was not encumbered by carriages—we had it all to ourselves. I suppose the reason was, that most people do not like to enjoy themselves too much, and therefore they do not go out to the Cliff House in the cold and the fog, and the dread silence and solitude of four o'clock in the morning. They are right. The impressive solemnity of such a pleasure trip is only equalled by an excursion to Lone Mountain in a hearse. Whatever of advantage there may be in having that Cliff House road all to yourself, we had—but to my mind a greater advantage would lie in dividing it up in small sections among the entire community; because, in consequence of the repairs in progress on it just now, it is as rough as a corduroy bridge—(in a good many places,) and consequently the less you have of it, the happier you are likely to be, and the less shaken up and disarranged on the inside. (Wherefore, when another early voyage is proposed to me, I want it understood that the road is not to be unencumbered with carriages, but just the reverse—so that the balance of the people shall be made to stand their share of the jolting and the desperate lonesomeness of the thing.)

From the moment we left the stable, almost, the fog was so thick that we could scarcely see fifty yards behind or before, or overhead; and for awhile, as we approached the Cliff House, we could not see the horse at all, and were obliged to steer by his ears, which stood up dimly out of the dense white mist that enveloped him. But for those friendly beacons, we must have been cast away and lost.

I have no opinion of a six-mile ride in the clouds; but if I ever have to take another, I want to leave the horse in the stable and go in a balloon. I shall prefer to go in the afternoon, also, when it is warm, so that

I may gape, and yawn, and stretch, if I am drowsy, without disarranging my horse-blanket and letting in a blast of cold wind.

We could scarcely see the sportive seals out on the rocks, writhing and squirming like exaggerated maggots, and there was nothing soothing in their discordant barking, to a spirit so depressed as mine was.

Harry took a cocktail at the Cliff House, but I scorned such ineffectual stimulus; I yearned for fire, and there was none there; they were about to make one, but the bar-keeper looked altogether too cheerful for me—I could not bear his unnatural happiness in the midst of such a ghastly picture of fog, and damp, and frosty surf, and dreary solitude. I could not bear the sacrilegious presence of a pleasant face at such a time; it was too much like sprightliness at a funeral, and we fled from it down the smooth and vacant beach.

We had that all to ourselves, too, like the road—and I want it divided up, also, hereafter. We could not drive in the roaring surf and seem to float abroad on the foamy sea, as one is wont to do in the sunny afternoon, because the very thought of any of that icy-looking water splashing on you was enough to congeal your blood, almost. We saw no white-winged ships sailing away on the billowy ocean, with the pearly light of morning descending upon them like a benediction— "because the fog had the bulge on the pearly light," as the Unreliable observed when I mentioned it to him afterwards; and we saw not the sun in the dawn of his glory, for the same reason. Hill and beach, and sea and sun were all wrapped in a ghostly mantle of mist, and hidden from our mortal vision. (When another early voyage is proposed to me, I want it understood that the sun in his glory, and the morning light, and the ships at sea, and all that sort of thing are to be left out of the programme, so that when we fail to see them, we shall not be so infernally disappointed.)

We were human icicles when we got to the Ocean House, and there was no fire there, either. I banished all hope, then, and succumbed to despair; I went back on my religion, and sought surcease of sorrow in soothing blasphemy. I am sorry I did it, now, but it was a great comfort to me, then. We could have had breakfast at the Ocean House, but we did not want it; can statues of ice feel hunger? But we adjourned to a private room and ordered red-hot coffee, and it was a sort of balm to my troubled mind to observe that the man who brought it was as cold, and as silent, and as solemn as the grave itself. His gravity was so impressive, and so appropriate and becoming to the melancholy surroundings, that it won upon me and thawed out some of the better instincts of my nature, and I told him he might ask a blessing if he thought it would lighten him up any—because he looked as if he wanted to, very bad—but he only shook his head resignedly and sighed.

That coffee did the business for us. It was made by a master-artist, and it had not a fault; and the cream that came with it was so rich and thick that you could hardly have strained it through a wire fence. As the generous beverage flowed down our frigid throats, our blood grew warm again, our muscles relaxed, our torpid bodies awoke to life and feeling, anger and uncharitableness departed from us and we were cheerful once more. We got good cigars, also, at the Ocean House, and drove into town over a smooth road, lighted by the sun and unclouded by fog.

Near the Jewish cemeteries we turned a corner too suddenly, and got upset, but sustained no damage, although the horse did what he honestly could to kick the buggy out of the State while we were grovelling in the sand. We went on down to the steamer, and while we were on board, the buggy was upset again by some outlaw, and an axle broken.

However, these little accidents, and all the deviltry and misfortune that preceded them, were only just and natural consequences of the absurd experiment of getting up at an hour in the morning when all God-fearing Christians ought to be in bed. I consider that the man who leaves his pillow, deliberately, at sun-rise, is taking his life in his own hands, and he ought to feel proud if he don't have to put it down again at the coroner's office before dark.

Now, for that early trip, I am not any healthier or any wealthier than I was before, and only wiser in that I know a good deal better than to go and do it again. And as for all those notable advantages, such as the sun in the dawn of his glory, and the ships, and the perfume of the flowers, etc., etc., etc., I don't see them, any more than myself and Washington see the soundness of Benjamin Franklin's attractive little poem.

If you go to the Cliff House at any time after seven in the morning, you cannot fail to enjoy it—but never start out there before daylight, under the impression that you are going to have a pleasant time and come back insufferably healthier and wealthier and wiser than your betters on account of it. Because if you do you will miss your cal-

culation, and it will keep you swearing about it right straight along for
a week to get even again.

Put no trust in the benefits to accrue from early rising, as set forth
by the infatuated Franklin—but stake the last cent of your substance on the judgment of old George Washington, the Father of his
Country, who said "he couldn't see it."

And you hear me endorsing that sentiment.

<hr>

FROM A LETTER TO HIS MOTHER, AUG. 12, 1864

My Dear Mother—You have portrayed to me so often & so
earnestly the benefit of taking frequent exercise, that I know it
will please you to learn that I belong to the San F. Olympic Club,
whose gymnasium is one of the largest & best appointed in the
United States. I am glad, now, that you put me in the notion
of it, Ma, because if you had not, I never would have thought
of it myself. I think it nothing but right to give you the whole credit
of it. It has been a great blessing to me. I feel like a new man. I
sleep better, I have a healthier appetite, my intellect is clearer, & I
have become so strong & hearty that I fully believe twenty years have
been added to my life. I feel as if I ought to be very well satisfied
with this result, when I reflect that I never was in that gymnasium
but once in my life, & that was over three months ago. . . .

<hr>

from CONCERNING THE ANSWER TO THAT CONUNDRUM
[*The Californian*, Oct. 8, 1864]

The day was excessively warm, and my comrade was an invalid;
consequently we travelled slowly, and conversed about distressing diseases and other such matters as I thought would be likely to interest
a sick man and make him feel cheerful. Instead of commenting on the
mild scenery we found on the route, we spoke of the ravages of the
cholera in the happy days of our boyhood; instead of talking about the
warm weather, we revelled in bilious fever reminiscences; instead of
boasting of the extraordinary swiftness of our horse, as most persons
similarly situated would have done, we chatted gaily of consumption;

and when we caught a glimpse of long white lines of waves rolling in silently upon the distant shore, our hearts were gladdened and our stomachs turned by fond memories of sea-sickness. It was a nice comfortable journey, and I could not have enjoyed it more if I had been sick myself.

———•———

FROM HOW TO CURE A COLD
[*Golden Era*, Sept. 20, 1863]

It is a good thing, perhaps, to write for the amusement of the public, but it is a far higher and nobler thing to write for their instruction — their profit — their actual and tangible benefit.

The latter is the sole object of this article.

If it prove the means of restoring to health one solitary sufferer among my race — of lighting up once more the fire of hope and joy in his faded eyes — of bringing back to his dead heart again the quick, generous impulses of other days — I shall be amply rewarded for my labor; my soul will be permeated with the sacred delight a Christian feels when he has done a good, unselfish deed.

Having led a pure and blameless life, I am justified in believing that no man who knows me will reject the suggestions I am about to make, out of fear that I am trying to deceive him.

Let the public do itself the honor to read my experience in doctoring a cold, as herein set forth, and then follow in my footsteps....

The first time I began to sneeze, a friend told me to go and bathe my feet in hot water and go to bed.

I did so.

Shortly afterward, another friend advised me to get up and take a cold shower-bath.

I did that also.

Within the hour, another friend assured me that it was policy to "feed a cold and starve a fever."

I had both.

I thought it best to fill myself up for the cold, and then keep dark and let the fever starve a while.

In a case of this kind, I seldom do things by halves; I ate pretty heartily; I conferred my custom upon a stranger who had just opened his restaurant that morning; he waited near me in respectful silence until I had finished feeding my cold, when he inquired if the people about Virginia were much afflicted by colds?

I told him I thought they were.

He then went out and took in his sign.

I started down toward the office, and on the way encountered another bosom friend, who told me that a quart of salt water, taken warm, would come as near curing a cold as anything in the world.

I hardly thought I had room for it, but I tried it anyhow.

The result was surprising; I must have vomited three-quarters of an hour; I believe I threw up my immortal soul.

Now, as I am giving my experience only for the benefit of those who are troubled with the distemper I am writing about, I feel that they will see the propriety of my cautioning them against following such portions of it as proved inefficient with me — and acting upon this conviction, I warn them against warm salt water.

It may be a good enough remedy, but I think it is too severe. If I had another cold in the head, and there was no course left me but to take either an earthquake or a quart of salt water, I would cheerfully take my chances on the earthquake.

After the storm which had been raging in my stomach had subsided, and no more good Samaritans happening along, I went on borrowing handkerchiefs again and blowing them to atoms, as had been my custom in the early stages of my cold, until I came across a lady who had just arrived from over the plains, and who said she had lived in a part of the country where doctors were scarce, and had from necessity acquired considerable skill in the treatment of simple "family complaints."

I knew she must have had much experience, for she appeared to be a hundred and fifty years old.

She mixed a decoction composed of molasses, aquafortis, turpentine, and various other drugs, and instructed me to take a wineglass full of it every fifteen minutes.

I never took but one dose; that was enough; it robbed me of all moral principle, and awoke every unworthy impulse of my nature.

Under its malign influence, my brain conceived miracles of meanness, but my hands were too feeble to execute them; at that time had it not been that my strength had surrendered to a succession of assaults from infallible remedies for my cold, I am satisfied that I would have tried to rob the graveyard.

Like most people, I often feel mean, and act accordingly, but until I took that medicine I had never reveled in such supernatural depravity and felt proud of it.

At the end of two days, I was ready to go to doctoring again. I took a few more unfailing remedies, and finally drove my cold from my head to my lungs.

I got to coughing incessantly, and my voice fell below Zero; I conversed in a thundering bass two octaves below my natural tone; I could only compass my regular nightly repose by coughing myself down to a state of utter exhaustion, and then the moment I began to talk in my sleep, my discordant voice woke me up again.

My case grew more and more serious every day.

Plain gin was recommended; I took it.

Then gin and molasses; I took that also.

Then gin and onions; I added the onions and took all three.

I detected no particular result, however, except that I had acquired a breath like a buzzard's.

I found I had to travel for my health.

I went to Lake Bigler with my reportorial comrade, Adair Wilson. It is gratifying to me to reflect that we traveled in considerable style; we went in the Pioneer coach, and my friend took all his baggage with him, consisting of two excellent silk handkerchiefs and a daguerreotype of his grandmother.

I had my regular gin and onions along.

Virginia, San Francisco, and Sacramento were well represented at the Lake House, and we had a very healthy time of it for a while. We sailed and hunted and fished and danced all day, and I doctored my cough all night.

By managing in this way, I made out to improve every hour in the twenty-four.

But my disease continued to grow worse.

A sheet-bath was recommended. I had never refused a remedy yet, and it seemed poor policy to commence then; therefore I determined to take a sheet-bath, notwithstanding I had no idea what sort of arrangement it was.

It was administered at midnight, and the weather was very frosty. My breast and back were bared, and a sheet (there appeared to be a thousand yards of it) soaked in ice-water, was wound around me until I resembled a swab for a Columbiad.

It is a cruel expedient. When the chilly rag touches one's warm flesh, it makes him start with sudden violence and gasp for breath just as men do in the death agony. It froze the marrow in my bones and stopped the beating of my heart.

I thought my time had come....

Never take a sheet-bath—never. Next to meeting a lady acquaintance, who, for reasons best known to herself, don't see you when she looks at you and don't know you when she does see you, it is the most uncomfortable thing in the world....

[W]hen the sheet-bath failed to cure my cough, a lady friend recommended the application of a mustard plaster to my breast.

I believe that would have cured me effectually, if it had not been for young Wilson.

When I went to bed I put my mustard plaster—which was a very gorgeous one, eighteen inches square—where I could reach it when I was ready for it.

But young Wilson got hungry in the night, and ate it up.

I never saw anybody have such an appetite; I am confident that lunatic would have eaten me if I had been healthy.

After sojourning a week at Lake Bigler, I went to Steamboat Springs, and besides the steam baths, I took a lot of the vilest medicines that were ever concocted. They would have cured me, but I had to go back to Virginia, where, notwithstanding the variety of new remedies I had absorbed every day, I managed to aggravate my disease by carelessness and undue exposure.

I finally concluded to visit San Francisco, and the first day I got here a lady at the Lick House told me to drink a quart of whisky every twenty-four hours, and a friend at the Occidental recommended precisely the same course.

Each advised me to take a quart—that makes half a gallon.

I calculate to do it or perish in the attempt.

Now, with the kindest motives in the world, I offer for the consideration of consumptive patients the variegated course of treatment I have lately gone through. Let them try it—if it don't cure them, it can't more than kill them.

———

MORE CEMETERIAL GHASTLINESS
[*Territorial Enterprise*, Feb. 3, 1866]

I spoke the other day of some singular proceedings of a firm of undertakers here, and now I come to converse about one or two more of the undertaker tribe. I begin to think this sort of people have no bowels—as the ancients would say—no heart, as we would express it. They appear to think only of business—business first, last, all the time. They trade in the woes of men as coolly as other people trade in candles and mackerel. Their hearts are ironclad, and they seem to have no sympathies in common with their fellow-men.

A prominent firm of undertakers here own largely in Lone Mountain Cemetery and also in the toll-road leading to it. Now if you or I owned that toll-road we would be satisfied with the revenue from a long funeral procession and would "throw in" the corpse—we would let him pass free of toll—we would wink placidly at the gate-keeper and say, "Never mind this gentleman in the hearse—this fellow's a dead-head." But the firm I am speaking of never do that—if a corpse starts to Paradise or perdition by their road he has got to pay his toll or else switch off and take some other route. And it is rare to see the pride this firm take in the popularity and respectability of their cemetery, and the interest and even enthusiasm which they display in their business.

A friend of mine was out at Lone Mountain the other day, and was moving sadly among the tombs thinking of departed comrades and recalling the once pleasant faces now so cold, and the once familiar voices now so still, and the once busy hands now idly crossed beneath the turf, when he came upon Mr. Smith, of the firm.

"Ah, good morning," says Smith, "come out to see us at last, have you?—glad you have! let me show you round—let me show you round. Pretty fine ain't it?—everything in apple pie order, eh? Everybody says so—everybody says mighty few graveyards go ahead of this. We are endorsed by the best people in San Francisco. We get 'em, sir, we get the pick and choice of the departed. Come, let me show you. Here's Major-General Jones—distinguished man, he was—very distinguished man—highsted him up on that mound, there, where he's prominent. And here's MacSpaden—rich?—Oh, my! And we've got Brigadier-General Jollopson here—there he is, over there—keep him trimmed up and spruce as a fresh "plant," all the time. And we've got Swimley, and Stiggers, the bankers, and Johnson and Swipe, the

railroad men, and m-o-r-e Admirals and them kind of people —
slathers of 'em! And bless you we've got as much as a whole block
planted in nothing but hundred-thousand-dollar fellows — and —"

(Here Mr. Smith's face lighted up suddenly with a blaze of enthusiasm, and he rubbed his hands together and ducked his head to get
a better view through the shrubbery of the distant toll-road, and then
exclaimed):

"Ah! is it another? Yes, I believe it is — yes it is! Third arrival today!
Long procession! 'George this is gay! Well, so-long, Thompson, I must
go and cache this party!"

And the happy undertaker skipped lightly away to offer the dismal
hospitalities of his establishment to the unconscious visitor in the
hearse.

POLITICS

It could probably be shown
by facts and figures that there is no
distinctly native American
Criminal class except Congress.

FROM THE GREAT PRIZE FIGHT
[*Golden Era*, Oct. 11, 1863]

THE ONLY TRUE AND RELIABLE ACCOUNT OF
THE GREAT PRIZE FIGHT FOR $100,000 AT
SEAL ROCK POINT, ON SUNDAY LAST, BETWEEN
HIS EXCELLENCY GOV. STANFORD AND
HON. F. F. LOW, GOVERNOR ELECT OF CALIFORNIA.

For the past month the sporting world has been in a state of feverish excitement on account of the grand prize fight set for last Sunday between the two most distinguished citizens of California, for a purse of a hundred thousand dollars. The high social standing of the competitors, their exalted position in the arena of politics, together with the princely sum of money staked upon the issue of the combat, all conspired to render the proposed prize fight a subject of extraordinary importance, and to give it an eclat never before vouchsafed to such a circumstance since the world began. Additional lustre was shed upon the coming contest by the lofty character of the seconds or bottle-holders chosen by the two champions, these being no other than Judge field (on the part of Gov. Low), Associate Justice of the Supreme Court of the United States, and Hon. Wm. M. Stewart, (commonly called "Bill Stewart," or "Bullyragging Bill Stewart,") of the city of Virginia, the most popular as well as the most distinguished lawyer in Nevada Territory, member of the Constitutional Convention, and future U.S.

Senator for the State of Washoe, as I hope and believe — on the part of Gov. Stanford. Principals and seconds together, it is fair to presume that such an array of talent was never entered for a combat of this description upon any previous occasion.

Stewart and Field had their men in constant training at the Mission during the six weeks preceding the contest, and such was the interest taken in the matter that thousands visited that sacred locality daily to pick up such morsels of information as they might, concerning the physical and scientific improvement being made by the gubernatorial acrobats. The anxiety manifested by the populace was intense. When it was learned that Stanford had smashed a barrel of flour to atoms with a single blow of his fist, the voice of the people was on his side. But when the news came that Low had caved in the head of a tubular boiler with one stroke of his powerful "mawley" (which term is in strict accordance with the language of the ring,) the tide of opinion changed again. These changes were frequent, and they kept the minds of the public in such a state of continual vibration that I fear the habit thus acquired is confirmed, and that they will never more cease to oscillate.

The fight was to take place on last Sunday morning at ten o'clock. By nine every wheeled vehicle and every species of animal capable of bearing burthens, were in active service, and the avenues leading to the Seal Rock swarmed with them in mighty processions whose numbers no man might hope to estimate.

I determined to be upon the ground at an early hour. Now I dislike to be exploded, as it were, out of my balmy slumbers, by a sudden, stormy assault upon my door, and an imperative order to "Get up!"—wherefore I requested one of the intelligent porters of the Lick House to call at my palatial apartments, and murmur gently through the keyhole the magic monosyllable "Hash!" That "fetched me"....

After an infinitude of fearful adventures, the history of which would fill many columns of this newspaper, I finally arrived at the Seal Rock Point at a quarter to ten — two hours and a half out from San Francisco, and not less gratified than surprised that I ever got there at all — and anchored my noble Morgan to a boulder on the hill-side. I had to swathe his head in blankets also, because, while my back was turned for a single moment, he developed another atrocious trait of his most remarkable character. He tried to eat little Augustus Maltravers Jackson, the "humbly" but interesting offspring of Hon. J.

Belvidere Jackson, a wealthy barber from San Jose. It would have been a comfort to me to leave the infant to his fate, but I did not feel able to pay for him.

When I reached the battle-ground, the great champions were already stripped and prepared for the "mill." Both were in splendid condition, and displayed a redundancy of muscle about the breast and arms which was delightful to the eye of the sportive connoisseur. They were well matched. Adepts said that Stanford's "heft" and tall stature were fairly offset by Low's superior litheness and activity. From their heads to the Union colors around their waists, their costumes were similar to that of the Greek Slave; from thence down they were clad in flesh-colored tights and grenadier boots.

The ring was formed upon the beautiful level sandy beach above the Cliff House, and within twenty paces of the snowy surf of the broad Pacific ocean, which was spotted here and there with monstrous sea-lions attracted shoreward by curiosity concerning the vast multitudes of people collected in the vicinity.

At five minutes past ten, Brigadier General Wright, the Referee, notified the seconds to bring their men "up to the scratch." They did so, amid the shouts of the populace, the noise whereof rose high above the roar of the sea.

FIRST ROUND.—The pugilists advanced to the centre of the ring, shook hands, retired to their respective corners, and at the call of the time-keeper, came forward and went at it. Low dashed out handsomely with his left and gave Stanford a paster in the eye, and at the same moment his adversary mashed him in the ear. (These singular phrases are entirely proper, Mr. Editor — I find them in the copy of "Bell's Life in London" now lying before me.) After some beautiful sparring, both parties went down — that is to say, they went down to the bottle-holders, Stewart and field, and took a drink.

SECOND ROUND.— Stanford launched out a well intended plunger, but Low parried it admirably and instantly busted him in the snoot. (Cries of "Bully for the Marysville Infant!") After some lively fibbing (both of them are used to it in political life) the combatants went to the grass. (See "Bell's Life.")

THIRD ROUND.— Both came up panting considerably. Low let go a terrific side-winder, but Stanford stopped it handsomely and replied with an earthquake on Low's bread-basket. (Enthusiastic shouts of "Sock it to him, my Sacramento Pet!") More fibbing — both

36

down.

FOURTH ROUND.—The men advanced and sparred warily for a few moments, when Stanford exposed his cocoanut an instant, and Low struck out from the shoulder and split him in the mug. (Cries of "Bully for the Fat Boy!")

FIFTH ROUND.— Stanford came up looking wicked, and let drive a heavy blow with his larboard flipper which caved in the side of his adversary's head. (Exclamations of "Hi! at him again Old Rusty!")

From this time until the end of the conflict, there was nothing regular in the proceedings. The two champions got furiously angry, and used up each other thus:

No sooner did Low realize that the side of his head was crushed in like a dent in a plug hat, than he "went after" Stanford in the most desperate manner. With one blow of his fist he mashed his nose so far into his face that a cavity was left in its place the size and shape of an ordinary soup-bowl. It is scarcely necessary to mention that in making room for so much nose, Gov. Stanford's eyes were crowded to such a degree as to cause them to "bug out" like a grasshopper's. His face was so altered that he scarcely looked like himself at all.

I never saw such a murderous expression as Stanford's countenance now assumed; you see it was so concentrated — it had such a small number of features to spread around over. He let fly one of his battering rams and caved in the other side of Low's head. Ah me, the latter was a ghastly sight to contemplate after that — one of the boys said it looked "like a beet which somebody had trod on it."

Low was "grit" though. He dashed out with his right and stove Stanford's chin clear back even with his ears. Oh, what a horrible sight he was, gasping and reaching after his tobacco, which was away back among his under-jaw teeth.

Stanford was unsettled for a while, but he soon rallied, and watching his chance, aimed a tremendous blow at his favorite mark, which crushed in the rear of Gov. Low's head in such a way that the crown thereof projected over his spinal column like a shed.

He came up to the scratch like a man, though, and sent one of his ponderous fists crashing through his opponent's ribs and in among his vitals, and instantly afterward he hauled out poor Stanford's left lung and smacked him in the face with it.

If ever I saw an angry man in my life it was Leland Stanford. He fairly raved. He jumped at his old speciality, Gov. Low's head; he tore it loose from his body and knocked him down with it. (Sensation in the crowd.)

Staggered by his extraordinary exertion, Gov. Stanford reeled, and before he could recover himself the headless but indomitable Low sprang forward, pulled one of his legs out by the roots, and dealt him a smashing paster over the eye with the end of it. The ever watchful Bill Stewart sallied out to the assistance of his crippled principal with a pair of crutches, and the battle went on again as fiercely as ever.

At this stage of the game the battle ground was strewn with a sufficiency of human remains to furnish material for the construction of three or four men of ordinary size, and good sound brains enough to stock a whole country like the one I came from in the noble old state of Missouri. And so dyed were the combatants in their own gore that they looked like shapeless, mutilated, red-shirted firemen.

The moment a chance offered, Low grabbed Stanford by the hair of the head, swung him thrice round and round in the air like a lasso, and then slammed him on the ground with such mighty force that he quivered all over, and squirmed painfully, like a worm; and behold, his body and such of his limbs as he had left, shortly assumed a swollen aspect like unto those of a rag doll-baby stuffed with saw-dust.

He rallied again, however, and the two desperadoes clinched and never left up until they had minced each other into such insignificant odds and ends that neither was able to distinguish his own remnants from those of his antagonist. It was awful.

Bill Stewart and Judge Field issued from their corners and gazed upon the sanguinary reminiscences in silence during several minutes. At the end of that time, having failed to discover that either champion had got the best of the fight, they threw up their sponges simultaneously, and Gen. Wright proclaimed in a loud voice that the battle was "drawn." May my ears never again be rent asunder with a burst of sound similar to that which greeted this announcement, from the multitude. Amen.

By order of Gen. Wright, baskets were procured, and Bill Stewart and Judge Field proceeded to gather up the fragments of their late principals, while I gathered up my notes and went after my infernal horse, who had slipped his blankets and was foraging among the neighboring children. I —* * * * * * *

P. S. — Messrs. Editors, I have been the victim of an infamous hoax. I have been imposed upon by that ponderous miscreant, Mr. Frank Lawler, of the Lick House. I left my room a moment ago, and the first man I met on the stairs was Gov. Stanford, alive and well, and as free from mutilation as you or I. I was speechless. Before I reached the street, I actually met Gov. Low also, with his own head on his own shoulders, his limbs intact, his inner mechanism in its proper place, and his cheeks blooming with gorgeous robustitude. I was amazed. But a word of explanation from him convinced me that I had been swindled by Mr. Lawler with a detailed account of a fight which had never occurred, and was never likely to occur; that I had believed him so implicitly as to sit down and write it out (as other reporters have done before me) in language calculated to deceive the public into the conviction that I was present at it myself, and to embellish it with a string of falsehoods intended to render that deception as plausible as possible. I ruminated upon my singular position for many minutes, arrived at no conclusion — that is to say, no satisfactory conclusion, except that Lawler was an accomplished knave and I was a consummate ass. I had suspected the first before, though, and been acquainted with the latter fact for nearly a quarter of a century.

In conclusion, permit me to apologize in the most abject manner to the present Governor of California, to Hon. Mr. Low, the Governor-elect, to Judge Field and to Hon. Wm. M. Stewart, for the great wrong which my natural imbecility has impelled me to do them in penning and publishing the foregoing sanguinary absurdity. If it were to do over again, I don't really know that I would do it. It is not possible for me to say how I ever managed to believe that refined and educated gentlemen like these could stoop to engage in the loathsome and degrading pastime of prize fighting. It was just Lawler's work, you understand — the lubberly, swelled-up effigy of a nine-days drowned man! But I shall get even with him for this. The only excuse he offers is that he got the story from John B. Winters, and thought of course it must be just so — as if a future Congressman for the State of Washoe could by any possibility tell the truth! Do you know that if either of these miserable scoundrels were to cross my path while I am in this mood I would scalp him in a minute? That's me — that's my style.

---

from THE SANDWICH ISLAND LEGISLATURE
[*Golden Era*, June 24, 1866]

I have seen a number of Legislatures, and there was a comfortable majority in each of them that knew just about enough to come in when it rained, and that was all. Few men of first class ability can afford to let their affairs go to ruin while they fool away their time in Legislatures for months on a stretch. Few such men care a straw for the small-beer distinctions one is able to achieve in such a place. But your chattering, one-horse village lawyer likes it, and your solemn ass from the cow-counties, who don't know the Constitution from the Lord's Prayer, enjoys it, and these you will always find in the Assembly; the one gabble, gabble, gabbling threadbare platitudes and "give-me-liberty-or-give-me-death" buncombe from morning till night and the other asleep, with his slab soled brogans set up like a couple of gravestones on the top of his desk.

——•——

BOB ROACH'S PLAN FOR CIRCUMVENTING A DEMOCRAT
[*Examiner*, Nov. 30, 1865]

Where did all these Democrats come from? They grow thicker and thicker and act more and more outrageously at each successive election. Now yesterday they had the presumption to elect S. H. Dwinelle to the Judgeship of the Fifteenth District Court, and not content with this, they were depraved enough to elect four out of the six Justices of the Peace! Oh, 'Enery Villiam, where is thy blush! Oh, Timothy Hooligan, where is thy shame? It's out. Democrats haven't got any. But Union men staid away from the election—they either did that or else they came to the election and voted Democratic tickets—I think it was the latter, though the Flag will doubtless say it was the former. But these Democrats didn't stay away—you never catch a Democrat staying away from an election. The grand end and aim of his life is to vote or be voted for, and he accommodates to circumstances and does one just as cheerfully as he does the other. The Democracy of America left their native wilds in England and Connaught to come here and vote— and when a man, and especially a foreigner, who don't have any voting at home any more than an Arkansas man has ice-cream for dinner, comes three or four thousand miles to luxuriate in occasional voting, he isn't going to stay away from an election any more than the Arkansas man will leave the hotel table in "Orleans" until he has destroyed most of the ice cream. The only man I ever knew who could counteract this passion on the part of Democrats for voting, was Robert Roach, carpenter of the steamer Aleck Scott, "plying to and from St. Louis to New Orleans and back," as her advertisement sometimes read. The Democrats generally came up as deck passengers from New Orleans, and the yellow fever used to snatch them right and left—eight or nine a day for the first six or eight hundred miles; consequently Roach would have a lot on hand to "plant" every time the boat landed to wood—"plant" was Roach's word. One day as Roach was superintending a burial the Captain came up and said:

"God bless my soul, Roach, what do you mean by shoving a corpse into a hole in the hill-side in this barbarous way, face down and its feet sticking out?"

"I always plant them foreign Democrats in that manner, sir, because, damn their souls, if you plant 'em any other way they'll dig out and vote the first time there's an election—but look at that fellow, now—you put 'em in head first and face down and the more they dig the deeper they'll go into the hill."

In my opinion, if we do not get Roach to superintend our cemeteries, enough Democrats will dig out at the next election to carry their entire ticket. It begins to look that way.

---

from ANSWERS TO CORRESPONDENTS
[*The Californian*, June 24, 1865]

TRUE SON OF THE UNION.... Here is a drudging public servant who has always served his masters patiently and faithfully, and although there was nothing in his instructions requiring him to get drunk on national holidays, yet with an unselfishness, and an enlarged public spirit, and a gushing patriotism that did him infinite credit, he did always get as drunk as a loon on these occasions — ay, and even upon any occasion of minor importance when an humble effort on his part could shed additional lustre upon his country's greatness, never did he hesitate a moment to go and fill himself full of gin. Now observe how his splendid services have been appreciated—behold how quickly the remembrance of them hath passed away—mark how the tried servant has been rewarded. This grateful officer—this pure patriot—has been known to get drunk five hundred times in a year for the honor and glory of his country and his country's flag, and no man cried "Well done, thou good and faithful servant...."

EARTHQUAKES

> I will set it down here as a maxim
> that the operations of the
> human intellect are much accelerated
> by an earthquake.

ANOTHER OF THEM
[*Morning Call*, June 23, 1864]

At five minutes to nine o'clock last night, San Francisco was favored by another earthquake. There were three distinct shocks, two of which were very heavy, and appeared to have been done on purpose, but the third did not amount to much. Heretofore our earthquakes — as all old citizens experienced in this sort of thing will recollect — have been distinguished by a soothing kind of undulating motion, like the roll of waves on the sea, but we are happy to state that they are shaking her up from below now. The shocks last night came straight up from that direction; and it is sad to reflect, in these spiritual times, that they might possibly have been freighted with urgent messages from some of our departed friends. The suggestion is worthy a moment's serious reflection, at any rate.

THE BOSS EARTHQUAKE
[*Morning Call*, July 22, 1864]

When we contracted to report for this newspaper, the important matter of two earthquakes a month was not considered in the salary. There shall be no mistake of that kind in the next contract, though. Last night, at twenty minutes to eleven, the regular semi monthly earthquake, due the night before, arrived twenty-four hours behind time, but it made up for the delay in uncommon and altogether unnecessary energy and enthusiasm. The first effort was so gentle as to move the inexperienced stranger to the expression of contempt and brave but very bad jokes; but the second was calculated to move him out of his boots, unless they fitted him neatly. Up in the third story of this building the sensation we experienced was as if we had been sent for and were mighty anxious to go. The house seemed to waltz from side to side with a quick motion, suggestive of sifting corn meal through a sieve; afterward it rocked grandly to and fro like a prodigious cradle, and in the meantime several persons started downstairs to see if there were anybody in the street so timid as to be frightened at a mere earthquake. The third shock was not important, as compared with the stunner that had just preceded it. That second shock drove people out of the theatres by dozens. At the Metropolitan, we are told that Franks, the comedian, had just come on the stage (they were playing the "Ticket-of-Leave Man,") and was about to express the unbounded faith he had in May; he paused until the jarring had subsided, and then improved and added force to the text by exclaiming, "It will take more than an earthquake to shake my faith in that woman!" And in that, Franks achieved a sublime triumph over the elements, for he "brought the house down," and the earthquake couldn't. From the time the shocks commenced last night, until the windows had stopped rattling, a minute and a half had elapsed.

***

EARTHQUAKE
[*Morning Call*, Sept. 8, 1864]

The regular semi-monthly earthquake arrived at ten minutes to ten o'clock, yesterday morning. Thirty-six hours ahead of time. It is supposed it was sent earlier, to shake up the Democratic State Convention, but if this was the case, the calculation was awkwardly made, for it fell short by about two hours. The Convention did not meet until noon. Either the earthquake or the Convention, or both combined, made the atmosphere mighty dense and sulphurous all day. If it was the Democrats alone, they do not smell good, and it certainly cannot be healthy to have them around.

***

RUEL EARTHQUAKE [OF OCTOBER, 1865]
[*Gold Hill News*, Oct. 13, 1865]

A MODEL ARTIST STRIKES AN ATTITUDE

A young gentleman who lives in Sacramento street, rushed down stairs and appeared in public with no raiment on save a knit undershirt, which concealed his person about as much as its tinfoil cap conceals a champagne bottle. He struck an attitude such as a man assumes when he is looking up, expecting danger from above, and bends his arm and holds it aloft to ward off possible missiles—and standing thus he glared fiercely up at the fire-wall of a tall building opposite, from which a few bricks had fallen. Men shouted at him to go in the house, people seized him by the arm and tried to drag him away—even tender-hearted women (O, Woman!—O ever noble, unselfish, angelic woman!—O, Woman, in our hours of ease uncertain, coy, and hard to please—when anything happens to go wrong with our harness, a ministering angel thou), women, I say, averted their faces, and nudging the paralyzed and impassible statue in the ribs with their elbows beseeched him to take their aprons—to take their shawls—to take their hoop-skirts—anything, anything, so that he would not stand there longer in such a plight and distract people's attention from the earthquake. But he wouldn't budge—he stood there in his naked majesty till the last tremor died away from the earth, and then looked around on the multitude—and stupidly enough, too, until his dull eye fell upon himself. He went back up stairs, then. He went up lively.

WHAT HAPPENED TO A FEW VIRGINIANS—
CHARLEY BRYAN CLIMBS A TELEGRAPH POLE.

But where is the use in dwelling on these incidents? There are enough of them to make a book. Joe Noques, of your city, was playing billiards in the Cosmopolitan Hotel. He went through a window into the court and then jumped over an iron gate eighteen feet high, and took his billiard cue with him. Sam Witgenstein took refuge in a church—probably the first time he was ever in one in his life. Judge Bryan climbed a telegraph pole. Pete Hopkins narrowly escaped injury. He was shaken abruptly from the summit of Telegraph Hill and fell on a three-story brick house ten feet below. I see that the morning papers (always ready to smooth over things), attribute the destruction of the house to the earthquake. That is newspaper magnanimity—but an earthquake has no friends. Extraordinary things happened to everybody except

me. No one even spoke to me — at least only one man did, I believe —
a man named Robinson — from Salt Lake, I think — who asked me to
take a drink. I refused.

—————•—•—————

THE GREAT EARTHQUAKE IN SAN FRANCISCO
[*New York Weekly Review*, Nov. 25, 1865]

San Francisco, Oct. 8, 1865

EDITORS REVIEW.

Long before this reaches your city, the telegraph will have mentioned
to you, casually, that San Francisco was visited by an earthquake to-
day, and the daily prints will have conveyed the news to their readers
with the same air of indifference with which it was clothed by the
unimpassioned lightning, and five minutes afterward the world will
have forgotten the circumstance, under the impression that just such
earthquakes are every-day occurrences here, and therefore not worth
remembering. But if you had been here you would have conceived
very different notions from these. To-day's earthquake was no ordinary
affair. It is likely that future earthquakes in this vicinity, for years to
come, will suffer by comparison with it.

I have tried a good many of them here, and of several varieties —
some that came in the form of a universal shiver; others that gave us
two or three sudden upward heaves from below; others that swayed
grandly and deliberately from side to side; and still others that came
rolling and undulating beneath our feet like a great wave of the sea.
But to-day's specimen belonged to a new, and, I hope, a very rare,
breed of earthquakes. first, there was a quick, heavy shock; three or
four seconds elapsed, and then the city and county of San Francisco
darted violently from north-west to south-east, and from south-east to
north-west five times with extraordinary energy and rapidity. I say
"darted," because that word comes nearest to describing the movement.

I was walking along Third street, and facing north, when the first
shock came; I was walking fast, and it "broke up my gait" pretty completely — checked me — just as a strong wind will do when you turn a
corner and face it suddenly. That shock was coming from the north-
west, and I met it half-way. I took about six or seven steps (went back
and measured the distance afterwards to decide a bet about the interval of time between the first and second shocks), and was just turning

the corner into Howard street when those five angry "darts" came. I suppose the first of them proceeded from the south-east, because it moved my feet toward the opposite point of the compass—to the left—and made me stagger against the corner house on my right. The noise accompanying the shocks was a tremendous rasping sound, like the violent shaking and grinding together of a block of brick houses. It was about the most disagreeable sound you can imagine.

I will set it down here as a maxim that the operations of the human intellect are much accelerated by an earthquake. Usually I do not think rapidly—but I did upon this occasion. I thought rapidly, vividly, and distinctly. With the first shock of the five, I thought—"I recognize that motion—this is an earthquake." With the second, I thought, "What a luxury this will be for the morning papers." With the third shock, I thought, "Well, my boy, you had better be getting out of this." Each of these thoughts was only the hundredth part of a second in passing through my mind. There is no incentive to rapid reasoning like an earthquake. I then sidled out toward the middle of the street—and I may say that I sidled out with some degree of activity, too. There is nothing like an earthquake to hurry a man up when he starts to go anywhere. As I went I glanced down to my left and saw the whole front of a large four-story brick building spew out and "splatter" abroad over the street in front of it. Another thought steamed through my brain. I thought this was going to be the greatest earthquake of the century, and that the city was going to be destroyed entirely, and I took out my watch and timed the event. It was twelve minutes to one o'clock, P. M. This showed great coolness and presence of mind on my part—most people would have been hunting for something to climb, instead of looking out for the best interests of history.

As I walked down the street—down the middle of the street—frequently glancing up with a sagacious eye at the houses on either side to see which way they were going to fall, I felt the earth shivering gently under me, and grew moderately sea-sick (and remained so for nearly an hour; others became excessively sleepy as well as sea-sick, and were obliged to go to bed, and refresh themselves with a sound nap.) A minute before the earthquake I had three or four streets pretty much to myself, as far as I could see down them (for we are a Sunday-respecting community, and go out of town to break the Sabbath) but five seconds after it I was lost in a swarm of crying children, and coat-less, hatless men and shrieking women. They were all in motion, too, and no two of them trying to run in the same direction. They charged simultaneously from opposite rows of houses, like opposing regiments from ambuscades, and came together with a crash and a yell in the centre of the street. Then came chaos and confusion, and a general digging out for somewhere else, they didn't know where, and didn't care.

Everything that *was* done, was done in the twinkling of an eye — there was no apathy visible anywhere. A street car stopped close at hand, and disgorged its passengers so suddenly that they all seemed to flash out at the self-same instant of time.

The crowd was in danger from outside influences for a while. A horse was coming down Third street, with a buggy attached to him, and following after him — either by accident or design — and the horse was either frightened at the earthquake or a good deal surprised — I cannot say which, because I do not know how horses are usually affected by such things — but at any rate he must have been opposed to earthquakes, because he started to leave there, and took the buggy and his master with him, and scattered them over a piece of ground as large as an ordinary park, and finally fetched up against a lamp-post with nothing hanging to him but a few strips of harness suitable for fiddle-strings. However he might have been affected previously, the expression upon his countenance at this time was one of unqualified surprise. The driver of the buggy was found intact and unhurt, but to the last degree dusty and blasphemous. As the crowds along the street had fortunately taken chances on the earthquake and opened out to let the horse pass, no one was injured by his stampede.

When I got to the locality of the shipwrecked four-story building before spoken of, I found that the front of it, from eaves to pavement, had fallen out, and lay in ruins on the ground. The roof and floors were broken down and dilapidated. It was a new structure and unoccupied, and by rare good luck it damaged itself alone by its fall. The walls were only three bricks thick, a fact which, taking into account the earthquakiness of the country, evinces an unquestioning trust in Providence, on the part of the proprietor, which is as gratifying as it is impolitic and reckless.

I turned into Mission street and walked down to Second without finding any evidences of the great ague, but in Second street itself I traveled half a block on shattered window glass. The large hotels, farther down town, were all standing, but the boarders were all in the

street. The plastering had fallen in many of the rooms, and a gentleman who was in an attic chamber of the Cosmopolitan at the time of
the quake, told me the water "sloshed" out of the great tanks on the
roof, and fell in sheets of spray to the court below. He said the huge
building rocked like a cradle after the first grand spasms; the walls
seemed to "belly" inward like a sail; and flakes of plastering began to
drop on him. He then went out and slid, feet foremost down one or
two hundred feet of banisters — partly for amusement, but chiefly
with an eye to expedition. He said he flashed by the frantic crowds in
each succeeding story like a telegraphic dispatch.

Several ladies felt a faintness and dizziness in the head, and one
(incredible as it may seem), weighing over two hundred and fifty
pounds, fainted all over. They hauled her out of her room, and deluged
her with water, but for nearly half an hour all efforts to resuscitate her
were fruitless. It is said that the noise of the earthquake on the ground
floor of the hotel, which is paved with marble, was as if forty freight
trains were thundering over it. The large billiard saloon in the rear of
the office was full of people at the time, but a moment afterward numbers of them were seen flying up the street with their billiard-cues in
their hands, like a squad of routed lancers. Three jumped out of a back
window into the central court, and found themselves imprisoned —
for the tall, spike-armed iron gate which bars the passage-way for coal
and provision wagons was locked.

"What did you do then?" I asked.

"Well, Conrad, from Humboldt — you know him — Conrad said,
'let's climb over, boys, and be devilish quick about it, too' — and he
made a dash for it — but Smith and me started in last and were first
over — because the seat of Conrad's pants caught on the spikes at the
top, and we left him hanging there and yelling like an Injun."

And then my friend called my attention to the gate and said:
"There's the gate — ten foot high, I should think, and nothing to catch
hold of to climb by — but don't you know I went over that gate like a
shot out of a shovel, and took my billiard-cue along with me? — I did
it, as certain as I am standing here — but if I could do it again for
fifteen hundred thousand dollars, I'll be d—— d — not unless there
was another earthquake, anyway."

From the fashionable barber-shops in the vicinity gentlemen
rushed into the thronged streets in their shirt-sleeves, with towels
round their necks, and with one side of their faces smoothly shaved,

and the other side foamy with lather.

One gentleman was having his corns cut by a barber, when the premonitory shock came. The barber's under-jaw dropped, and he stared aghast at the dancing furniture. The gentleman winked complacently at the by-standers, and said with fine humor, "Oh, go on with your surgery, John—it's nothing but an earthquake; no use to run, you know, because if you're going to the devil anyhow, you might as well start from here as outside." Just then the earth commenced its hideous grinding and surging movement, and the gentleman retreated toward the door, remarking, "However, John, if we've *got* to go, perhaps we'd as well start from the street, after all."

On North Beach, men ran out of the bathing houses attired like the Greek slave, and mingled desperately with ladies and gentlemen who were as badly frightened as themselves, but more elaborately dressed.

The City Hall which is a large building, was so dismembered, and its walls sprung apart from each other, that the structure will doubtless have to be pulled down. The earthquake rang a merry peal on the City Hall bell, the "clapper" of which weighs seventy-eight pounds. It is said that several engine companies turned out, under the impression that the alarm was struck by the fire-telegraph.

Bells of all sorts and sizes were rung by the shake throughout the city, and from what I can learn the earthquake formally announced its visit on every door-bell in town. One gentleman said: "My door-bell fell to ringing violently, but I said to myself, 'I know *you*—you are an Earthquake; and you appear to be in a hurry; but you'll jingle that bell considerably before *I* let you in—on the contrary, I'll crawl under this sofa and get out of the way of the plastering.'"

I went down toward the city front and found a brick warehouse mashed in as if some foreigner from Brobdignag had sat down on it.

All down Battery street the large brick wholesale houses were pretty universally shaken up, and some of them badly damaged, the roof of one being crushed in, and the fire-walls of one or two being ripped off even with the tops of the upper windows, and dumped into the street below.

The tall shot tower in First street weathered the storm, but persons who watched it respectfully from a distance said it swayed to and fro like a drunken giant.

I saw three chimneys which were broken in two about three feet from the top, and the upper sections slewed around until they sat corner-wise on the lower ones.

The damage done to houses by this earthquake is estimated at over half a million of dollars.

But I had rather talk about the "incidents." The Rev. Mr. Harmon, Principal of the Pacific Female Seminary, at Oakland, just across the Bay from here, had his entire flock of young ladies at church — and also his wife and children — and was watching and protecting them jealously, like one of those infernal scaly monsters with a pestilential breath that were employed to stand guard over imprisoned heroines in the days of chivalry, and who always proved inefficient in the hour of danger — he was watching them, I say, when the earthquake came, and what do you imagine he did, then? Why that confiding trust in Providence which had sustained him through a long ministerial career all at once deserted him, and he got up and ran like a quarter-horse. But that was not the misfortune of it. The exasperating feature of it was that his wife and children and all the school-girls remained bravely in their seats and sat the earthquake through without flinching. Oakland talks and laughs again at the Pacific Female Seminary.

The Superintendent of the Congregational Sunday School in Oakland had just given out the text, "And the earth shook and trembled," when the earthquake came along and took up the text and preached the sermon for him.

The Pastor of Starr King's church, the Rev. Mr. Stebbins, came down out of his pulpit after the first shock and embraced a woman. It was an instance of great presence of mind. Some say the woman was his wife, but I regard the remark as envious and malicious. Upon occasions like this, people who are too much scared to seize upon an offered advantage, are always ready to depreciate the superior judgment and sagacity of those who profited by the opportunity they lost themselves.

In a certain aristocratic locality up-town, the wife of a foreign dignitary is the acknowledged leader of fashion, and whenever she emerges from her house all the ladies in the vicinity fly to the windows to see what she has "got on," so that they may make immediate arrangements to procure similar costumes for themselves. Well, in the midst of the earthquake, the beautiful foreign woman (who had just indulged in a bath) appeared in the street *with a towel around her neck*. It was all the raiment she had on. Consequently, in that vicinity, a towel around the neck is considered the only orthodox "earthquake costume." Well, and why not? It is elegant, and airy, and simple, and graceful, and pretty, and are not these the chief requisites in female dress? If it were generally adopted it would go far toward reconciling some people to these dreaded earthquakes.

An enterprising barkeeper down town who is generally up with the times, has already invented a sensation drink to meet the requirements of our present peculiar circumstances. A friend in whom I have confidence, thus describes it to me: "A tall ale-glass is nearly filled with California brandy and Angelica wine—one part of the former to two of the latter; fill to the brim with champagne; charge the drink with electricity from a powerful galvanic battery, and swallow it before the lightning cools. Then march forth—and before you have gone a hundred yards you will think you are occupying the whole street; a parlor clock will look as big as a church; to blow your nose will astonish you like the explosion of a mine, and the most trivial abstract matter will seem as important as the Day of Judgment. When you want this extraordinary drink, disburse your twenty-five cents, and call for an 'EARTHQUAKE.'" MARK TWAIN.

EARTHQUAKE ALMANAC
[*Dramatic Chronicle*, Oct. 17, 1865]

EDS. CHRONICLE:—At the instance of several friends who feel a boding anxiety to know beforehand what sort of phenomena we may expect the elements to exhibit during the next month or two, and who have lost all confidence in the various patent medicine almanacs, because of the unaccountable reticence of those works concerning the extraordinary event of the 8th inst., I have compiled the following almanac expressly for this latitude:

Oct. 17.—Weather hazy; atmosphere murky and dense. An expression of profound melancholy will be observable upon most countenances.

Oct. 18.—Slight earthquake. Countenances grow more melancholy.

Oct. 19.—Look out for rain. It would be absurd to look in for it. The general depression of spirits increased.

Oct. 20.—More weather.

Oct. 21.—Same.

Oct. 22.—Light winds, perhaps. If they blow, it will be from the "east'ard, or the nor'ard, or the west'ard, or the suth'ard," or from some general direction approximating more or less to these points of the compass or otherwise. Winds are uncertain—more especially when they blow from whence they cometh and whither they listeth. N. B.—Such is the nature of winds.

Oct. 23. — Mild, balmy earthquakes.

Oct. 24. — Shaky.

Oct. 25. — Occasional shakes, followed by light showers of bricks and plastering. N. B. — Stand from under.

Oct. 26. — Considerable phenomenal atmospheric foolishness About this time expect more earthquakes, but do not look out for them, on account of the bricks.

Oct. 27. — Universal despondency, indicative of approaching disaster. Abstain from smiling, or indulgence in humorous conversation, or exasperating jokes.

Oct. 28. — Misery, dismal forebodings and despair. Beware of all light discourse — a joke uttered at this time would produce a popular outbreak.

Oct. 29. — Beware!

Oct. 30. — Keep dark!

Oct. 31. — Go slow!

Nov. 1. — Terrific earthquake. This is the great earthquake month. More stars fall and more worlds are slathered around carelessly and destroyed in November than in any other month of the twelve.

Nov. 2. — Spasmodic but exhilarating earthquakes, accompanied by occasional showers of rain, and churches and things.

Nov. 3. — Make your will.

Nov. 4. — Sell out.

Nov. 5. — Select your "last words." Those of John Quincy Adams will do, with the addition of a syllable, thus: "This is the last of earth-quakes."

Nov. 6. — Prepare to shed this mortal coil.

Nov. 7. — Shed!

Nov. 8. — The sun will rise as usual, perhaps; but if he does he will doubtless be staggered some to find nothing but a large round hole eight thousand miles in diameter in the place where he saw this world serenely spinning the day before. MARK TWAIN.

No Earthquake
[*Morning Call*, Aug. 23, 1864]

In consequence of the warm, close atmosphere which smothered the city at two o'clock yesterday afternoon, everybody expected to be shaken out of their boots by an earthquake before night, but up to the hour of our going to press the supernatural boot-jack had not arrived yet. That is just what makes it so unhealthy — the earthquakes are getting so irregular. When a community get used to a thing, they suffer when they have to go without it. However, the trouble cannot be remedied; we know of nothing that will answer as a substitute for one of those convulsions — to an unmarried man.

from ROUGHING IT

A month afterward I enjoyed my first earthquake. It was one which was long called the "great" earthquake, and is doubtless so distinguished till this day. It was just after noon, on a bright October day. I was coming down Third street. The only objects in motion anywhere in sight in that thickly built and populous quarter, were a man in a buggy behind me, and a street car wending slowly up the cross street. Otherwise, all was solitude and a Sabbath stillness. As I turned the corner, around a frame house, there was a great rattle and jar, and it occurred to me that here was an item! — no doubt a fight in that house. Before I could turn and seek the door, there came a really terrific shock; the ground seemed to roll under me in waves, interrupted by a violent joggling up and down, and there was a heavy grinding noise as of brick houses rubbing together. I fell up against the frame house and hurt my elbow. I knew what it was, now, and from mere reportorial instinct, nothing else, took out my watch and noted the time of day; at that moment a third and still severer shock came, and as I reeled about on the pavement trying to keep my footing, I saw a sight! The entire front of a tall four-story brick building in Third street sprung outward like a door and fell sprawling across the street, raising a dust like a great volume of smoke! And here came the buggy — overboard went the man, and in less time than I can tell it the vehicle was distributed in small fragments along three hundred yards of street. One could have fancied that somebody had fired a charge of chair-rounds and rags down the thoroughfare. The street car had stopped, the horses were rearing and plunging, the passengers were pouring out at both ends, and one fat man had crashed half way through a glass window on one side of the car, got wedged fast and was squirming and screaming like an impaled madman. Every door, of every house, as far as the eye could reach, was vomiting a stream of human beings; and almost before one could execute a wink and begin another, there was a massed multitude of people stretching in endless procession down every street my position commanded. Never was solemn solitude turned into teeming life quicker.

Of the wonders wrought by "the great earthquake," these were all that came under my eye; but the tricks it did, elsewhere, and far and wide over the town, made toothsome gossip for nine days. The destruction of property was trifling—the injury to it was wide-spread and somewhat serious.

The "curiosities" of the earthquake were simply endless. Gentlemen and ladies who were sick, or were taking a siesta, or had dissipated till a late hour and were making up lost sleep, thronged into the public streets in all sorts of queer apparel, and some without any at all. One woman who had been washing a naked child, ran down the street holding it by the ankles as if it were a dressed turkey. Prominent citizens who were supposed to keep the Sabbath strictly, rushed out of saloons in their shirt-sleeves, with billiard cues in their hands. Dozens of men with necks swathed in napkins, rushed from barber-shops, lathered to the eyes or with one cheek clean shaved and the other still bearing a hairy stubble. Horses broke from stables, and a frightened dog rushed up a short attic ladder and out on to a roof, and when his scare was over had not the nerve to go down again the same way he had gone up. A prominent editor flew down stairs, in the principal hotel, with nothing on but one brief undergarment—met a chambermaid, and exclaimed:

"Oh, what *shall* I do! Where shall I go!"

She responded with naive serenity:

"If you have no choice, you might try a clothing-store!"...

The plastering that fell from ceilings in San Francisco that day, would have covered several acres of ground. For some days afterward, groups of eyeing and pointing men stood about many a building, looking at long zig-zag cracks that extended from the eaves to the ground. Four feet of the tops of three chimneys on one house were broken square off and turned around in such a way as to completely stop the draft. A crack a hundred feet long gaped open six inches wide in the middle of one street and then shut together again with such force, as to ridge up the meeting earth like a slender grave. A lady sitting in her rocking and quaking parlor, saw the wall part at the ceiling, open and shut twice, like a mouth, and then drop the end of a brick on the floor like a tooth. She was a woman easily disgusted with foolishness, and she arose and went out of there. One lady who was coming down stairs was astonished to see a bronze Hercules lean forward on its pedestal as if to strike her with its club. They both reached the bottom of the flight at the same time,—the woman insensible from the fright. Her child, born some little time afterward, was club-footed. However— on second thought,—if the reader sees any coincidence in this, he must do it at his own risk.

The first shock brought down two or three huge organ-pipes in one of the churches. The minister, with uplifted hands, was just closing the services. He glanced up, hesitated, and said:

"However, we will omit the benediction!"—and the next instant there was a vacancy in the atmosphere where he had stood.

After the first shock, an Oakland minister said:

"Keep your seats! There is no better place to die than this"—

And added, after the third:

"But outside is good enough!" He then skipped out at the back door.

Such another destruction of mantel ornaments and toilet bottles as the earthquake created, San Francisco never saw before. There was hardly a girl or a matron in the city but suffered losses of this kind. Suspended pictures were thrown down, but oftener still, by a curious freak of the earthquake's humor, they were whirled completely around with their faces to the wall! There was a great difference of opinion, at first, as to the course or direction the earthquake traveled, but water that splashed out of various tanks and buckets settled that. Thousands of people were made so sea-sick by the rolling and pitching of floors and streets that they were weak and bed-ridden for hours, and some few for even days afterward. Hardly an individual escaped nausea entirely.

The queer earthquake-episodes that formed the staple of San Francisco gossip for the next week would fill a much larger book than this, and so I will diverge from the subject.

SOCIETY PAGES

> Fashions? It is out of my line, Maria.
> How am I to know anything about such
> mysteries—I that languish alone?

A LOVE OF A BONNET DESCRIBED.
[*Evening Bulletin*, Oct. 30, 1865]

Well, you ought to see the new style of bonnets, and then die. You see, everybody has discarded ringlets and bunches of curls, and taken to the clod of compact hair on the "after-guard," which they call a "waterfall," though why they name it so I cannot make out, for it looks no more like one's general notion of a waterfall than a cabbage looks like a cataract. Yes, they have thrown aside the bunches of curls which necessitated the wearing of a bonnet with a back-door to it, or rather, a bonnet without any back to it at all, so that the curls bulged out from under an overhanging spray of slender feathers, sprigs of grass, etc. You know the kind of bonnet I mean; it was as if a lady spread a diaper on her head, with two of the corners brought down over her ears, and the other trimmed with a bunch of graceful flummery and allowed to hang over her waterfall—fashions are mighty tanglesome things to write—but I am coming to it directly. The diaper was the only beautiful bonnet women have worn within my recollection—but as they have taken exclusively to the waterfalls, now, they have thrown it aside and adopted, ah me, the infernalest, old-fashionedest, ruralest atrocity in its stead you ever saw. It is perfectly plain and hasn't a ribbon, or a flower, or any ornament whatever about it; it is severely shaped like the half of a lady's thimble split in two lengthwise—or would be if that thimble had a perfectly square end instead of a rounded one— just imagine it—glance at it in your mind's eye—and recollect, no ribbons, no flowers, no filagree — only the plainest kind of plain straw or plain black stuff. It don't come forward as far as the hair, and it fits to the head as tightly as a thimble fits, folded in a square mass against the back of the head, and the square end of the bonnet half covers it and fits as square and tightly against it as if somebody had hit the woman in the back of the head with a tombstone or some other heavy and excessively flat projectile. And a woman looks as distressed in it as a cat with her head fast in a tea-cup. It is infamous.

MORE FASHIONS—EXIT "WATERFALL."
[*Territorial Enterprise*, Oct. 1865]

I am told that the Empress Eugenie is growing bald on the top of her head, and that to hide this defect she now combs her "back-hair" forward in such a way as to make her look all right. I am also told that this mode of dressing the hair is already fashionable in all the great civilized cities of the world, and that it will shortly be adopted here. Therefore let your ladies "stand-by" and prepare to drum their ringlets to the front when I give the word. I shall keep a weather eye out for this fashion, for I am an uncompromising enemy of the popular "waterfall," and I yearn to see it in disgrace. Just think of the disgusting shape and appearance of the thing. The hair is drawn to a slender neck at the back, and then commences a great fat, oblong ball, like a kidney covered with a net; and sometimes this net is so thickly bespangled with white beads that the ball looks soft, and fuzzy, and filmy and gray at a little distance — so that it vividly reminds you of those nauseating garden spiders in the States that go about dragging a pulpy, grayish bagfull of young spiders slung to them behind; and when I look at these suggestive waterfalls and remember how sea-sick it used to make me to mash one of those spider-bags, I feel sea-sick again, as a general thing. Its shape alone is enough to turn one's stomach. Let's have the back-hair brought forward as soon as convenient. N. B. — I shall feel much obliged to you if you can aid me in getting up this panic. I have no wife of my own and therefore as long as I have to make the most of other people's it is a matter of vital importance to me that they should dress with some degree of taste.

from **MARK TWAIN ON FASHIONS**
[*Golden Era*, Feb. 25, 1866]

I once made up my mind to keep the ladies of the State of Nevada posted upon the fashions, but I found it hard to do. The fashions got so shaky that it was hard to tell what was good orthodox fashion, and what was heretical and vulgar. This shakiness still obtains in everything pertaining to a lady's dress except her bonnet and her shoes. Some wear waterfalls, some wear nets, some wear cataracts of curls, and a few go bald, among the old maids; so no man can swear to any particular "fashion" in the matter of hair.

The same uncertainty seems to prevail regarding hoops. Little "highflyer" schoolgirls of bad associations, and a good many women of full growth, wear no hoops at all. And we suspect these, as quickly and as naturally as we suspect a woman who keeps a poodle. Some who I know to be ladies, wear the ordinary moderate-sized hoops, and some who I also know to be ladies, wear the new hoop of the "spread-eagle" pattern—and some wear the latter who are not elegant and virtuous ladies—but that is a thing that may be said of any fashion whatever, of course. The new hoops with a spreading base look only tolerably well. They are not bell-shaped—the "spread" is much more abrupt than that. It is tent-shaped; I do not mean an army tent, but a circus tent—which comes down steep and small half way and then shoots suddenly out horizontally and spreads abroad. To critically examine these hoops—to get the best effect—one should stand on the corner of Montgomery and look up a steep street like Clay or Washington. As the ladies loop their dresses up till they lie in folds and festoons on the spreading hoop, the effect presented by a furtive glance up a steep street is very charming. It reminds me of how I used to peep under circus tents when I was a boy and see a lot of mysterious legs tripping about with no visible bodies attached to them. And what handsome varicolored, gold-clasped garters they wear now-a-days! But for the new spreading hoops, I might have gone on thinking ladies still tied up their stockings with common strings and ribbons as they used to do when I was a boy and they presumed upon my youth to indulge in little freedoms in the way of arranging their apparel which they do not dare to venture upon in my presence now. . . .

THE PIONEERS' BALL
[*The Californian*, Nov. 25, 1865]

It was estimated that four hundred persons were present at the ball. The gentlemen wore the orthodox costume for such occasions, and the ladies were dressed the best they knew how. N. B. — Most of these ladies were pretty, and some of them absolutely beautiful. Four out of every five ladies present were pretty. The ratio at the Colfax party was two out of every five. I always keep the run of these things. While upon this department of the subject, I may as well tarry a moment and furnish you with descriptions of some of the most noticeable costumes.

Mrs. W. M. was attired in an elegant *pate de foi gras*, made expressly for her, and was greatly admired.

Miss S. had her hair done up. She was the centre of attraction for the gentlemen, and the envy of all the ladies.

Miss G. W. was tastefully dressed in a *tout ensemble*, and was greeted with deafening applause wherever she went.

Mrs. C. N. was superbly arrayed in white kid gloves. Her modest and engaging manner accorded well with the unpretending simplicity of her costume, and caused her to be regarded with absorbing interest by every one.

The charming Miss M. M. B. appeared in a thrilling waterfall, whose exceeding grace and volume compelled the homage of pioneers and emigrants alike. How beautiful she was!

The queenly Mrs. L. R. was attractively attired in her new and beautiful false teeth, and the *bon jour* effect they naturally produced was heightened by her enchanting and well-sustained smile. The manner of this lady is charmingly pensive and melancholy, and her troops of admirers desired no greater happiness than to get on the scent of her sozodont-sweetened sighs and track her through her sinuous course among the gay and restless multitude.

Miss R. P., with that repugnance to ostentation in dress which is so peculiar to her, was attired in a simple white lace collar, fastened with a neat pearl-button solitaire. The fine contrast between the sparkling vivacity of her natural optic and the steadfast attentiveness of her placid glass eye was the subject of general and enthusiastic remark.

The radiant and sylph-like Mrs. T., late of your State, wore hoops. She showed to good advantage, and created a sensation wherever she appeared. She was the gayest of the gay.

Miss C. L. B. had her fine nose elegantly enameled, and the easy grace with which she blew it from time to time, marked her as a cultivated and accomplished woman of the world; its exquisitely modulated tone excited the admiration of all who had the happiness to hear it.

Being offended with Miss X., and our acquaintance having ceased permanently, I will take this opportunity of observing to her that it is of no use for her to be slopping off to every ball that takes place, and flourishing around with a brass oyster-knife skewered through her waterfall, and smiling her sickly smile through her decayed teeth, with her dismal pug nose in the air. There is no use in it—she don't fool anybody. Everybody knows she is old; everybody knows she is repaired (you might almost say built) with artificial bones and hair and muscles and things, from the ground up—put together scrap by scrap—and everybody knows, also, that all one would have to do would be to pull out her key-pin and she would go to pieces like a Chinese puzzle. There, now, my faded flower, take that paragraph home with you and amuse yourself with it; and if ever you turn your wart of a nose up at me again I will sit down and write something that will just make you rise up and howl.

CHILDREN & OTHER ANIMALS

**Familiarity breeds contempt—
and children.**

FROM **ANSWERS TO CORRESPONDENTS**
[*The Californian*, June 24, 1865]

YOUNG MOTHER.—And so you think a baby is a thing of beauty and a joy forever? Well, the idea is pleasing, but not original—every cow thinks the same of its own calf. Perhaps the cow may not think it so elegantly, but still she thinks it, nevertheless. I honor the cow for it. We all honor this touching maternal instinct wherever we find it, be it in the home of luxury or in the humble cow-shed. But really, madam, when I come to examine the matter in all its bearings, I find that the correctness of your assertion does not manifest itself in all cases. A sore-faced baby with a neglected nose cannot be conscientiously regarded as a thing of beauty, and inasmuch as babyhood spans but three short years, no baby is competent to be a joy "forever." It pains me thus to demolish two-thirds of your pretty sentiment in a single sentence, but the position I hold in this chair requires that I shall not permit you to deceive and mislead the public with your plausible figures of speech. I know a female baby aged eighteen months, in this city, which cannot hold out as a "joy" twenty-four hours on a stretch, let alone "forever." And it possesses some of the most remarkable eccentricities of character and appetite that have ever fallen under my notice. I will set down here a statement of this infant's operations, (conceived, planned and carried out by itself, and without suggestion or assistance from its mother or any one else,) during a single day— and what I shall say can be substantiated by the sworn testimony of witnesses. It commenced by eating one dozen large blue-mass pills, box and all; then it fell down a flight of stairs, and arose with a bruised and purple knot on its forehead, after which it proceeded in quest of further refreshment and amusement. It found a glass trinket ornamented with brass-work—mashed up and ate the glass, and then swallowed the brass. Then it drank about twenty or thirty drops of laudanum, and more than a dozen table-spoonsful of strong spirits of camphor. The reason why it took no more laudanum was, because there was no more to take. After this it lay down on its back, and shoved five or six inches of a silver-headed whalebone cane down its throat; got it fast there, and it was all its mother could do to pull the cane out again, without pulling out some of the child with it. Then, being hungry for glass again, it broke up several wine glasses, and fell to eating and swallowing the fragments, not minding a cut or two. Then it ate a quantity of butter, pepper, salt and California matches, actually taking a spoonful of butter, a spoonful of salt, a spoonful of pepper, and three or four lucifer matches, at each mouthful. (I will remark here that this thing of beauty likes painted German lucifers, and eats all she can get of them; but she infinitely prefers California matches—which I regard as a compliment to our home manufactures of more than ordinary value, coming, as it does, from one who is too young to flatter.) Then she washed her head with soap and water, and afterwards ate what soap was left, and drank as much of the suds as she had room for, after which she sallied forth and took the cow familiarly by the tail, and got kicked heels over head. At odd times during the day, when this joy forever happened to have nothing particular on hand, she put in the time by climbing up on places and falling down off them, uniformly damaging herself in the operation. As young as she is, she speaks many words tolerably distinctly, and being plain-spoken in other respects, blunt and to the point, she opens conversation with all strangers, male or female, with the same formula—"How do, Jim?" Not being familiar with the ways of children, it is possible that I have been magnifying into matter of surprise things which may not strike any one who is familiar with infancy as being at all astonishing. However, I cannot believe that such is the case, and so I repeat that my report of this baby's performances is strictly true—and if any one doubts it, I can produce the child. I will further engage that she shall devour anything that is given her, (reserving to myself only the right to exclude anvils,) and fall down from any place to which she may be elevated, (merely stipulating that her preference for alighting on her head shall be respected, and, therefore, that the elevation chosen shall be high enough to enable her to accomplish this to her satisfaction.) But I find I have wandered from my subject—so, without further argument, I will reiterate my conviction that not all babies are things of beauty and joys forever.

MORE CHILDREN
[*Morning Call*, Sept. 30, 1864]

It would have worried the good King Herod to see the army of school children that swarmed into the [Mechanics'] Fair yesterday, if he could have been there to suffer the discomfort of knowing he could not slaughter them under our eccentric system of government without getting himself into trouble. There were about eight hundred pupils of the Public Schools in the building at one time.

THE CHRISTMAS FIRESIDE
[*The Californian*, Dec. 23, 1865]

FOR GOOD LITTLE BOYS AND GIRLS.
By Grandfather Twain.
THE STORY OF A BAD LITTLE BOY THAT BORE A CHARMED LIFE.

Once there was a bad little boy, whose name was Jim—though, if you will notice, you will find that bad little boys are nearly always called James in your Sunday-school books. It was very strange, but still it was true, that this one was called Jim.

He didn't have a sick mother, either—a sick mother who was pious and had the consumption, and would be glad to lie down in the grave and be at rest, but for the strong love she bore her boy, and the anxiety she felt that the world would be harsh and cold toward him when she was gone. Most bad boys in the Sunday books are named James, and have sick mothers who teach them to say, "Now, I lay me down," etc., and sing them to sleep with sweet plaintive voices, and then kiss them good-night, and kneel down by the bedside and weep. But it was different with this fellow. He was named Jim, and there wasn't anything the matter with his mother—no consumption, or anything of that kind. She was rather stout than otherwise, and she was not pious; moreover, she was not anxious on Jim's account; she said if he were to break his neck, it wouldn't be much loss; she always spanked him to sleep, and she never kissed him good-night; on the contrary, she boxed his ears when she was ready to leave him.

Once, this little bad boy stole the key of the pantry and slipped in there and helped himself to some jam, and filled up the vessel with tar, so that his mother would never know the difference; but all at once a terrible feeling didn't come over him, and something didn't seem to whisper to him, "Is it right to disobey my mother? Isn't it sinful to do this? Where do bad little boys go who gobble up their good kind mother's jam?" and then he didn't kneel down all alone and promise never to be wicked any more, and rise up with a light, happy heart, and go and tell his mother all about it and beg her forgiveness, and be blessed by her with tears of pride and thankfulness in her eyes. No; that is the way with all other bad boys in the books, but it happened otherwise with this Jim, strangely enough. He ate that jam, and said it was bully, in his sinful, vulgar way; and he put in the tar, and said that was bully also, and laughed, and observed that "the old woman would get up and snort" when she found it out; and when she did find it out he denied knowing anything about it, and she whipped him severely, and he did the crying himself. Everything about this boy was curious—everything turned out differently with him from the way it does to the bad Jameses in the books.

Once he climbed up in Farmer Acorn's apple tree to steal apples, and the limb didn't break and he didn't fall and break his arm, and get torn by the farmer's great dog, and then languish on a sick bed for weeks and repent and become good. Oh, no—he stole as many apples as he wanted, and came down all right, and he was all ready for the dog, too, and knocked him endways with a rock when he came to tear him. It was very strange—nothing like it ever happened in those mild little books with marbled backs, and with pictures in them of men with swallow-tailed coats and bell-crowned hats and pantaloons that are short in the legs, and women with the waists of their dresses under their arms and no hoops on. Nothing like it in any of the Sunday-school books.

Once he stole the teacher's penknife, and when he was afraid it would be found out and he would get whipped, he slipped it into

George Wilson's cap—poor Widow Wilson's son, the moral boy, the good little boy of the village, who always obeyed his mother, and never told an untruth, and was fond of his lessons and infatuated with Sunday-school. And when the knife dropped from the cap and poor George hung his head and blushed, as if in conscious guilt, and the grieved teacher charged the theft upon him, and was just in the very act of bringing the switch down upon his trembling shoulders, a white-haired improbable justice of the peace did not suddenly appear in their midst and strike an attitude and say, "Spare this noble boy—there stands the cowering culprit! I was passing the school door at recess, and, unseen myself, I saw the theft committed!" And then Jim didn't get whaled, and the venerable justice didn't read the tearful school a homily, and take George by the hand and say such a boy deserved to be exalted, and then tell him to come and make his home with him, and sweep out the office, and make fires, and run errands, and chop wood, and study law, and help his wife to do household labors, and have all the balance of the time to play, and get forty cents a month, and be happy. No, it would have happened that way in the books, but it didn't happen that way to Jim. No meddling old clam of a justice dropped in to make trouble, and so the model boy George got threshed, and Jim was glad of it. Because, you know, Jim hated moral boys. Jim said he was "down on them milksops." Such was the coarse language of this bad, neglected boy.

But the strangest things that ever happened to Jim was the time he went boating on Sunday and didn't get drowned, and that other time that he got caught out in the storm when he was fishing on Sunday, and didn't get struck by lightning. Why, you might look, and look, and look through the Sunday-school books, from now till next Christmas, and you would never come across anything like this. Oh, no—you would find that all the bad boys who go boating on Sunday invariably get drowned, and all the bad boys who get caught out in storms, when they are fishing on Sunday, infallibly get struck by lightning. Boats with bad boys in them always upset on Sunday, and it always storms when bad boys go fishing on the Sabbath. How this Jim ever escaped is a mystery to me.

This Jim bore a charmed life—that must have been the way of it. Nothing could hurt him. He even gave the elephant in the menagerie a plug of tobacco, and the elephant didn't knock the top of his head off with his trunk. He browsed around the cupboard after essence of peppermint, and didn't make a mistake and drink aqua fortis. He stole his father's gun and went hunting on the Sabbath, and didn't shoot three or four of his fingers off. He struck his little sister on the temple with his fist when he was angry, and she didn't linger in pain through long summer days and die with sweet words of forgiveness upon her lips that redoubled the anguish of his breaking heart. No—she got over it. He ran off and went to sea at last, and didn't come back and find himself sad and alone in the world, his loved ones sleeping in the quiet church-yard, and the vine-embowered home of his boyhood tumbled down and gone to decay. Ah, no—he came home drunk as a piper, and got into the station house the first thing.

And he grew up, and married, and raised a large family, and brained them all with an axe one night, and got wealthy by all manner of cheating and rascality, and now he is the infernalest wickedest scoundrel in his native village, and is universally respected, and belongs to the Legislature.

So you see there never was a bad James in the Sunday-school books that had such a streak of luck as this sinful Jim with the charmed life.

<hr />

THE STORY OF THE GOOD LITTLE BOY
[*Sketches, New and Old*]

Once there was a good little boy by the name of Jacob Blivens. He always obeyed his parents, no matter how absurd and unreasonable their demands were; and he always learned his book, and never was late at Sabbath-school. He would not play hookey, even when his sober judgment told him it was the most profitable thing he could do. None of the other boys could ever make that boy out, he acted so strangely. He wouldn't lie, no matter how convenient it was. He just said it was wrong to lie, and that was sufficient for him. And he was so honest that he was simply ridiculous. The curious ways that that Jacob had, surpassed everything. He wouldn't play marbles on Sunday, he wouldn't rob birds' nests, he wouldn't give hot pennies to organ-grinders' monkeys; he didn't seem to take any interest in any kind of rational amusement. So the other boys used to try to reason it out and come to an understanding of him, but they couldn't arrive at any satisfactory conclusion. As I said before, they could only figure out a sort of vague idea that he was "afflicted," and so they took him under their protection, and never allowed any harm to come to him.

This good little boy read all the Sunday-school books; they were his greatest delight. This was the whole secret of it. He believed in the good little boys they put in the Sunday-school books; he had every confidence in them. He longed to come across one of them alive once; but he never did. They all died before his time, maybe. Whenever he read about a particularly good one he turned over quickly to the end to see what became of him, because he wanted to travel thousands of miles and gaze on him; but it wasn't any use; that good little boy always died in the last chapter, and there was a picture of his funeral, with all his relations and the Sunday-school children standing around the grave in pantaloons that were too short, and bonnets that were too large, and everybody crying into handkerchiefs that had as much as a yard and a half of stuff in them. He was always headed off in this way. He never could see one of those good little boys on account of his always dying in the last chapter.

Jacob had a noble ambition to be put in a Sunday-school book. He wanted to be put in, with pictures representing him gloriously declining to lie to his mother, and her weeping for joy about it; and pictures representing him standing on the doorstep giving a penny to a poor beggar-woman with six children, and telling her to spend it freely, but not to be extravagant, because extravagance is a sin; and pictures of him magnanimously refusing to tell on the bad boy who always lay in wait for him around the corner as he came from school, and welted him over the head with a lath, and then chased him home, saying, "Hi! hi!" as he proceeded. That was the ambition of young Jacob Blivens. He wished to be put in a Sunday-school book. It made him feel a little uncomfortable sometimes when he reflected that the good little boys always died. He loved to live, you know, and this was the most unpleasant feature about being a Sunday-school book boy. He knew it was not healthy to be good. He knew it was more fatal than consumption to be so supernaturally good as the boys in the books were; he knew that none of them had ever been able to stand it long, and it pained him to think that if they put him in a book he wouldn't ever see it, or even if they did get the book out before he died it wouldn't be popular without any picture of his funeral in the back part of it. It couldn't be much of a Sunday-school book that couldn't tell about the advice he gave to the community when he was dying. So at last, of course, he had to make up his mind to do the best he could under the circumstances—to live right, and hang on as long as he could, and have his dying speech all ready when his time came.

But somehow nothing ever went right with this good little boy; nothing ever turned out with him the way it turned out with the good little boys in the books. They always had a good time, and the bad boys had the broken legs; but in his case there was a screw loose somewhere, and it all happened just the other way. When he found Jim Blake stealing apples, and went under the tree to read to him about the bad little boy who fell out of a neighbor's apple tree and broke his arm, Jim fell out of the tree, too, but he fell on *him* and broke *his* arm, and Jim wasn't hurt at all. Jacob couldn't understand that. There wasn't anything in the books like it.

And once, when some bad boys pushed a blind man over in the mud, and Jacob ran to help him up and receive his blessing, the blind man did not give him any blessing at all, but whacked him over the head with his stick and said he would like to catch him shoving *him* again, and then pretending to help him up. This was not in accordance with any of the books. Jacob looked them all over to see.

One thing that Jacob wanted to do was to find a lame dog that hadn't any place to stay, and was hungry and persecuted, and bring him home and pet him and have that dog's imperishable gratitude. And at last he found one and was happy; and he brought him home and fed him, but when he was going to pet him the dog flew at him and tore all the clothes off him except those that were in front, and made a spectacle of him that was astonishing. He examined authorities, but he could not understand the matter. It was of the same breed of dogs that was in the books, but it acted very differently. Whatever this boy did he got into trouble. The very things the boys in the books got rewarded for turned out to be about the most unprofitable things he could invest in.

Once, when he was on his way to Sunday-school, he saw some bad boys starting off pleasuring in a sailboat. He was filled with consternation, because he knew from his reading that boys who went sailing on Sunday invariably got drowned. So he ran out on a raft to warn them, but a log turned with him and slid him into the river. A man got him out pretty soon, and the doctor pumped the water out of him, and gave him a fresh start with his bellows, but he caught cold and lay sick abed nine weeks. But the most unaccountable thing about it was that the bad boys in the boat had a good time all day, and then reached home alive and well in the most surprising manner. Jacob Blivens said there was nothing like these things in the books. He was perfectly dumbfounded.

When he got well he was a little discouraged, but he resolved to keep on trying anyhow. He knew that so far his experiences wouldn't do to go in a book, but he hadn't yet reached the allotted term of life for good little boys, and he hoped to be able to make a record yet if he could hold on till his time was fully up. If everything else failed he had his dying speech to fall back on.

He examined his authorities, and found that it was now time for him to go to sea as a cabin-boy. He called on a ship captain and made his application, and when the captain asked for his recommendations he proudly drew out a tract and pointed to the words, "To Jacob Blivens, from his affectionate teacher." But the captain was a coarse, vulgar man, and he said, "Oh, that be blowed! *that* wasn't any proof that he knew how to wash dishes or handle a slush-bucket, and he guessed he didn't want him." This was altogether the most extraordinary thing that ever happened to Jacob in all his life. A compliment from a teacher, on a tract, had never failed to move the tenderest emotions of ship captains, and open the way to all offices of honor and profit in their gift—it never had in any book that ever *he* had read. He could hardly believe his senses.

This boy always had a hard time of it. Nothing ever came out according to the authorities with him. At last, one day, when he was around hunting up bad little boys to admonish, he found a lot of them in the old iron foundry fixing up a little joke on fourteen or fifteen dogs, which they had tied together in a long procession, and were going to ornament with empty nitro-glycerine cans made fast to their tails. Jacob's heart was touched. He sat down on one of those cans (for he never minded grease when duty was before him), and he took hold of the foremost dog by the collar, and turned his reproving eye upon wicked Tom Jones. But just at that moment Alderman McWelter, full of wrath, stepped in. All the bad boys ran away, but Jacob Blivens rose in conscious innocence and began one of those stately little Sunday-school book speeches which always commence with "Oh, sir!" in dead opposition to the fact that no boy, good or bad, ever starts a remark with "Oh, sir." But the alderman never waited to hear the rest. He took Jacob Blivens by the ear and turned him around, and hit him a whack in the rear with the flat of his hand; and in an instant that good little boy shot out through the roof and soared away toward the sun, with the fragments of those fifteen dogs stringing after him like the tail of a kite. And there wasn't a sign of that alderman or that old iron foundry left on the face of the earth; and, as for young Jacob Blivens, he never got a chance to make his last dying speech after all his trouble fixing it up, unless he made it to the birds; because, although the bulk of him came down all right in a tree-top in an adjoining county, the rest of him was apportioned around among four townships, and so they had to hold five inquests on him to find out whether he was dead or not, and how it occurred. You never saw a boy scattered so.[*]

Thus perished the good little boy who did the best he could, but didn't come out according to the books. Every boy who ever did as he did prospered except him. His case is truly remarkable. It will probably never be accounted for.

ADVICE FOR GOOD LITTLE BOYS
[*San Francisco Youths' Companion*, July 1, 1865]

You ought never to take anything that don't belong to you—if you can not carry it off.

If you unthinkingly set up a tack in another boy's seat, you ought never to laugh when he sits down on it—unless you can't "hold in."

Good little boys must never tell lies when the truth will answer just as well. In fact, real good little boys will never tell lies at all—not at all—except in case of the most urgent necessity.

It is wrong to put a sheepskin under your shirt when you know that you are going to get a licking. It is better to retire swiftly to a secret place and weep over your bad conduct until the storm blows over.

You should never do anything wicked and then lay it on your brother, when it is just as convenient to lay it on another boy.

---

[*]This glycerine catastrophe is borrowed from a floating newspaper item, whose author's name I would give if I knew it.—[M. T.]

You ought never to call your aged grandpapa a "rum old file"—except when you want to be unusually funny.

You ought never to knock your little sisters down with a club. It is better to use a cat, which is soft. In doing this you must be careful to take the cat by the tail in such a manner that she cannot scratch you.

—•—

ADVICE FOR GOOD LITTLE GIRLS
[*San Francisco Youths' Companion*, July 1 or 8, 1865]

Good little girls ought not to make mouths at their teachers for every trifling offense. This kind of retaliation should only be resorted to under peculiarly aggravating circumstances.

If you have nothing but a rag doll stuffed with saw-dust, while one of your more fortunate playmates has a costly china one, you should treat her with a show of kindness, nevertheless. And you ought not to attempt to make a forcible swap with her unless your conscience would justify you in it, and you know you are able to do it.

You ought never to take your little brother's "chawing-gum" away from him by main force; it is better to rope him in with the promise of the first two dollars and a half you find floating down the river on a grindstone. In the artless simplicity natural to his time of life, he will regard it as a perfectly fair transaction. In all ages of the world this eminently plausible fiction has lured the obtuse infant to financial ruin and disaster.

If at any time you find it necessary to correct your brother, do not correct him with mud—never on any account throw mud at him, because it will soil his clothes. It is better to scald him a little; for then you attain two desirable results—you secure his immediate attention to the lesson you are inculcating, and, at the same time, your hot water will have a tendency to remove impurities from his person—and possibly the skin also, in spots.

If your mother tells you to do a thing, it is wrong to reply that you won't. It is better and more becoming to intimate that you will do as she bids you, and then afterward act quietly in the matter according to the dictates of your better judgment.

You should ever bear in mind that it is to your kind parents that you are indebted for your food and your nice bed and your beautiful clothes, and for the privilege of staying home from school when you let on that you are sick. Therefore you ought to respect their little prejudices and humor their little whims and put up with their little foibles until they get to crowding you too much.

Good little girls should always show marked deference for the aged. You ought never to "sass" old people—unless they "sass" you first.

LOST CHILD
[*Morning Call*, Sept. 2, 1864]

A fat, chubby infant, about two years old, was found by the police yesterday evening, lying fast asleep in the middle of Folsom street, between Sixth and Seventh, and in dangerous proximity to the railroad track. We saw the cheerful youngster in the city jail last night, sitting contentedly in the arms of a negro man who is employed about the establishment. He had been taking another sleep by the stove in the jail kitchen. Possibly the following description of the waif may be recognized by some distressed mother who did not rest well last night: A fat face, serious countenance; considerable dignity of bearing; flaxen hair; eyes dark bluish gray, (by gaslight, at least;) a little soiled red jacket; brown frock, with pinkish squares on it half an inch across; kid gaiter shoes and red-striped stockings; evidently admires his legs, and answers "Dah-dah" to each and all questions, with strict impartiality. Any one having lost an offspring of the above description can get it again by proving property and paying for this advertisement.

FROM "THOSE BLASTED CHILDREN"
[*Golden Era*, March 27, 1864]

Lick House, San Francisco
Wednesday, 1864

No. 165 is a pleasant room. It is situated at the head of a long hall, down which, on either side, are similar rooms occupied by sociable bachelors, and here and there one tenanted by an unsociable nurse or so. Charley Creed sleeps in No. 157. He is my timepiece—or, at least, his boots are. If I look down the hall and see Charley's boots still before his door, I know it is early yet, and I may hie me sweetly to bed again. But if those unerring boots are gone, I know it is after eleven o'clock, and time for me to be rising with the lark.

This reminds me of the lark of yesterday and last night, which was altogether a different sort of bird from the one I am talking about now. Ah me! Summer girls and summer dresses, and summer scenes at the "Willows", Seal Rock Point, and the grim sea-lions wallowing in the angry surf; glimpses through the haze of stately ships far away at sea; a dash along the smooth beach, and the exhilaration of watching the white waves come surging ashore, and break into seething foam about the startled horse's feet; reveries beside the old wreck, half buried in sand, and compassion for the good ship's fate; home again in a soft twilight, oppressed with the odor of flowers—home again to San Francisco, drunk, perhaps, but not disorderly. Dinner at six, with ladies and gentlemen dressed with faultless taste and elegance, and all drunk, apparently, but very quiet and well-bred—unaccountably so, under the circumstances, it seemed to my cloudy brain. Many things happened after that, I remember—such as visiting some of their haunts with those dissipated *Golden Era* fellows, and—

Here come those young savages again—those noisy and inevitable children. God be with them!—or they with him, rather, if it be not asking too much. They are another time-piece of mine. It is two o'clock now; they are invested with their regular lunch, and have come up here to settle it. I will soothe my troubled spirit with a short season of blasphemy, after which I will expose their infamous proceedings with a relentless pen. They have driven me from labor many and many a time; but behold! the hour of retribution is at hand.

That is young Washington Billings, now—a little dog in long flaxen curls and Highland costume.

"Hi, Johnny! look through the keyhole! here's that feller with a long nose, writing again—less stir him up!" (A double kick against the door—a grand infant war-whoop in full chorus—and then a clatter of scampering feet....)

"You, Bob Miller, you leg go that string—I'll smack you in the eye." "You will, will you? I'd like to see you try it. You jes' hit me if you dare!" "You lay your hands on me, 'n I will hit you." "Now I've laid my hand on you, why don't you hit?" "Well, I mean, if you lay 'em on me so's to hurt." "Ah-h! you're afraid, that's the reason!" "No I ain't, neither, you big fool." (Ah, now they're at it. Discord shall invade the ranks of my foes, and they shall fall by their own hands. It appears from the sound without that two nurses have made a descent upon the combatants, and are bearing them from the field. The nurses are abusing each other. One boy proclaims that the other struck him when he wasn't doin' nothin'; and the other boy says he was called a big fool. Both are going right straight, and tell their pa's. Verily, things are going along as comfortably as I could wish, now.) "Sandy Baker, I know what makes your pa's hair kink so; it's cause he's a mulatter; I heard my ma say so." "It's a lie!" (Another row, and more skirmishing with the nurses. Truly, happiness flows in upon me most bountifully this day.) "Hi, boys! here comes a Chinaman!" (God pity any Chinaman who chances to come in the way of the boys hereabout, for the eye of the law regardeth him not, and the youth of California in their generation are down upon him.) "Now, boys! grab his clothes basket — take him by the tail!" (There they go, now, like a pack of young demons; they have confiscated the basket, and the dismayed Chinaman is towing half the tribe down the hall by his cue. Rejoice, O my soul, for behold, all things are lovely, etc. — to speak after the manner of the vulgar.) "Oho, Miss Susy Badger, my uncle Tom's goin' across the bay to Oakland, 'n' down to Santa Clara, 'n' Alamedy, 'n' San Leandro, 'n' everywheres — all over the world, 'n' he's goin' to take me with him — he said so." "Humph! that ain't noth'n — I been there. My aunt Mary'd take me to any place I wanted to go, if I wanted her to, but I don't; she's got horses 'n' things — O, ever so many! — millions of 'em; but my ma says it don't look well for little girls to be always gadd'n about. That's why you don't ever see me goin' to places like some girls do. I despise to —" (The end is at hand; the nurses have massed themselves on the left; they move in serried phalanx on my besiegers; they surround them, and capture the last miscreant — horse, foot, and dragoons, munitions of war, and camp equipage. The victory is complete. They are gone — my castle is no longer menaced, and the rover is free. I am here, staunch and true!)

It is a living wonder to me that I haven't scalped some of those children before now. I expect I would have done it, but then I hardly felt well enough acquainted with them. I scarcely ever show them any attention anyhow, unless it is to throw a boot-jack at them or some little nonsense of that kind when I happen to feel playful. I am confident I would have destroyed several of them though, only it might appear as if I were making most too free.

I observe that that young officer of the Pacific squadron—the one with his nostrils turned up like port-holes—has become a great favorite with half the mothers in the house, by imparting to them much useful information concerning the manner of doctoring children among the South American savages.... Now, I am no peanut. I have an idea that I could invent some little remedies that would stir up a commotion among these women, if I chose to try. I always had a good general notion of physic, I believe. It is one of my natural gifts, too, for I have never studied a single day under a regular physician. I will jot down a few items here, just to see how likely I am to succeed.

In the matter of measles, the idea is, to bring it out—bring it to the surface. Take the child and fill it up with saffron tea. Add something to make the patient sleep—say a tablespoonful of arsenic. Don't rock it—it will sleep anyhow.

As far as brain fever is concerned: This is a very dangerous disease, and must be treated with decision and dispatch. In every case where it has proved fatal, the sufferer invariably perished. You must strike at the root of the distemper. Remove the brains; and then — Well, that will be sufficient—that will answer—just remove the brains. This remedy has never been known to fail. It was invented by the lamented J. W. Macbeth, Thane of Cawdor, Scotland, who refers to it thus: "Time was, that when the brains were out, the man would die; but, under different circumstances, I think not; and, all things being equal, I believe you, my boy." Those were his last words.

Concerning worms: Administer a catfish three times a week. Keep the room very quiet; the fish won't bite if there is the least noise.

When you come to fits, take no chances on fits. If the child has them bad, soak it in a barrel of rain-water over night, or a good article of vinegar. If this does not put an end to its troubles, soak it a week. You can't soak a child too much when it has fits.

In cases wherein an infant stammers, remove the under-jaw. In proof of the efficacy of this treatment, I append the following certificate, voluntarily forwarded to me by Mr. Zeb. Leavenworth, of St. Louis, Mo.

St. Louis, May 26, 1863
"Mr. Mark Twain—Dear Sir:—Under Providence, I am beholden to you for the salvation of my Johnny. For a matter of three years, that

suffering child stuttered to that degree that it was a pain and a sorrow to me to hear him stagger over the sacred name of 'p-p-p-pap.' It troubled me so that I neglected my business; I refused food; I took no pride in my dress, and my hair actually began to fall off. I could not rest; I could not sleep. Morning, noon, and night, I did nothing but moan pitifully, and murmur to myself: 'Hell's fire, what am I going to do about my Johnny?' But in a blessed hour you appeared unto me like an angel from the skies; and without hope of reward, revealed your sovereign remedy—and that very day, I sawed off my Johnny's under-jaw. May Heaven bless you, noble Sir. It afforded instant relief; and my Johnny has never stammered since. I honestly believe he never will again. As to disfigurement, he does seem to look sorter ornery and hog-mouthed, but I am too grateful in having got him effectually saved from that dreadful stuttering, to make much account of small matters. Heaven speed you in your holy work of healing the afflictions of humanity. And if my poor testimony can be of any service to you, do with it as you think will result in the greatest good to our fellow-creatures. Once more, Heaven bless you. *Zeb. Leavenworth.*"

Now, that has such a plausible ring about it, that I can hardly keep from believing it myself. I consider it a very fair success.

Regarding Cramps. Take your offspring—let the same be warm and dry at the time—and immerse it in a commodious soup-tureen filled with the best quality of camphene. Place it over a slow fire, and add reasonable quantities of pepper, mustard, horse-radish, saltpetre, strychnine, blue vitriol, aqua fortis, a quart of flour, and eight or ten fresh eggs, stirring it from time to time, to keep up a healthy reaction. Let it simmer fifteen minutes. When your child is done, set the tureen off, and allow the infallible remedy to cool. If this does not confer an entire insensibility to cramps, you must lose no time, for the case is desperate. Take your offspring, and parboil it. The most vindictive cramps cannot survive this treatment; neither can the subject, unless it is endowed with an iron constitution. It is an extreme measure, and I always dislike to resort to it. I never parboil a child until everything else has failed to bring about the desired end.

Well, I think those will do to commence with. I can branch out, you know, when I get more confidence in myself.

O infancy! thou are beautiful, thou art charming, thou art lovely to contemplate! But thoughts like these recall sad memories of the past, of the halcyon days of my childhood, when I was a sweet, prattling innocent, the pet of a dear home-circle, and the pride of the village.

Enough, enough! I must weep, or this bursting heart will break. MARK TWAIN.

MOSES IN THE BULRUSHES AGAIN
[*Morning Call*, July 16, 1864]

On Thursday evening, officers John Conway and King had their attention attracted by the crying of a child at the Catholic Orphan Asylum door; where, upon examination, they discovered an infant, apparently but a few days old, wrapped up in a shawl. It was delivered to the care of the benevolent Sisters at the Institution. It appeared to be a good-enough baby—nothing the matter with it—and it has been unaccountable to all who have heard of the circumstance, what the owner wanted to throw it away for.

FROM MARK TWAIN'S INTERIOR NOTES—NO. 2
[*Bulletin*, Dec. 6, 1866]

We visited the mining camps of Red Dog and You Bet, and returned to Nevada in the night, through a forest country cut up into innumerable roads. In our simplicity we depended on the horses to choose the route for themselves, because by many romantic books we had been taught a wild and absurd admiration for the instinct of that species of brute. The only instinct ours had was one which moved them to hunt for places where there wasn't any road, and it was unerring—it never failed them. However, our horses did not go lame. It was very singular. My experience of horses is that they never throw away a chance to go lame, and that in all respects they are well meaning and unreliable animals. I have also observed that if you refuse a high price for a favorite horse, he will go and lay down somewhere and die.

On or about the 21st of the present month, it became apparent to me that the forthcoming race between *Norfolk* and *Lodi* was awakening extraordinary attention all over the Pacific coast, and even far away in the Atlantic States. I saw that if I failed to see this race I might live a century, perhaps, without ever having an opportunity to see its equal. I went at once to a livery stable — the man said his teams had all been engaged a week before I called. I got the same answer at all the other livery stables, except one. They told me there that they had a nice dray, almost new, and a part of a horse — they said part of a horse because a good deal of him was gone, in the way of a tail, and one ear and a portion of the other, and his upper lip, and one eye; and, inasmuch as his teeth were exposed, and he had a villainous cast in his remaining eye, these defects, added to his damaged ears and departed tail, gave him an extremely "gallus" and unprepossessing aspect-but they only asked two hundred and forty dollars for the turn-out for the day.

I resisted the yearning I felt to hire this unique establishment.

Then they said they had a capacious riding-horse left, but all the seats on him except one had been engaged; they said he was an unusually long horse, and he could seat seven very comfortably; and that he was very gentle, and would not kick up behind; and that one of the choicest places on him for observation was still vacant, and I could have it for nineteen dollars — and so on and so on; and while the passenger agent was talking, he was busy measuring off a space of nine inches for me pretty high up on the commodious animal's neck.

It seemed to me that the prospect of going to the races was beginning to assume a very "neck-or-nothing" condition, but nevertheless I steadfastly refused the supercargo's offer, and he sold the vacancy to a politician who was used to being on the fence and would naturally consider a seat astride a horse's neck in the light of a pleasant variety.

SABBATH REFLECTIONS
[*Territorial Enterprise*, Jan. 28, 1866]

This is the Sabbath to-day. This is the day set apart by a benignant Creator for rest — for repose from the wearying toils of the week, and for calm and serious (Brown's dog has commenced to howl again — I wonder why Brown persists in keeping that dog chained up?) meditation upon those tremendous subjects pertaining to our future existence. How thankful we ought to be (There goes that rooster, now.) for this sweet respite; how fervently we ought to lift up our voice and (Confound that old hen — lays an egg every forty minutes, and then cackles until she lays the next one.) testify our gratitude. How sadly, how soothingly the music of that deep-toned bell floats up from the distant church! How gratefully we murmur (Scat! — that old gray tomcat is always bully-ragging that other one — got him down now, and digging the hair out of him by the handful.) thanksgiving for these Sabbath blessings. How lovely the day is! ("Buy a broom! buy a broom!") How wild and beautiful the ("*Golden Era* 'n' Sund' *Mercry*, two for a bit apiece!") sun smites upon the tranquil ("*Alta*, Mon' *Call*, an' *Merican Flag!*") city! ("Po-ta-to-o-o-es, ten pounds for two bits — po-ta-to-o-o-es, ten pounds for quart-va-dollar!")

However, never mind these Sunday reflections — there are too many distracting influences abroad. This people have forgotten San Francisco is not a ranch — or rather, that it ought not properly to be a ranch. It has got all the disagreeable features of a ranch, though. Every citizen keeps from ten to five hundred chickens, and these crow and cackle all day and all night; they stand watches, and the watch on duty makes a racket while the off-watch sleeps. Let a stranger get outside of Montgomery and Kearny from Pacific to Second, and close his eyes, and he can imagine himself on a well-stocked farm, without an effort, for his ears will be assailed by such a vile din of gobbling of turkeys, and crowing of hoarse-voiced roosters, and cackling of hens, and howling of cows, and whinnying of horses, and braying of jackasses, and yowling of cats, that he will be driven to frenzy, and may look to perform prodigies of blasphemy such as he never knew himself capable of before.

Sunday reflections! A man might as well try to reflect in Bedlam as in San Francisco when her millions of livestock are in tune. Being calm, now, I will call down no curse upon these dumb brutes (as they are called by courtesy), but I will go so far as to say I wish they may all die without issue, and that a sudden and violent death may overtake any person who afterwards attempts to reinstate the fowl and brute nuisance.

from RUNAWAY
[*Morning Call*, July 14, 1864]

Yesterday morning, a horse and cart were carelessly left unhitched and unwatched in Dupont street. The horse, being of the Spanish persuasion and not to be depended on, finally got tired standing idle, and ran away. He ran into Berry street, ran half a square and upset the cart, and fell, helplessly entangled in the harness. The vehicle was somewhat damaged, but two or three new wheels, some fresh sides, and a new bottom, will make it all right again. Considering the fact that little short narrow Berry street contains as many small children as all the balance of San Francisco put together, it is strange the frantic horse did not hash up a dozen or two of them in his reckless career. They all escaped, however, by the singular accident of being out of the way at the time, and they visited the wreck in countless swarms, after the disaster, and examined it with unspeakable satisfaction. . . .

HOW TO CURE HIM OF IT
[*Morning Call*, Aug. 27, 1864]

In a court in Minna street, between First and Second, they keep a puppy tied up which is insignificant as to size, but formidable as to yelp. We are unable to sleep after nine o'clock in the morning on account of it. Sometimes the subject of these remarks begins at three in the morning and yowls straight ahead for a week. We have lain awake many mornings out of pure distress on account of that puppy— because we know that if he does not break himself of that habit it will kill him; it is bound to do it—we have known thousands and thousands of cases like it. But it is easily cured. Give the creature a double handful of strychnine, dissolved in a quart of Prussic acid, and it will soo-oothe him down and make him as quiet and docile as a dried herring. The remedy is not expensive, and is at least worthy of a trial, even for the novelty of the thing.

from MARK TWAIN ON THE DOG QUESTION
[*Morning Call*, Dec. 9, 1866]

The presence of the dog is often betrayed to the Policeman by his bark. Remove the bark from his system and your dog is safe. This may be done by mixing a spoonful of the soother called strychnine in his rations. It will be next to impossible to ever get that dog to bark any more.

THE POLICE

California had a population then that "inflicted" justice after a fashion that was simplicity and primitiveness itself....

WHAT HAVE THE POLICE BEEN DOING?
[*Golden Era*, Jan. 21, 1866]

Ain't they virtuous? Don't they take good care of the city? Is not their constant vigilance and efficiency shown in the fact that roughs and rowdies here are awed into good conduct?—isn't it shown in the fact that ladies even on the back streets are safe from insult in the day-time, when they are under the protection of a regiment of soldiers?—isn't it shown in the fact that although many offenders of importance go unpunished, they infallibly snaffle every Chinese chicken-thief that attempts to drive his trade, and are duly glorified by name in the papers for it?—isn't it shown in the fact that they are always on the look-out and keep out of the way and never get run over by wagons and things? And ain't they spry?—ain't they energetic?—ain't they frisky?—Don't they parade up and down the sidewalk at the rate of a block an hour and make everybody nervous and dizzy with their fright-ful velocity? Don't they keep their clothes nice—and ain't their hands soft? And don't they work?—don't they work like horses?—don't they, now? Don't they smile sweetly on the women?—and when they are fatigued with their exertions, don't they back up against a lamp-post and go on smiling till they break plumb down? But ain't they nice?—that's it, you know!—ain't they nice? They don't sweat—you never see one of those fellows sweat. Why, if you were to see a policeman sweating you would say, "oh, here, this poor man is going to die—because this sort of thing is unnatural, you know." Oh, no—you never see one of those fellows sweat. And ain't they easy and comfortable and happy—always leaning up against a lamp-post in the sun, and scratching one shin with the other foot and enjoying themselves? Serene?— I reckon not.

I don't know anything the matter with the Department, but may be Dr. Rowell does. Now when Ziele broke that poor wretch's skull the other night for stealing six bits' worth of flour sacks, and had him taken to the Station House by a policeman, and jammed into one of the cells in the most humorous way, do you think there was anything wrong there? I don't. Why should they arrest Ziele and say, "Oh come, now, you *say* you found this stranger stealing on your premises, and we know you knocked him on the head with your club—but then you better go in a cell, too, till we see whether there's going to be any other account of the thing—any account that mightn't jibe with yours altogether, you know—you go in for confessed assault and battery, you know." Why should they do that? Well, nobody ever said they did.

And why shouldn't they shove that half-senseless wounded man into a cell without getting a doctor to examine and see how badly he was hurt, and consider that next day would be time enough, if he chanced to live that long? And why shouldn't the jailor let him alone when he found him in a dead stupor two hours after—let him alone because he couldn't wake him—couldn't wake a man who was sleeping and with that calm serenity which is peculiar to men whose heads have been caved in with a club—couldn't wake such a subject, but never suspected that there was anything unusual in the circumstance? Why shouldn't the jailor do so? Why certainly—why shouldn't he?— the man was an infernal stranger. He had no vote. Besides, had not a gentleman just said he stole some flour sacks? Ah, and if he stole flour sacks, did he not deliberately put himself outside the pale of humanity and Christian sympathy by that hellish act? I think so. The Department think so. Therefore, when the stranger died at 7 in the morning, after four hours of refreshing slumber in that cell, with his skull actually split in twain from front to rear, like an apple, as was ascertained by post mortem examination, what the very devil do you want to go and find fault with the prison officers for? You are *always* putting in your shovel. Can't you find somebody to pick on besides the police? It takes all my time to defend them from people's attacks.

I know the Police Department is a kind, humane and generous institution. Why, it was no longer ago than yesterday that I was reminded of that time Captain Lees broke his leg. Didn't the free-handed, noble Department shine forth with a dazzling radiance then? Didn't the Chief detail officers Shields, Ward and two others to watch over him and nurse him and look after all his wants with motherly solicitude — four of them, you know — four of the very biggest and ablest-bodied men on the force —when less generous people would have thought two nurses sufficient — had these four acrobats in active hospital service that way in the most liberal manner, at a cost to the city of San Francisco of only the trifling sum of five hundred dollars a month — the same being the salaries of four officers of the regular police force at $125 a month each. But don't you know there are people mean enough to say that Captain Lees ought to have paid his own nurse bills, and that if he had had to do it may be he would have managed to worry along on less than five hundred dollars worth of nursing a month? And don't you know that they say also that interested parties are always badgering the Supervisors with petitions for an increase of the police force, and showing such increase to be a terrible necessity, and yet they have always got to be hunting up and creating new civil offices and berths, and making details for nurse service in order to find something for them to do after they get them appointed? And don't you know that they say that they wish to God the city would hire a detachment of nurses and keep them where they will be handy in case of accident, so that property will not be left unprotected while policemen are absent on duty in sick rooms. You can't think how it aggravates me to hear such harsh remarks about our virtuous police force. Ah, well, the police will have their reward hereafter — no doubt.

———◆———

OUR ACTIVE POLICE
[*Dramatic Chronicle*, Dec. 12, 1865]

The *Call* gives an account of an unoffending Chinese rag-picker being set upon by a gang of boys and nearly stoned to death. It concludes the paragraph thus: "He was carried to the City and County Hospital in an insensible condition, his head having been split open and his body badly bruised. The young ruffians scattered, and it is doubtful if any of them will be recognized and punished." If that unoffending man dies, and a murder has consequently been committed, it is doubtful whether his murderers will be recognized and punished, is it? And yet if a Chinaman steals a chicken he is sure to be recognized and punished, through the efforts of one of our active police force. If our active police force are not too busily engaged in putting a stop to petty thieving by Chinamen, and fraternizing with newspaper reporters, who hold up their wonderful deeds to the admiration of the community, let it be looked to that the boys who were guilty of this murderous assault on an industrious and unoffending man are recognized and punished. The Call says "some philanthropic gentlemen dispersed the miscreants;" these philanthropic gentlemen, if the police do their duty and arrest the culprits, can probably recognize them.

THIEF-CATCHING
[*Territorial Enterprise*, Dec. 19, 1865]

One may easily find room to abuse as many as several members of Chief Burke's civilian army for laziness and uselessness, but the detective department is supplied with men who are sharp, shrewd, always on the alert and always industrious. It is only natural that this should be so. An ordinary policemen is chosen with especial reference to large stature and powerful muscle, and he only gets $125 a month, but the detective is chosen with especial regard to brains, and the position pays better than a lucky faro-bank. A shoemaker can tell by a single glance at a boot whose shop it comes from, by some peculiarity of workmanship; but to a bar-keeper all boots are alike; a printer will take a number of newspaper scraps, that show no dissimilarity to each other, and name the papers they were cut from; to a man who is accustomed to being on the water, the river's surface is a printed book which never fails to divulge the hiding place of the sunken rock, or betray the presence of the treacherous shoal. In ordinary men, this quality of detecting almost imperceptible differences and peculiarities is acquired by long practice, and goes not beyond the limits of their own occupation—but in the detective it is an instinct, and discovers to him the secret signs of all trades, and the faint shades of difference between things which look alike to the careless eye.

Detective Rose can pick up a chicken's tail feather in Montgomery street and tell in a moment what roost it came from at the Mission; and if the theft is recent, he can go out there and take a smell of the premises and tell which block in Sacramento street the Chinaman lives in who committed it, by some exquisite difference in the stink left, and which he knows to be peculiar to one particular block of buildings.

Mr. McCormick, who should be on the detective force regularly, but as yet is there only by brevet, can tell an obscene photograph by the back, as a sport tells an ace from a jack.

Detective Blitz can hunt down a transgressing hack-driver by some peculiarity in the style of his blasphemy.

The forte of Lees and Ellis, is the unearthing of embezzlers and forgers. Each of these men are best in one particular line, but at the same time they are good in all. And now we have Piper, who takes a cake, dropped in the Lick House by a coat-thief, and sits down to read it as another man would a newspaper. It informs him who baked the cake; who bought it; where the purchaser lives; that he is a Mexican; that his name is Salcero; that he is a thief by profession—and then Piper marches away two miles, to the Presidio, and grabs this foreigner, and convicts him with the cake that cannot lie, and makes him shed his boots and finds $200 in greenbacks in them, and makes him shuck himself and finds upon him store of stolen gold. And so Salcero goes to the station-house. The detectives are smart, but I remarked to a friend that some of the other policemen were not. He said the remark was unjust—that those "other policemen were as smart as they could afford to be for $125 a month." It was not a bad idea. Still, I contend that some of them could not afford to be Daniel Websters, maybe, for any amount of money.

FROM **FUNNY**
[*Territorial Enterprise*, Feb. 15, 1866]

Chief Burke's Star Chamber Board of Police Commissioners is the funniest institution extant, and the way he conducts it is the funniest theatrical exhibition in San Francisco. Now to see the Chief fly around and snatch up accuser and accused before the Commission when any policeman is charged with misconduct in the public prints, you would imagine that fearful Commission was really going to raise the very devil. But it is all humbug, display, fuss and feathers. The Chief brings his policeman out as sinless as an angel, unless the testimony be heavy enough and strong enough, almost, to hang an ordinary culprit, in which case a penalty of four or five days' suspension is awarded.

Wouldn't you call that Legislature steeped in stupidity which appointed a father to try his own son for crimes against the State? Of course. And knowing that the father must share the disgrace if the son is found guilty, would you ever expect a conviction? Certainly not. And would you expect the father's blind partiality for his own offspring to weigh heavily against evidence given against that son. Assuredly you would. Well, this Police Commission is a milder form of that same principle. Chief Burke makes all these policemen, by appointment — breeds them — and feels something of a parent's solicitude for them; and yet, if any charge is brought against them, he is the judge before whom they are tried! Isn't it perfectly absurd? I think so. It takes all three of those Commissioners to convict — the verdict must be unanimous — therefore, since every conviction of one of the Chief's offspring must in the nature of things be a sort of reflection upon himself, you cannot be surprised to know that police officers are very seldom convicted before the Police Commissioners. Though the man's sins were blacker than night, the Chief can always prevent conviction by simply withholding his consent. And this extraordinary power works both ways, too. See how simple and easy a matter it was for the Chief to say to a political obstruction in his path: "You are dismissed, McMillan; I know of nothing to your discredit as an officer, but you are an aspirant to my position and I won't keep a stick to break my own back with." He simply said "Go," and he had to shove! If he had been one of the Chief's pets, he might have committed a thousand rascalities, but the powerful Commission would have shielded and saved him every time. Nay, more — it would have made a tremendous hubbub, and a showy and noisy pretense of trying him — and then brought him out blameless and shown him to be an abused and persecuted innocent and entitled to the public commiseration.

Why, the other day, in one of the Commission trials, where a newspaper editor was summoned as a prosecutor, they detailed a substitute for the real delinquent, and tried *him!* There may be more joke than anything else about that statement, but I heard it told, anyhow. And then it is plausible — it is just characteristic of Star Chamber tactics.

You ought to see how it makes the Chief wince for any one to say a word against a policeman; they are his offspring, and he feels all a father's sensitiveness to remarks affecting their good name. It is natural that he should, and it is wrong to do violence to this purely human trait by making him *swear* that he will impartially try them for their crimes, when the thing is perfectly impossible. He *cannot* be impartial—is it human nature to judge with strict impartiality his own friends, his own dependent, his own offspring?...

There is a bill in the hands of a San Francisco legislator which proposes to put the police appointing power in the hands of the Mayor, the District Attorney, and the city and county attorney; and the trial of policemen and power to punish or dismiss them, in the hands of the county and police court prosecuting attorney. This would leave Chief Burke nothing to do but attend to his own legitimate business of keeping the police department up to their work all the time, and is just the kind of bill that ought to pass. It would reduce the Chief from autocrat of San Francisco, with absolute power, to the simple rank of Chief of Police with no power to meddle in outside affairs or do anything but mind his own particular business. He told me, not more than a week ago, that such an arrangement would exactly suit him. Now we shall see if it suits him. Don't you dare to send any log-rolling, wire-pulling squads of policemen to Sacramento, Mr. Burke.

CULTURE

> A "connoisseur" should
> never be in doubt about anything.
> It is ruinous.

A TOUCHING STORY OF GEORGE WASHINGTON'S BOYHOOD
[*The Californian*, Oct. 29, 1864]

If it please your neighbor to break the sacred calm of night with the snorting of an unholy trombone, it is your duty to put up with his wretched music and your privilege to pity him for the unhappy instinct that moves him to delight in such discordant sounds. I did not always think thus; this consideration for musical amateurs was born of certain disagreeable personal experiences that once followed the development of a like instinct in myself. Now this infidel over the way, who is learning to play on the trombone, and the slowness of whose progress is almost miraculous, goes on with his harrowing work every night, uncursed by me, but tenderly pitied. Ten years ago, for the same offence, I would have set fire to his house. At that time I was a prey to an amateur violinist for two or three weeks, and the sufferings I endured at his hands are inconceivable. He played "Old Dan Tucker," and he never played anything else — but he performed that so badly that he could throw me into fits with it if I were awake, or into a nightmare if I were asleep. As long as he confined himself to "Dan Tucker," though, I bore with him and abstained from violence; but when he projected a fresh outrage, and tried to do "Sweet Home," I went over and burnt him out. My next assailant was a wretch who felt a call to play the clarionet. He only played the scale, however, with his distressing instrument, and I let him run the length of his tether, also; but finally, when he branched out into a ghastly tune, I felt my reason deserting me under the exquisite torture, and I sallied forth and burnt him out likewise. During the next two years I burned out an amateur cornet-player, a bugler, a bassoon-sharp, and a barbarian whose talents ran in the bass-drum line. I would certainly have scorched this trombone man if he had moved into my neighborhood in those days. But as I said before, I leave him to his own destruction now, because I have had experience as an amateur myself, and I feel nothing but compassion for that kind of people. Besides, I have learned that there lies dormant in the souls of all men a penchant for some particular musical instrument, and an unsuspected yearning to learn to play on it, that are bound to wake up and demand attention some day. Therefore, you who rail at such as disturb your slumbers with unsuccessful and demoralizing attempts to subjugate a fiddle, beware! for sooner or later your own time will come. It is customary and popular to curse these amateurs when they wrench you out of a pleasant dream at night with a peculiarly diabolical note, but seeing that we are all made alike, and must all develop a distorted talent for music in the fullness of time, it is not right. I am charitable to my trombone maniac; in a moment of inspiration he fetches a snort, sometimes, that brings me to a sitting posture in bed, broad awake and weltering in a cold perspiration. Perhaps my first thought is that there has been an earthquake; perhaps I hear the trombone, and my next thought is that suicide and the silence of the grave would be a happy release from this nightly agony; perhaps the old instinct comes strong upon me to go after my matches; but my first cool, collected thought is that the trombone man's destiny is upon him, and he is working it out in suffering and tribulation; and I banish from me the unworthy instinct that would prompt me to burn him out.

After a long immunity from the dreadful insanity that moves a man to become a musician in defiance of the will of God that he should confine himself to sawing wood, I finally fell a victim to the instrument they call the Accordeon. At this day I hate that contrivance as fervently as any man can, but at the time I speak of I suddenly acquired a disgusting and idolatrous affection for it. I got one of powerful capacity and learned to play "Auld Lang Syne" on it. It seems to me, now, that I must have been gifted with a sort of inspiration to be enabled, in the state of ignorance in which I then was, to select out of the whole range of musical composition the one solitary tune that sounds vilest and most distressing on the accordeon. I do not suppose there is another tune in the world with which I could have inflicted so much anguish upon my race as I did with that one during my short musical career.

After I had been playing "Lang Syne" about a week, I had the vanity to think I could improve the original melody, and I set about adding some little flourishes and variations to it, but with rather indifferent success, I suppose, as it brought my landlady into my presence with an expression about her of being opposed to such desperate enterprises. Said she, "Do you know any other tune but that, Mr. Twain?" I told her, meekly, that I did not. "Well, then," said she, "stick to it just as it is; don't put any variations to it, because it's rough enough on the boarders the way it is now."

The fact is, it was something more than simply "rough enough" on them; it was altogether too rough; half of them left, and the other half would have followed, but Mrs. Jones saved them by discharging me from the premises.

I only stayed one night at my next lodging-house. Mrs. Smith was after me early in the morning. She said, "You can go, sir; I don't want you here; I have had one of your kind before—a poor lunatic, that played the banjo and danced breakdowns, and jarred the glass all out of the windows; you kept me awake all night, and if you was to do it again I'd take and mash that thing over your head!" I could see that this woman took no delight in music, and I moved to Mrs. Brown's.

For three nights in succession I gave my new neighbors "Auld Lang Syne," plain and unadulterated, save by a few discords that rather improved the general effect than otherwise. But the very first time I tried the variations the boarders mutinied. I never did find anybody that would stand those variations. I was very well satisfied with my efforts in that house, however, and I left it without any regrets; I drove one boarder as mad as a March hare, and another one tried to scalp his mother. I reflected, though, that if I could only have been allowed to give this latter just one more touch of the variations, he would have finished the old woman.

I went to board at Mrs. Murphy's, an Italian lady of many excellent qualities. The very first time I struck up the variations, a haggard, care-worn, cadaverous old man walked into my room and stood beaming upon me a smile of ineffable happiness. Then he placed his hand upon my head, and looking devoutly aloft, he said with feeling unction, and in a voice trembling with emotion, "God bless you, young man! God bless you! for you have done that for me which is beyond all praise. For years I have suffered from an incurable disease, and knowing my doom was sealed and that I must die, I have striven with all my power to resign myself to my fate, but in vain — the love of life was too strong within me. But Heaven bless you, my benefactor! for since I heard you play that tune and those variations, I do not want to live any longer — I am entirely resigned — I am willing to die — I am anxious to die." And then the old man fell upon my neck and wept a flood of happy tears. I was surprised at these things, but I could not help feeling a little proud at what I had done, nor could I help giving the old gentleman a parting blast in the way of some peculiarly lacerating variations as he went out at the door. They doubled him up like a jack-knife, and the next time he left his bed of pain and suffering, he was all right, in a metallic coffin.

My passion for the accordeon finally spent itself and died out, and I was glad when I found myself free from its unwholesome influence. While the fever was upon me, I was a living, breathing calamity wherever I went, and desolation and disaster followed in my wake. I bred discord in families, I crushed the spirits of the light-hearted, I drove the melancholy to despair, I hurried invalids to premature dissolution, and I fear me I disturbed the very dead in their graves. I did incalculable harm and inflicted untold suffering upon my race with my execrable music, and yet to atone for it all, I did but one single blessed act, in making that weary old man willing to go to his long home.

Still, I derived some little benefit from that accordeon, for while I continued to practice on it, I never had to pay any board — landlords were always willing to compromise, on my leaving before the month was up.

Now, I had two objects in view, in writing the foregoing, one of which, was to try and reconcile people to those poor unfortunates who feel that they have a genius for music, and who drive their neighbors crazy every night in trying to develop and cultivate it, and the other was to introduce an admirable story about Little George Washington, who could Not Lie, and the Cherry Tree — or the Apple Tree, I have forgotten now, which, although it was told me only yesterday. And writing such a long and elaborate introductory has caused me to forget the story itself; but it was very touching.

FROM **ANSWERS TO CORRESPONDENTS**
[*The Californian*, June 10, 1865]

AMATEUR SERENADER.—Yes, I will give you some advice, and do it with a good deal of pleasure. I live in a neighborhood which is well stocked with young ladies, and consequently I am excruciatingly sensitive upon the subject of serenading. Sometimes I suffer. In the first place, always tune your instruments before you get within three hundred yards of your destination—this will enable you to take your adored unawares, and create a pleasant surprise by launching out at once upon your music; it astonishes the dogs and cats out of their presence of mind, too, so that if you hurry you can get through before they have a chance to recover and interrupt you; besides, there is nothing captivating in the sounds produced in tuning a lot of melancholy guitars and fiddles, and neither does a group of able-bodied, sentimental young men so engaged look at all dignified. Secondly, clear your throats and do all the coughing you have got to do before you arrive at the seat of war— I have known a young lady to be ruthlessly startled out of her slumbers by such a sudden and direful blowing of noses and "h'm-h'm-ing" and coughing, that she imagined the house was beleaguered by victims of consumption from the neighboring hospital; do you suppose the music was able to make her happy after that? Thirdly, don't stand right under the porch and howl, but get out in the middle of the street, or better still, on the other side of it—distance lends enchantment to the sound; if you have previously transmitted a hint to the lady that she is going to be serenaded, she will understand who the music is for; besides, if you occupy a neutral position in the middle of the street, may be all the neighbors round will take stock in your serenade and invite you in to take wine with them. Fourthly, don't sing a whole opera through—enough of a thing's enough. Fifthly, don't sing "Lilly Dale"—the profound satisfaction that most of us derive from the reflection that the girl treated of in that song is dead, is constantly marred by the resurrection of the lugubrious ditty itself by your kind of people. Sixthly, don't let your screaming tenor soar an octave above all the balance of the chorus, and remain there setting everybody's teeth on edge for four blocks around; and, above all, don't let him sing a solo; probably there is nothing in the world so suggestive of serene contentment and perfect bliss as the spectacle of a calf chewing a dish-rag, but the nearest approach to it is your reedy tenor, standing apart, in sickly attitude, with head thrown back and eyes uplifted to the moon, piping his distressing solo: now do not pass lightly over this matter, friend, but ponder it with that seriousness which its importance entitles it to. Seventhly, after you have run all the chickens and dogs and cats in the vicinity distracted, and roused them into a frenzy of crowing, and cackling, and yowling, and caterwauling, put up your dreadful instruments and go home. Eighthly, as soon as you start, gag your tenor—otherwise he will be letting off a screech every now and then to let the people know he is around; your amateur tenor singer is notoriously the most self-conceited of all God's creatures. Tenthly, don't go serenading at all—it is a wicked, unhappy and seditious practice, and a calamity to all souls that are weary and desire to slumber and be at rest. Eleventhly and lastly, the father of the young lady in the next block says that if you come prowling around his neighborhood again with your infamous scraping and tooting and yelling, he will sally forth and deliver you into the hands of the police. As far as I am concerned myself, I would like to have you come, and come often, but as long as the old man is so prejudiced, perhaps you had better serenade mostly in Oakland, or San Jose, or around there somewhere.

FROM **FINE PICTURE OF REV. MR. KING**
[*Morning Call*, Sept. 1, 1864]

California and Nevada Territory are flooded with distressed-looking abortions done in oil, in water-colors, in crayon, in lithography, in photography, in sugar, in plaster, in marble, in wax, and in every substance that is malleable or chiselable, or that can be marked on, or scratched on, or painted on, or which by its nature can be compelled to lend itself to a relentless and unholy persecution and distortion of the features of the great and good man who is gone from our midst—Rev. Thomas Starr King. We do not believe these misguided artistic lunatics meant to confuse the lineaments, and finally destroy and drive out from our memories the cherished image of our lost orator, but just the contrary. We believe their motive was good, but we know their execution was atrocious. We look upon these blank, monotonous, over-fed and sleepy-looking pictures, and ask, with Dr. Bellows, "Where was the seat of this man's royalty?" But we ask in vain of these wretched counterfeits. There is no more life or expression in them than you may find in the soggy, upturned face of a pickled infant, dangling by the neck in a glass jar among the trophies of a doctor's back office. . . .

———

FROM **ANSWERS TO CORRESPONDENTS**
[*Morning Call*, July 6, 1865]

AGNES ST. CLAIR SMITH.—This correspondent writes as follows: "I suppose you have seen the large oil painting (entitled 'St. Patrick preaching at Tara, A. D. 432,') by J. Harrington, of San Francisco, in the window of the picture store adjoining the Eureka Theatre, on Montgomery street. What do you think of it?"

Yes, I have seen it. I think it is a petrified nightmare. I have not time to elaborate my opinion.

———

FROM **AN UNBIASED CRITICISM**
[*The Californian*, March 18, 1865]

THE CALIFORNIA ART UNION—ITS MORAL EFFECTS UPON THE
YOUTH OF BOTH SEXES
CAREFULLY CONSIDERED AND CANDIDLY COMMENTED UPON.

The Editor of THE CALIFORNIAN ordered me to go to the rooms of the California Art Union and write an elaborate criticism upon the pictures upon exhibition there, and I beg leave to report that the result is hereunto appended, together with bill for same.

I do not know anything about Art and very little about music or anatomy, but nevertheless I enjoy looking at pictures and listening to operas, and gazing at handsome young girls, about the same as people do who are better qualified by education to judge of merit in these matters.

After writing the above rather neat heading and preamble on my foolscap, I proceeded to the new Art Union rooms last week, to see the paintings, about which I had read so much in the papers during my recent three months' stay in the Big Tree region of Calaveras county; (up there, you know, they read *everything*, because in most of those little camps they have no libraries, and no books to speak of, except now and then a patent-office report, or a prayer-book, or literature of that kind, in a general way, that will hang on and last a good while when people are careful with it, like miners; but as for novels, they pass them around and wear them out in a week or two. Now there was Coon, a nice bald-headed man at the hotel in Angel's Camp. I asked him to lend me a book, one rainy day: he was silent a moment, and a shade of melancholy flitted across his fine face, and then he said, "Well, I've got a mighty responsible old Webster-Unabridged, what there is left of it, but they started her sloshing around, and sloshing around, and sloshing around the camp before I ever got a chance to read her myself, and next she went to Murphy's, and from there she went to Jackass, and now, by G——d, she's gone to San Andreas, and I don't expect I'll ever see that book again; but what makes me mad, is that for all they're so handy about keeping her sashshaying around from shanty to shanty and from camp to camp, none of 'em's ever got a good word for her. Now Coddington had her a week, and she was too many for *him*—he couldn't spell the words; he tackled some of them regular busters, tow'rd the middle, you know, and they throwed him; next, Dyer, he tried her a jolt, but he couldn't *pronounce* 'em— Dyer can hunt quail or play seven-up as well as any man, understand me, but he can't *pronounce* worth a d——n; he used to worry along well enough, though, till he'd flush one of them rattlers with a clatter of syllables as long as a string of sluice-boxes, and then he'd lose his grip and throw up his hand; and so, finally, Dick Stoker harnessed her, up there at his cabin, and sweated over her, and cussed over her, and rastled with her for as much as three weeks, night and day, till he got as far as R, and then passed her over to 'Lige Pickerell, and said she was the all-firedest dryest reading that ever *he* struck; well, well, if she's come back from San Andreas, you can get her and prospect her, but I don't reckon there's a good deal left of her by this time; though time was when she was as likely a book as any in the State, and as hefty, and had an amount of general information in her that was aston- ishing, if any of these cattle had known enough to get it out of her;" and ex-corporal Coon proceeded cheerlessly to scout with his brush after the straggling hairs on the rear of his head and drum them to the front for inspection and roll-call, as was his usual custom before turn- ing in for his regular afternoon nap:) but as I was saying, they read everything, up there. . . .

But I digress to some extent, for maybe it was not really necessary to be quite so elaborate as I have been in order to enable the reader to understand that we were in the habit of reading everything thoroughly that fell in our way at Angel's, and that consequently we were familiar with all that had appeared in print about the new Art Union rooms. They get all the papers regularly every evening there, 24 hours out from San Francisco.

However, now that I have got my little preliminary point established to my satisfaction, I will proceed with my Art criticism.

The rooms of the California Art Union are pleasantly situated over the picture store in Montgomery street near the Eureka Theatre, and the first thing that attracts your attention when you enter is a beautiful and animated picture representing the Trial Scene in the *Merchant of Venice.* They did not charge me anything for going in there, because the Superintendent was not noticing at the time, but it is likely he would charge you or another man twenty-five cents — I think he would, because when I tried to get a dollar and a half out of a fellow I took for a stranger, the new-comer said the usual price was only two bits, and besides he was a heavy life-member and not obliged to pay anything at all — so I had to let him in for a quarter, but I had the satisfaction of telling him we were not letting life-members in free, now, as much as we *were.* It touched him on the raw. I let another fellow in for nothing, because I had cabined with him a few nights in Esmeralda [County, Nevada] several years ago, and I thought it only fair to be hospitable with him now that I had a chance. He introduced me to a friend of his named Brown, (I was hospitable to Brown also,) and me and Brown sat down on a bench and had a long talk about Washoe and other things, and I found him very entertaining for a stranger. He said his mother was a hundred and thirteen years old, and he had an aunt who died in her infancy, who, if she had lived, would have been older than his mother, now. He judged so because, originally, his aunt was born before his mother was. That was the first thing he told me, and then we were friends in a moment. It could not but be flattering to me, a stranger, to be made the recipient of information of so private and sacred a nature as the age of his mother and the early decease of his aunt, and I naturally felt drawn towards him and bound to him by a stronger and a warmer tie than the cold, formal introduction that had previously passed between us. I shall cherish the memory of the ensuing two hours as being among the purest and happiest of my checkered life. I told him frankly who I was, and where I came from, and where I was going to, and when I calculated to start, and all about my uncle Ambrose, who was an Admiral, and was for a long time in

command of a large fleet of canal boats, and about my gifted aunt
Martha, who was a powerful poetess, and a dead shot with a brickbat
at forty yards, and about myself and how I was employed at good pay
by the publishers of The Californian to come up there and write an
able criticism upon the pictures in the Art Union — indeed I concealed nothing from Brown, and in return he concealed nothing from
me, but told me everything he could recollect about his rum old
mother, and his grandmother, and all his relations, in fact. And so we
talked, and talked, and exchanged these tender heart-reminiscences
until the sun drooped far in the West, and then Brown said, "Let's go
down and take a drink."

----

from STILL FURTHER CONCERNING THAT CONUNDRUM
[The Californian, Oct. 15, 1864]

In accordance with your desire, I went to the Academy of Music on
Monday evening, to take notes and prepare myself to write a careful
critique upon the opera of the *Crown Diamonds*. That you considered me able to acquit myself creditably in this exalted sphere of literary labor, was gratifying to me, and I should even have felt flattered
by it had I not known that I was so competent to perform the task well,
that to set it for me could not be regarded as a flattering concession,
but, on the contrary, only a just and deserved recognition of merit.

Now, to throw disguise aside and speak openly, I have long
yearned for an opportunity to write an operatic diagnostical and ana-
lytical dissertation for you. I feel the importance of carefully-digested
newspaper criticism in matters of this kind — for I am aware that by
it the dramatic and musical tastes of a community are moulded, cultivated and irrevocably fixed — that by it these tastes are vitiated and
debased, or elevated and ennobled, according to the refinement or
vulgarity, and the competency or incompetency of the writers to whom
this department of the public training is entrusted. If you would see
around you a people who are filled with the keenest appreciation of
perfection in musical execution and dramatic delineation, and
painfully sensitive to the slightest departures from the true standard
of art in these things, you must employ upon your newspapers critics
capable of discriminating between merit and demerit, and alike fearless in praising the one and condemning the other. Such a person —

although it may be in some degree immodest in me to say so — I claim to be. You will not be surprised, then, to know that I read your boshy criticisms on the opera with the most exquisite anguish — and not only yours, but those which I find in every paper in San Francisco.

You do nothing but sing one everlasting song of praise; when an artist, by diligence and talent, makes an effort of transcendent excellence, behold, instead of receiving marked and cordial attention, both artist and effort sink from sight, and are lost in the general slough of slimy praise in which it is your pleasure to cause the whole company, good, bad, and indifferent, to wallow once a week. With this brief but very liberal and hearty expression of sentiment, I will drop the subject and leave you alone for the present, for it behooves me now to set you a model in criticism.

The opera of the *Crown Diamonds* was put upon the stage in creditable shape on Monday evening, although I noticed that the curtains of the "Queen of Portugal's" drawing-room were not as gorgeous as they might have been, and that the furniture had a second-hand air about it, of having seen service in the preceding reign. The acting and the vocalization, however, were, in the main, good. I was particularly charmed by the able manner in which Signor Bellindo Alphonso Cellini, the accomplished basso-relievo furniture-scout and sofa-shifter performed his part. I have before observed that this rising young artist gave evidence of the rarest genius in his peculiar department of operatic business, and have been annoyed at noticing with what studied care a venomous and profligate press have suppressed his name and suffered his sublimest efforts to pass unnoticed and unglorified. Shame upon such grovelling envy and malice! But, with all your neglect, you have failed to crush the spirit of the gifted furniture-scout, or seduce from him the affectionate encouragement and appreciation of the people. The moment he stepped upon the stage on Monday evening, to carry out the bandit chieftain's valise, the upper circles, with one accord, shouted, "Supe! supe!" and greeted him with warm and generous applause. It was a princely triumph for Bellindo; he told me afterwards it was the proudest moment of his life.

I watched Alphonso during the entire performance and was never so well pleased with him before, although I have admired him from the first. In the second act, when the eyes of the whole audience were upon him—when his every movement was the subject of anxiety and suspense—when everything depended upon his nerve and self-possession, and the slightest symptom of hesitation or lack of confidence would have been fatal—he stood erect in front of the cave, looking calmly and unflinchingly down upon the camp-stool for several moments, as one who has made up his mind to do his great work or perish in the attempt, and then seized it and bore it in triumph to the foot-lights! It was a sublime spectacle. There was not a dry eye in the house. In that moment, not even the most envious and uncharitable among the noble youth's detractors would have had the hardihood to say he was not endowed with a lofty genius.

Again, in the scene where the Prime Minister's nephew is imploring the female bandit to fly to the carriage and escape impending wrath, and when dismay and confusion ruled the hour, how quiet, how unmoved, how grandly indifferent was Bellindo in the midst of it all!— what stolidity of expression lay upon his countenance! While all save himself were unnerved by despair, he serenely put forth his finger and mashed to a shapeless pulp a mosquito that loitered upon the wall, yet betrayed no sign of agitation the while. Was there nothing in this lofty contempt for the dangers which surrounded him that marked the actor destined hereafter to imperishable renown?

Possibly upon that occasion when it was necessary for Alphonso to remove two chairs and a table during the shifting of the scenes, he performed his part with undue precipitation; with the table upside down upon his head, and grasping the corners with hands burdened with the chairs, he appeared to some extent undignified when he galloped across the stage. Generally his conception of his part is excellent, but in this case I am satisfied he threw into it an enthusiasm not required and also not warranted by the circumstances. I think that careful study and reflection will convince him that I am right, and that the author of the opera intended that in this particular instance the furniture should be carried out with impressive solemnity. That he had this in view is evidenced by the slow and stately measure of the music played by the orchestra at that juncture.

But the crowning glory of Cellini's performance that evening was the placing of a chair for the Queen of Portugal to sit down in after she had become fatigued by earnestly and elaborately abusing the Prime Minister for losing the Crown Diamonds. He did not grab the chair by the hind leg and shove it awkwardly at her Majesty; he did not seize it by the seat and thrust it ungracefully toward her; he did not handle it as though he was undecided about the strict line of his duty or ignorant of the proper manner of performing it. He did none of these things. With a coolness and confidence that evinced the most perfect conception and the most consummate knowledge of his part, he came gently forward and laid hold of that chair from behind, set it in its proper place with a movement replete with grace, and then leaned upon the back of it, resting his chin upon his hand, and in this position smiled a smile of transfigured sweetness upon the audience over the Queen of Portugal's head. There shone the inspired actor! and the people saw and acknowledged him; they waited respectfully for Miss Richings to finish her song, and then with one impulse they poured forth upon him a sweeping tempest of applause.

At the end of the piece the idolized furniture-scout and sofa-skirmisher was called before the curtain by an enthusiastic shouting and clapping of hands, but he was thrust aside, as usual, and other artists, (who chose to consider the compliment as intended for themselves,) swept bowing and smirking along the footlights and received it. I swelled with indignation, but I summoned my fortitude and resisted the pressure successfully. I am still intact.

Take it altogether, the *Crown Diamonds* was really a creditable performance. I feel that I would not be doing my whole duty if I closed this critique without speaking of Miss Caroline Richings, Miss Jenny Kempton, Mr. Hill, Mr. Seguin and Mr. Peakes, all of whom did fair justice to their several parts, and deserve a passing notice. With study, perseverance and attention, I have no doubt these vocalists will in time achieve a gratifying success in their profession.

I believe I have nothing further to say. I will call around, tomorrow, after you have had time to read, digest and pass your judgment upon my criticism, and, if agreeable, I will hire out to you for some years in that line. MARK TWAIN....

ON CALIFORNIA CRITICS
[*Golden Era*, Feb. 25, 1866]

Edwin Forrest [popular Shakespearean tragedian] is coming here. Very well — good bye, Mr. Forrest. Our critics will make you sing a lively tune. They will soon let you know that your great reputation cannot protect you on this coast. You have passed muster in New York, but they will show you up here. They will make it very warm for you. They will make you understand that a man who has served a lifetime as dramatic critic on a New York paper may still be incompetent, but that a California critic knows it all, notwithstanding he may have been in the shoemaking business most of his life, or a plow-artist on a ranch. You will be the sickest man in America before you get through with this trip. They will set up Frank Mayo for your model as soon as you get here, and they will say you don't play up to him, whether you do or not. And then they will decide that you are a "bilk." That is the grand climax of all criticism. They will say it here, first, and the country papers will endorse it afterwards. It will then be considered proven. You might as well quit, then.

You see, they always go into ecstasies with an actor the first night he plays, and they call him the most gifted in America the next morning. Then they think they have not acted with metropolitan coolness and self possession, and they slew around on the other tack and abuse him like a pickpocket to get even. This was Bandman's experience, Menken's, Heron's, Vestali's, Boniface's, and many others I could name. It will be yours also. You had better stay where you are. You will regret it if you come here. How would you feel if they told you your playing might answer in places of small consequence but wouldn't do in San Francisco? They will tell you that, as sure as you live. And then say, in the most crushing way:

"Mr. Forrest has evidently mistaken the character of this people. We will charitably suppose that this is the case, at any rate. We make no inquiry as to what kind of people he has been in the habit of playing before, but we simply inform him that he is now in the midst of a refined and cultivated community, and one which will not tolerate such indelicate allusions as were made use of in the play of 'Othello' last night. If he would not play to empty benches, this must not be repeated." They always come the "refined and cultivated" dodge on a new actor — look out for it, Mr. Forrest, and do not let it floor you. The boys know enough that it is one of the most effective shots that can be fired at a stranger. Come on, Forrest — I will write your dramatic obituary, gratis.

The other day I was looking through that autobiography, which I am building for the instruction of the world, when I came across an incident that I had written several years before. It was something that happened in San Francisco a long time ago.

At that time I was a newspaperman. I was out of a job. There was a friend of mine, a poet, but, as he could not sell his poems, he also had nothing to do for a living, and he was having a hard time of it, too. There was a love passage in it, too, but I will spare you that and leave you to read it in my book. Well, my friend, the poet, said to me that his life was a failure, and I told him I thought it was, and then he said he thought he ought to commit suicide, and I said, "All right," which was disinterested advice to a friend in trouble. My advice was positive. It was somewhat disinterested, but there were a few selfish motives behind it. As a reporter, I knew that a good "scoop" would get me employment, and so I wanted him to kill himself without letting anybody but me know about the deed. Then I could sell the news and get a new start in life. The poet could be spared, and so, largely for his own good and partly for mine, I urged him not to delay in doing the thing. I kept the idea in his mind. You know, there is no dependence in a suicide—he may change his mind.

He had a preference for a pistol, which was an extravagance, for we hadn't enough between us to hire a pistol. A fork would have been easier. I told him that, as we were financially crippled, we could not buy a revolver. Then he wanted a knife. To that I objected, too, on the same grounds. At last he mentioned drowning, and asked me what I thought of it. I said that it was a very good way, except that he was a fine swimmer, and I did not know whether it would turn out well on this account. But I consented to the plan, seeing no better one in sight.

So we went down to the beach. I went with him because I wanted to see that the thing was done right. You know the curiosity some people have. When we reached the shore of the sea a wonderful thing happened.

He was all ready to take the fatal leap. I was ready to see him do it. Providence interposed. From out the ocean, borne, perhaps, from the other side of the Pacific, there was washed up on the sand at our feet a gift—a gift that the sea had been tossing around for weeks, maybe, waiting for us to come down to the coast and receive it. What was it? It was a life preserver.

Now, you can imagine the complications that arose. The plan to do the suicide act by the drowning method fell through with a crash. With that life preserver, you see, he might have stayed in the water for weeks. I couldn't afford to wait that long. Suddenly I had an idea. That was no trouble for me, for I have the habit of having them often. He never had any, especially when he was going to write poetry. I suggested that he pawn the life preserver and get a revolver. The preserver was a good one. To be sure, the ocean had kept it for us a long time, and it had a few holes in it, but yet it was good enough to pawn somewhere. We sought the pawnbroker. He wanted ten percent a month on the loan from the life preserver. I didn't object, for I never expected to try to get it out again. All I wanted was a revolver — quick.

The pawnbroker gave us an old derringer, which is a kind of pistol that has but one barrel and shoots a bullet as big as a hickory nut. It was the only firearm he would let us have. Then he grew suspicious, wanted to know what we were going to do with the derringer. I drew him aside. "My friend is a poet," I said, "and he wants to kill himself with it." Upon which he replied, "Oh, well, if he is only a poet, it is well. God speed him."

We went out and loaded the pistol. Just then I had some qualms about staying to see the act of my friend. I hadn't objected to witnessing a drowning, but this shooting was different; the drowning might have been looked upon as accidental, but not so with this. But I calmed myself, for when I suggested that I might go away he grew uneasy and acted as though he would not carry out his purpose if I did not stay beside him. So I stayed. He placed the barrel at his temple. He hesitated. In spite of all I could do I waxed impatient. "Pull the trigger!" I cried. He pulled it. The ball went clean through his head. I held my breath. Then I found that the bullet had cleaned out all the gray matter. It had made a new man of him. Before he shot that shot he was nothing but a poet. Now he is a useful citizen. The ball just carried the poetic faculty out of the back door. Ever since then, although I am aware that I assisted him in the crime for selfish ends, I have been wishing that I might again help some other poet, or many of them, in the same way. . . .

FORTY-NINERS

{ I have had a sufficiently variegated
time of it to enable me to talk
Pioneer like a native,
and feel like a Forty-Niner. }

FROM ROUGHING IT

It was in this Sacramento Valley, just referred to, that a deal of the most lucrative of the early gold mining was done, and you may still see, in places, its grassy slopes and levels torn and guttered and disfigured by the avaricious spoilers of fifteen and twenty years ago. You may see such disfigurements far and wide over California — and in some such places, where only meadows and forests are visible — not a living creature, not a house, no stick or stone or remnant of a ruin, and not a sound, not even a whisper to disturb the Sabbath stillness — you will find it hard to believe that there stood at one time a fiercely-flourishing little city, of two thousand or three thousand souls, with its newspaper, fire company, brass band, volunteer militia, bank, hotels, noisy Fourth of July processions and speeches, gambling hells crammed with tobacco smoke, profanity, and rough-bearded men of all nations and colors, with tables heaped with gold dust sufficient for the revenues of a German principality — streets crowded and rife with business — town lots worth four hundred dollars a front foot — labor, laughter, music, dancing, swearing, fighting, shooting, stabbing — a bloody inquest and a man for breakfast every morning — *everything* that delights and adorns existence — all the appointments and appurtenances of a thriving and prosperous and promising young city, — and *now* nothing is left of it all but a lifeless, homeless solitude. The men are gone, the houses have vanished, even the *name* of the place is forgotten. In no other land, in modern times, have towns so absolutely died and disappeared, as in the old mining regions of California.

It was a driving, vigorous, restless population in those days. It was a *curious* population. It was the *only* population of the kind that the world has ever seen gathered together, and it is not likely that the world will ever see its like again. For, observe, it was an assemblage of two hundred thousand *young* men — not simpering, dainty, kid-gloved weaklings, but stalwart, muscular, dauntless young braves, brim full of push and energy, and royally endowed with every attribute that goes to make up a peerless and magnificent manhood — the very pick and choice of the world's glorious ones. No women, no children, no gray and stooping veterans, — none but erect, bright-eyed, quick-moving, strong-handed young giants — the strangest population, the finest population, the most gallant host that ever trooped down the startled solitudes of an unpeopled land. And where are they now? Scattered to the ends of the earth — or prematurely aged and decrepit — or shot or stabbed in street affrays — or dead of disappointed hopes and broken hearts — all gone, or nearly all — victims devoted upon the altar of the golden calf — the noblest holocaust that ever wafted its sacrificial incense heavenward. It is pitiful to think upon.

It was a splendid population — for all the slow, sleepy, sluggish-brained sloths staid at home — you never find that sort of people among pioneers — you cannot build pioneers out of that sort of material. It was that population that gave to California a name for getting up astounding enterprises and rushing them through with a magnificent dash and daring and a recklessness of cost or consequences, which she bears unto this day — and when she projects a new surprise, the grave world smiles as usual, and says, "Well, that is California all over."

JIM SMILEY AND HIS JUMPING FROG*
[*New York Saturday Press*, Nov. 18, 1865]

Mr. A. Ward,

Dear Sir:—Well, I called on good-natured, garrulous old Simon Wheeler, and I inquired after your friend Leonidas W. Smiley, as you requested me to do, and I hereunto append the result. If you can get

---

*First published version of the short story later titled "The Celebrated Jumping Frog of Calaveras County."

any information out of it you are cordially welcome to it. I have a lurking suspicion that your Leonidas W. Smiley is a myth — that you never knew such a personage, and that you only conjectured that if I asked old Wheeler about him it would remind him of his infamous Jim Smiley, and he would go to work and bore me nearly to death with some infernal reminiscence of him as long and tedious as it should be useless to me. If that was your design, Mr. Ward, it will gratify you to know that it succeeded.

I found Simon Wheeler dozing comfortably by the bar-room stove of the little old dilapidated tavern in the ancient mining camp of Boomerang, and I noticed that he was fat and bald-headed, and had an expression of winning gentleness and simplicity upon his tranquil countenance. He roused up and gave me good-day. I told him a friend of mine had commissioned me to make some inquiries about a cherished companion of his boyhood named Leonidas W. Smiley — Rev. Leonidas W. Smiley — a young minister of the gospel, who he had heard was at one time a resident of this village of Boomerang. I added that if Mr. Wheeler could tell me anything about this Rev. Leonidas W. Smiley, I would feel under many obligations to him.

Simon Wheeler backed me into a corner and blockaded me there with his chair — and then sat down and reeled off the monotonous narrative which follows this paragraph. He never smiled, he never frowned, he never changed his voice from the quiet, gently-flowing key to which he turned the initial sentence, he never betrayed the slightest suspicion of enthusiasm — but all through the interminable narrative there ran a vein of impressive earnestness and sincerity, which showed me plainly that so far from his imagining that there was anything ridiculous or funny about his story, he regarded it as a really important matter, and admired its two heroes as men of transcendent genius in finesse. To me, the spectacle of a man drifting serenely along through such a queer yarn without ever smiling was exquisitely absurd. As I said before, I asked him to tell me what he knew of Rev. Leonidas W. Smiley, and he replied as follows. I let him go on in his own way, and never interrupted him once:

There was a feller here once by the name of *Jim* Smiley, in the winter of '49 — or maybe it was the spring of '50 — I don't recollect exactly, some how, though what makes me think it was one or the other is because I remember the big flume wasn't finished when he first come to the camp; but anyway, he was the curiosest man about always betting on anything that turned up you ever see, if he could get anybody to bet on the other side, and if he couldn't he'd change sides — any way that suited the other man would suit *him* — any way just so's he got a bet, *he* was satisfied. But still, he was lucky — uncommon lucky; he most always come out winner. He was always ready and laying for a chance; there couldn't be no solitry thing mentioned but what that feller'd offer to bet on it — and take any side you please, as I was just telling you: if there was a horse race, you'd find him flush or you find him busted at the end of it; if there was a dog-fight, he'd bet on it; if there was a cat-fight, he'd bet on it; if there was a chicken-fight, he'd bet on it; why if there was two birds setting on a fence, he would bet you which one would fly first — or if there was a camp-meeting he would be there reglar to bet on parson Walker, which he judged to be the best exhorter about here, and so he was, too, and a good man; if he even see a straddle-bug start to go any wheres, he would bet you how long it would take him to get wherever he was going to, and if you took him up he would foller that straddle-bug to Mexico but what he would find out where he was bound for and how long he was on the road. Lots of the boys here has seen that Smiley and can tell you about him. Why, it never made no difference to *him* — he would bet on *anything* — the dangdest feller. Parson Walker's wife laid very sick, once, for a good while, and it seemed as if they warn't going to save her; but one morning he come in and Smiley asked him how she was, and he said she was considerable better — thank the Lord for his inf'nit mercy — and coming on so smart that with the blessing of Providence she'd get well yet — and Smiley, before he thought, says, "Well, I'll resk two-and-a-half that she don't, anyway."

Thish-yer Smiley had a mare — the boys called her the fifteen-minute nag, but that was only in fun, you know, because, of course, she was faster than that — and he used to win money on that horse, for all she was so slow and always had the asthma, or the distemper, or the consumption, or something of that kind. They used to give her two or three hundred yards' start, and then pass her under way; but always at the fag-end of the race she'd get excited and desperate-like, and come cavorting and spraddling up, and scattering her legs around limber, sometimes in the air, and sometimes out to one side amongst the fences, and kicking up m-o-r-e dust, and raising m-o-r-e racket with her coughing and sneezing and blowing her nose—and always fetch up at the stand just about a neck ahead, as near as you could cipher it down.

And he had a little small bull-pup, that to look at him you'd think he warn't worth a cent, but to set around and look ornery, and lay for a chance to steal something. But as soon as money was up on him he was a different dog—his under-jaw'd begin to stick out like the for'castle of a steamboat, and his teeth would uncover, and shine savage like the furnaces. And a dog might tackle him, and bully-rag him, and bite him, and throw him over his shoulder two or three times, and Andrew Jackson—which was the name of the pup—Andrew Jackson would never let on but what he was satisfied, and hadn't expected nothing else—and the bets being doubled and doubled on the other side all the time, till the money was all up—and then all of a sudden he would grab that other dog just by the joint of his hind legs and freeze to it— not chaw, you understand, but only just grip and hang on till they throwed up the sponge, if it was a year. Smiley always came out winner on that pup till he harnessed a dog once that didn't have no hind legs, because they'd been sawed off in a circular saw, and when the thing had gone along far enough, and the money was all up, and he came to make a snatch for his pet holt, he saw in a minute how he'd been imposed on, and how the other dog had him in the door, so to speak, and he 'peared surprised, and then he looked sorter discouraged like, and didn't try no more to win the fight, and so he got shucked out bad. He gave Smiley a look as much as to say his heart was broke, and it was his fault, for putting up a dog that hadn't no hind legs for him to take holt of, which was his main dependence in a fight, and then he limped off a piece, and laid down and died. It was a good pup, was that Andrew Jackson, and would have made a name for hisself if he'd lived, for the stuff was in him, and he had genius—I know it, because he hadn't had no opportunities to speak of, and it don't stand to reason that a dog could make such a fight as he could under them circumstances, if he hadn't no talent. It always makes me feel sorry when I think of that last fight of his'on, and the way it turned out.

Well, thish-yer Smiley had rat-terriers and chicken cocks, and tomcats, and all them kind of things, till you couldn't rest, and you couldn't fetch nothing for him to bet on but he'd match you. He ketched a frog one day and took him home and said he cal'lated to educate him; and so he never done nothing for three months but set in his back yard and learn that frog to jump. And you bet you he *did* learn him, too. He'd give him a little hunch behind, and the next minute you'd see that frog whirling in the air like a doughnut—see him turn one summerset, or maybe a couple, if he got a good start, and come down flat-footed and all right, like a cat. He got him up so in the matter of ketching flies, and kept him in practice so constant, that he'd nail a fly every time as far as he could see him. Smiley said all a frog wanted was education, and he could do most anything—and I believe him. Why, I've seen him set Dan'l Webster down here on this floor—Dan'l Webster was the name of the frog—and sing out, "Flies! Dan'l, flies," and quicker'n you could wink, he'd spring straight up, and snake a fly off'n the counter there, and flop down on the floor again as solid as a gob of mud, and fall to scratching the side of his head with his hind foot as indifferent as if he hadn't no idea he'd done any more'n any frog might do. You never see a frog so modest and straightfor'ard as he was, for all he was so gifted. And when it come to fair-and-square jumping on a dead level, he could get over more ground at one straddle than any animal of his breed you ever see. Jumping on a dead level was his strong suit, you understand, and when it come to that, Smiley would ante up money on him as long as he had a red. Smiley was monstrous proud of his frog, and well he might be, for fellers that had travelled and ben everywheres all said he laid over any frog that ever *they* see.

Well, Smiley kept the beast in a little lattice box, and he used to fetch him down town sometimes and lay for a bet. One day a feller—a stranger in the camp, he was—come across him with his box, and says:

"What might it be that you've got in the box?"

And Smiley says, sorter indifferent like, "It might be a parrot, or it might be a canary, maybe, but it ain't—it's only just a frog."

And the feller took it, and looked at it careful, and turned it round this way and that, and says, "H'm—so 'tis. Well, what's *he* good for?"

"Well," Smiley says, easy and careless, "He's good enough for *one* thing I should judge—he can out-jump ary frog in Calaveras county."

The feller took the box again, and took another long, particular look, and give it back to Smiley and says, very deliberate, "Well—I don't see no points about that frog that's any better'n any other frog."

"Maybe you don't," Smiley says. "Maybe you understand frogs, and maybe you don't understand 'em; maybe you've had experience, and maybe you ain't only a amature, as it were. Anyways, I've got my opinion, and I'll resk forty dollars that he can outjump ary frog in Calaveras county."

And the feller studied a minute, and then says, kinder sad, like, "Well—I'm only a stranger here, and I ain't got no frog—but if I had a frog I'd bet you."

And then Smiley says, "That's all right—that's all right—if you'll hold my box a minute I'll go and get you a frog;" and so the feller took the box, and put up his forty dollars along with Smiley's, and set down to wait.

So he set there a good while thinking and thinking to hisself, and then he got the frog out and prized his mouth open and took a tea-spoon and filled him full of quail-shot—filled him pretty near up to his chin—and set him on the floor. Smiley he went out to the swamp and slopped around in the mud for a long time, and finally he ketched a frog and fetched him in and give him to this feller and says:

"Now if you're ready, set him alongside of Dan'l, with his fore-paws just even with Dan'l's, and I'll give the word." Then he says, "one—two—three—jump!" and him and the feller touched up the frogs from behind, and the new frog hopped off lively, but Dan'l give a heave, and hysted up his shoulders—so—like a Frenchman, but it wasn't no use—he couldn't budge; he was planted as solid as a anvil, and he couldn't no more stir than if he was anchored out. Smiley was a good deal surprised, and he was disgusted too, but he didn't have no idea what the matter was, of course.

The feller took the money and started away, and when he was going out at the door he sorter jerked his thumb over his shoulder—this way—at Dan'l, and says again, very deliberate, "Well—I don't see no points about that frog that's any better'n any other frog."

Smiley he stood scratching his head and looking down at Dan'l a long time, and at last he says, "I do wonder what in the nation that frog throwed off for—I wonder if there ain't something the matter with him—he 'pears to look mighty baggy, somehow"—and he ketched Dan'l by the nap of the neck, and lifted him up and says, "Why blame my cats if he don't weigh five pound"—and turned him upside down, and he belched out about a double-handful of shot. And then he see how it was, and he was the maddest man—he set the frog down and took out after that feller, but he never ketched him. And—

(Here Simon Wheeler heard his name called from the front-yard, and got up to go and see what was wanted.) And turning to me as he moved away, he said: "Just sit where you are, stranger, and rest easy—I ain't going to be gone a second."

But by your leave, I did not think that a continuation of the history of the enterprising vagabond Jim Smiley would be likely to afford me much information concerning the Rev. Leonidas W. Smiley, and so I started away.

At the door I met the sociable Wheeler returning, and he buttonholed me and recommenced:

"Well, thish-yer Smiley had a yaller one-eyed cow that didn't have no tail only just a short stump like a bannanner, and —"

"O, curse Smiley and his afflicted cow!" I muttered, good-naturedly, and bidding the old gentleman good-day, I departed.

Yours, truly,
MARK TWAIN.

from ROUGHING IT

But they were rough in those times! They fairly reveled in gold, whisky, fights and fandangoes, and were unspeakably happy. The honest miner raked from a hundred to a thousand dollars out of his claim a day, and what with the gambling dens and the other entertainments, he hadn't a cent the next morning, if he had any sort of luck. They cooked their own bacon and beans, sewed on their own buttons, washed their own shirts—blue woolen ones; and if a man wanted a fight on his hands without any annoying delay, all he had to do was to appear in public in a white shirt or a stove-pipe hat, and he would be accommodated. For those people hated aristocrats. They had a particular and malignant animosity toward what they called a "biled shirt."

It was a wild, free, disorderly, grotesque society! Men—only swarming hosts of stalwart *men*—nothing juvenile, nothing feminine, visible anywhere!

In those days miners would flock in crowds to catch a glimpse of that rare and blessed spectacle, a woman! Old inhabitants tell how, in a certain camp, the news went abroad early in the morning that a woman was come! They had seen a calico dress hanging out of a wagon down at the camping-ground — sign of emigrants from over the great Plains. Everybody went down there, and a shout went up when an actual, bona fide dress was discovered fluttering in the wind! The male emigrant was visible. The miners said:

"Fetch her out!"

He said: "It is my wife, gentlemen—she is sick—we have been robbed of money, provisions, everything, by the Indians—we want to rest."

"Fetch her out! We've got to see her!"

"But, gentlemen, the poor thing, she—"

"FETCH HER OUT!"

He "fetched her out," and they swung their hats and sent up three rousing cheers and a tiger; and they crowded around and gazed at her, and touched her dress, and listened to her voice with the look of men who listened to a *memory* rather than a present reality—and then they collected twenty-five hundred dollars in gold and gave it to the man, and swung their hats again and gave three more cheers, and went home satisfied.

Once I dined in San Francisco with the family of a pioneer, and talked with his daughter, a young lady whose first experience in San Francisco was an adventure, though she herself did not remember it, as she was only two or three years old at the time. Her father said that, after landing from the ship, they were walking up the street, a servant leading the party with the little girl in her arms. And presently a huge miner, bearded, belted, spurred, and bristling with deadly weapons— just down from a long campaign in the mountains, evidently—barred the way, stopped the servant, and stood gazing, with a face all alive with gratification and astonishment. Then he said, reverently:

"Well, if it ain't a child!" And then he snatched a little leather sack out of his pocket and said to the servant:

"There's a hundred and fifty dollars in dust, there, and I'll give it to you to let me kiss the child!"

That anecdote is *true*.

But see how things change. Sitting at that dinner table, listening to that anecdote, if I had offered double the money for the privilege of kissing the same child, I would have been refused. Seventeen added years have far more than doubled the price.

And while upon this subject I will remark that once in Star City, in the Humboldt Mountains, I took my place in a sort of long, post-office single file of miners, to patiently await my chance to peep through a crack in the cabin and get a sight of the splendid new sensation—a genuine, live Woman! And at the end of half of an hour my turn came, and I put my eye to the crack, and there she was, with one arm akimbo, and tossing flap-jacks in a frying-pan with the other. And she was one hundred and sixty-five° years old, and hadn't a tooth in her head.

By and by, an old friend of mine, a miner, came down from one of the decayed mining camps of Tuolumne, California, and I went back with him. We lived in a small cabin on a verdant hillside, and there were not five other cabins in view over the wide expanse of hill and forest. Yet a flourishing city of two or three thousand population had occupied this grassy dead solitude during the flush times of twelve or fifteen years before, and where our cabin stood had once been the heart of the teeming hive, the centre of the city. When the mines gave out the town fell into decay, and in a few years wholly disappeared — streets, dwellings, shops, everything — and left no sign. The grassy slopes were as green and smooth and desolate of life as if they had never been disturbed. The mere handful of miners still remaining, had seen the town spring up, spread, grow, and flourish in its pride; and they had seen it sicken and die, and pass away like a dream. With it their hopes had died, and their zest of life. They had long ago resigned themselves to their exile, and ceased to correspond with their distant friends or turn longing eyes toward their early homes. They had accepted banishment, forgotten the world and been forgotten of the world. They were far from telegraphs and railroads, and they stood, as it were, in a living grave, dead to the events that stirred the globe's great populations, dead to the common interests of men, isolated and outcast from brotherhood with their kind. It was the most singular, and almost the most touching and melancholy exile that fancy can imagine.

I had three hundred dollars left and nowhere in particular to lay my head. I went to Jackass Gulch and cabined for a while with some

---

°Being in calmer mood, now, I voluntarily knock off a hundred from that. — M.T.

friends of mine, surface miners. They were lovely fellows; charming comrades in every way and honest and honorable men; their credit was good for bacon and beans and this was fortunate because their kind of mining was a peculiarly precarious one; it was called pocket-mining, and so far as I have been able to discover, pocket-mining is confined and restricted on this planet to a very small region around about Jackass Gulch.

A "pocket" is a concentration of gold dust in one little spot on the mountainside; it is close to the surface; the rains wash its particles down the mountainside, and they spread, fan-shape, wider and wider as they go. The pocket-miner washes a pan of dirt, finds a speck or two of gold in it, makes a step to the right or the left, washes another pan, finds another speck or two, and goes on washing to the right or to the left until he knows when he has reached the limits of the fan by the best of circumstantial evidence, to wit—that his pan-washings furnish no longer the speck of gold. The rest of his work is easy—he washes along up the mountainside, tracing the narrowing fan by his washings, and at last he reaches the gold deposit. It may contain only a few hundred dollars, which he can take out with a couple of dips of his shovel; also it may contain a concentrated treasure worth a fortune. It is the fortune he is after and he will seek it with a never-perishing hope as long as he lives.

These friends of mine had been seeking that fortune daily for eighteen years; they had never found it but they were not at all discouraged; they were quite sure they would find it some day. . . .

FROM **MARK TWAIN'S NOTEBOOKS & JOURNALS**

Jan. 23, 1865—Angels [Camp]—Rainy, stormy—Beans & dishwater for breakfast at the Frenchman's; dishwater & beans for dinner, and both articles warmed over for supper.

24th—Rained all day—meals as before.

25th—Same as above.

26th—Rain, beans & dishwater—tapidaro [*tapidara:* part of a Mexican stirrup] beefsteak for a change—no use, could not bite it.

27th—Same old diet—same old weather—went out to the "pocket" claim—had to rush back.

28th—Rain & wind all day & all night. Chili beans & dishwater

three times today, as usual, & some kind of "slum" which the Frenchman called "hash." Hash be d — d.

29th — The old, old thing. We shall *have* to stand the weather, but
as J says, we *won't* stand this dishwater & beans any longer, by G —.

30th Jan. — Moved to the new hotel, just opened — good fare, &
coffee that a Christian may drink without jeopardizing his eternal
soul. . . .

Feb. 3 — Dined at the Frenchman's, in order to let Dick see how
he does things. Had Hellfire soup & the old regular beans & dishwater. The Frenchman has 4 kinds of soup which he furnishes to customers only on great occasions. They are popularly known among the
Boarders as Hellfire, General Debility, Insanity & Sudden Death, but
it is not possible to describe them.

---

from THE AUTOBIOGRAPHY OF MARK TWAIN

Our clothes were pretty shabby but that was no matter; we were in the
fashion; the rest of the slender population were dressed as we were.
Our boys hadn't had a cent for several months and hadn't needed one,
their credit being perfectly good for bacon, coffee, flour, beans and
molasses. If there was any difference, Jim [Gillis] was the worst
dressed of the three of us; if there was any discoverable difference in
the matter of age, Jim's shreds were the oldest; but he was a gallant
creature and his style and bearing could make any costume regal. One
day we were in the decayed and naked and rickety inn when a couple
of musical tramps appeared; one of them played the banjo and the
other one danced unscientific clog-dances and sang comic songs that
made a person sorry to be alive. They passed the hat and collected
three or four dimes from the dozen bankrupt pocket-miners present.
When the hat approached Jim he said to me, with his fine millionaire
air, "Let me have a dollar."

I gave him a couple of halves. Instead of modestly dropping them
into the hat, he pitched them into it at the distance of a yard, just as
in the ancient novels milord the Duke doesn't hand the beggar a bene-
faction but "tosses" it to him or flings it at his feet — and it is always a
"purse of gold." In the novel, the witnesses are always impressed; Jim's
great spirit was the spirit of the novel; to him the half-dollars were a
purse of gold; like the Duke he was playing to the gallery, but the par-

allel ends there. In the Duke's case, the witnesses knew he could afford the purse of gold, and the largest part of their admiration consisted in envy of the man who could throw around purses of gold in that fine and careless way. The miners admired Jim's handsome liberality but they knew he couldn't afford what he had done, and that fact modified their admiration.

——•——

Perhaps the reader has visited Utah, Nevada, or California, even in these latter days, and while communing with himself upon the sorrowful banishment of those countries from what he considers "the world," has had his wings clipped by finding that *he* is the one to be pitied, and that there are entire populations around him ready and willing to do it for him—yea, who are complacently doing it for him already, wherever he steps his foot. Poor thing, they are making fun of his hat; and the cut of his New York coat; and his conscientiousness about his grammar; and he feeble profanity; and his consumingly ludicrous ignorance of ores, shafts, tunnels, and other things which he never saw before, and never felt enough interest in to read about. And all the time that he is thinking what a sad fate it is to be exiled to that far country, that lonely land, the citizens around him are looking down on him with a blighting compassion because he is an "emigrant" instead of that proudest and blessedest creature that exists on all the earth, a "FORTY-NINER."

THE ROMANTIC ITCH

{ ...[A] sweetheart of mine whose breath was so sweet it decayed her teeth... }

FROM **A NOTABLE CONUNDRUM**
[*The Californian*, Oct. 1, 1864]

The [Mechanics'] Fair continues, just the same. It is a nice place to hunt for people in. I have hunted for a friend there for as much as two hours of an evening, and at the end of that time found the hunting just as good as it was when I commenced.

If the projectors of this noble Fair never receive a dollar or even a kindly word of thanks for the labor of their hands, the sweat of their brows and the wear and tear of brain it has cost them to plan their work and perfect it, a consciousness of the incalculable good they have conferred upon the community must still give them a placid satisfaction more precious than money or sounding compliments. They have been the means of bringing many a pair of loving hearts together that could not get together anywhere else on account of parents and other obstructions. When you see a young lady standing by the sanitary scarecrow which mutely appeals to the public for quarters and swallows them, you may know by the expectant look upon her face that a young man is going to happen along there presently; and, if you have my luck, you will notice by that look still remaining upon her face that you are not the young man she is expecting. They court a good deal at the Fair, and the young fellows are always exchanging notes with the girls. For this purpose the business cards scattered about the place are found very convenient. I picked up one last night which was printed on both sides, but had been interlined in pencil, by somebody's Arabella, until one could not read it without feeling dizzy. It ran about in this wise — though the interlineations were not in parentheses in the original:

"John Smith, (My Dearest and Sweetest:) Soap Boiler and Candle Factor; (If you love me, if you love) Bar Soap, Castile Soap and Soft Soap, peculiarly suitable for (your Arabella, fly to the) Pacific coast, because of its non-liability to be affected by the climate. Those who may have kitchen refuse to sell, can leave orders, and our soap-fat carts will visit the (Art Gallery. I will be in front of the big mirror in an hour from now, and will go with you to the) corner designated. For the very best Soap and Candles the market affords, apply at the (Academy of Music. And from there, O joy! how my heart thrills with rapture at the prospect! with souls sur-charged with bliss, we will wander forth to the) Soap Factory, or to the office, which is located on the (moon-lit beach,) corner of Jackson street, near the milk ranch. (From Arabella, who sends kisses to her darling) JOHN SMITH, Pioneer Soap Boiler and Candle Factor."

Sweethearts usually treasure up these little affectionate billets, and that this one was lost in the Pavilion, seemed proof to me that its contents were rather distracting to the mind of the young man who received it. He never would have lost it if he had not felt unsettled about something. I think it is likely he got mixed, so to speak, as to whether he was the lucky party, or whether it was the soap-boiler. However, I have possession of her extraordinary document now, and this is to inform Arabella that, in the hope that I may answer for the other young man, and do to fill a void or so in her aching heart, I am drifting about, in an unsettled way, on the look-out for her — sometimes on the Pacific Coast, sometimes at the Art Gallery, sometimes at the soap factory, and occasionally at the moonlit beach and the milk ranch. If she happen to visit either of those places shortly, and will have the goodness to wait a little while, she can calculate on my drifting around in the course of an hour or so.

I cannot say that all visitors to the Fair go there to make love, though I have my suspicions that a good many of them do. Numbers go there to look at the machinery and misunderstand it, and still greater numbers, perhaps, go to criticise the pictures. There is a handsome portrait in the Art Gallery of a pensive young girl. Last night it fell under the critical eye of a connoisseur from Arkansas. She examined it in silence for many minutes, and then she blew her nose calmly, and, says she, "I like it—it is so sad and thinkful."

Somebody knocked Weller's bust down from its shelf at the Fair, the other night, and destroyed it. It was wrong to do it, but it gave rise to a very able pun by a young person who has had much experience in such things, and was only indifferently proud of it. He said it was Weller enough when it was a bust, but just the reverse when it was busted. Explanation: He meant that it looked like Weller in the first place, but it did not after it was smashed to pieces. He also meant that it was well enough to leave it alone and not destroy it. The Author of this fine joke is among us yet, and I can bring him around if you would like to look at him. One would expect him to be haughty and ostentatious, but you would be surprised to see how simple and unpretending he is and how willing to take a drink.

... But the conundrum I have alluded to in the heading of this article, was the best thing of the kind that has ever fallen under my notice. It was projected by a young man who has hardly any education at all, and whose opportunities have been very meagre, even from his childhood up. It was this: "Why was Napoleon when he crossed the Alps, like the Sanitary cheese at the Mechanics' Fair?"

It was very good for a young man just starting in life; don't you think so? He has gone away now to Sacramento. Probably we shall never see him more. He did not state what the answer was.

—•—

from ANSWERS TO CORRESPONDENTS
[*The Californian*, June 10, 1865]

ST. CLAIR HIGGINS, *Los Angeles.*—"My life is a failure; I have adored, wildly, madly, and she whom I love has turned coldly from me and shed her affections upon another; what would you advise me to do?" You should shed your affections on another, also—or on several, if there are enough to go round. Also, do everything you can to make your former flame unhappy. There is an absurd idea disseminated in novels, that the happier a girl is with another man, the happier it makes the old lover she has blighted. Don't you allow yourself to believe any such nonsense as that. The more cause that girl finds to regret that she did not marry you, the more comfortable you will feel over it. It isn't poetical, but it is mighty sound doctrine.

—•—

MORE ROMANCE
[*Territorial Enterprise*, Dec. 11, 1865]

The pretty waiter girls are always getting people into trouble. But I beg pardon—I should say "ladies," not "girls." I learned this lesson "in the days when I went gypsying," which was a long time ago. I said to one of these self-important hags, "Mary, or Julia, or whatever your name may be, who is that old slab singing at the piano—the girl with the 'bile' on her nose?" Her eyes snapped. "You call her *girl!*—you shall find out yourself—she is a *lady*, if you please!" They are all "ladies," and they take it as an insult when they are called anything else. It was one of these charming ladies who got shot, by an ass of a lover from the wilds of Arizona, yesterday in the Thunderboldt Saloon, but unhappily not killed. The fellow had enjoyed so long the society of ill-favored squaws who have to be scraped before one can tell the color of their complexions, that he was easily carried away with the well sea-soned charms of "French Mary" of the Thunderboldt Saloon, and got so "spooney" in his attentions that he hung around her night after night, and breathed her garlicky sighs with ecstasy. But no man can be honored with a beer girl's society without paying for it. French Mary made this man Vernon buy basket after basket of cheap champagne and got a heavy commission, which is usually their privilege; in the saloon her company always cost him five or ten dollars an hour, and she was doubtless a still more expensive luxury out of it.

It is said that he was always insisting upon her marrying him, and threatening to leave and go back to Arizona if she did not. She could not afford to let the goose go until he was completely plucked, and so she would consent, and set the day, and then the poor devil, in a burst of generosity, would celebrate the happy event with a heavy outlay of cash. This ruse was played until it was worn out, until Vernon's patience was worn out, until Vernon's purse was worn out also. Then there was no use in humbugging the poor numscull any longer, of course; and so French Mary deserted him, to wait on customers who had cash—the unfeeling practice always observed by lager beer ladies under sim-ilar circumstances. She told him she would not marry him or have anything more to do with him, and he very properly tried to blow her brains out. But he was awkward, and only wounded her dangerously. He killed himself, though, effectually, and let us hope that it was the wisest thing he could have done, and that he is better off now, poor fellow.

———◄•►———

AURELIA'S UNFORTUNATE YOUNG MAN
[*The Californian*, Oct. 22, 1864]

The facts in the case come to me by letter from a young lady who lives in the beautiful city of San José; she is personally unknown to me, and simply signs herself "Aurelia Maria," which may possibly be a fictitious name. But no matter, the poor girl is almost heart-broken by the misfortunes she has undergone, and so confused by the conflicting counsels of misguided friends and insidious enemies, that she does not know what course to pursue in order to extricate herself from the web of difficulties in which she seems almost hopelessly involved. In this dilemma she turns to me for help, and supplicates for my guidance and instruction with a moving eloquence that would touch the heart of a statue. Hear her sad story:

She says that when she was sixteen years old she met and loved with all the devotion of a passionate nature a young man from New Jersey, named Williamson Breckinridge Caruthers, who was some six years her senior. They were engaged, with the free consent of their friends and relatives, and for a time it seemed as if their career was destined to be characterized by an immunity from sorrow beyond the usual lot of humanity. But at last the tide of fortune turned; young Caruthers became infected with smallpox of the most virulent type, and when he recovered from his illness, his face was pitted like a waffle-mould, and his comeliness gone forever. Aurelia thought to break off the engagement at first, but pity for her unfortunate lover caused her to postpone the marriage-day for a season, and give him another trial. The very day before the wedding was to have taken place, Breckinridge, while absorbed in watching the flight of a balloon, walked into a well and fractured one of his legs, and it had to be taken off above the knee. Again Aurelia was moved to break the engagement, but again love triumphed, and she set the day forward and gave him another chance to reform. And again misfortune overtook the unhappy youth. He lost one arm by the premature discharge of a Fourth of July cannon, and within three months he got the other pulled out by a carding-machine. Aurelia's heart was almost crushed by these latter calamities. She could not but be deeply grieved to see her lover passing from her piecemeal, feeling, as she did, that he could not last forever under this disastrous process of reduction, yet knowing of no way to stop its dreadful career, and in her tearful despair she almost regretted, like brokers who hold on and lose, that she had not taken him at first, before he had suffered such an alarming depreciation. Still, her brave soul bore her up, and she resolved to bear with her friend's unnatural disposition yet a little longer. Again the wedding-day approached, and again disappointment overshadowed it; Caruthers fell ill with the erysipelas, and lost the use of one of his eyes entirely. The friends and relatives of the bride, considering that she had already put up with more than could reasonably be expected of her, now came forward and insisted that the match should be broken off; but after wavering awhile, Aurelia, with a generous spirit which did her credit, said she had reflected calmly upon the matter and could not discover that Breckinridge was to blame. So she extended the time once more, and he broke his other leg. It was a sad day for the poor girl when she saw the surgeons reverently bearing away the sack whose uses she had learned by previous experience, and her heart told her the bitter truth that some more of her lover was gone. She felt that the field of her affections was growing more and more circumscribed every day, but once more she frowned down her relatives and renewed her betrothal. Shortly before the time set for the nuptials another disaster occurred. There was but one man scalped by the Owens River Indians last year. That man was Williamson Breckinridge Caruthers, of New Jersey. He was hurrying home with happiness in his heart, when he lost his hair forever, and in that hour of bitterness he almost cursed the mistaken mercy that had spared his head.

At last Aurelia is in serious perplexity as to what she ought to do. She still loves her Breckinridge, she writes, with truly womanly feeling—she still loves what is left of him—but her parents are bitterly opposed to the match, because he has no property and is disabled from working, and she has not sufficient means to support both comfortably. "Now, what should she do?" she asks with painful and anxious solicitude.

It is a delicate question; it is one which involves the life-long happiness of a woman, and that of nearly two-thirds of a man, and I feel that it would be assuming too great a responsibility to do more than make a mere suggestion in the case. How would it do to build to him?

If Aurelia can afford the expense, let her furnish her mutilated lover with wooden arms and wooden legs, and a glass eye and a wig, and give him another show; give him ninety days, without grace, and if he does not break his neck in the meantime, marry him and take the chances. It does not seem to me that there is much risk, any way, because if he sticks to his singular propensity for damaging himself every time he sees a good opportunity, his next experiment is bound to finish him, and then you are all right, you know, married or single. If married, the wooden legs and such other valuables as he may possess, revert to the widow, and you see you sustain no actual loss save the cherished fragment of a noble but most unfortunate husband, who honestly strove to do right, but whose extraordinary instincts were against him. Try it, Maria! I have thought the matter over carefully and well, and it is the only chance I see for you. It would have been a happy conceit on the part of Caruthers if he had started with his neck and broken that first, but since he has seen fit to choose a different policy and string himself out as long as possible, I do not think we ought to upbraid him for it if he has enjoyed it. We must do the best we can under the circumstances, and try not to feel exasperated at him.

ONE REPORTER'S LIFE

The old saw says,
'Let a sleeping dog lie.' Right.
Still, when there
is much at stake it is better to
get a newspaper to do it.

FROM **THE AUTOBIOGRAPHY OF MARK TWAIN**

After leaving Nevada I was a reporter on the *Morning Call* of San Francisco. I was more than that—I was *the* reporter. There was no other. There was enough work for one and a little over, but not enough for two—according to Mr. Barnes' idea, and he was the proprietor and therefore better situated to know about it than other people.

By nine in the morning I had to be at the police court for an hour and make a brief history of the squabbles of the night before. They were usually between Irishmen and Irishmen, and Chinamen and Chinamen, with now and then a squabble between the two races for a change. Each day's evidence was substantially a duplicate of the evidence of the day before, therefore the daily performance was killingly monotonous and wearisome. So far as I could see there was only one man connected with it who found anything like a compensating interest in it, and that was the court interpreter. He was an Englishman who was glibly familiar with fifty-six Chinese dialects. He had to change from one to another of them every ten minutes and this exercise was so energizing that it kept him always awake, which was not the case with the reporters. Next we visited the higher courts and made notes of the decisions which had been rendered the day before. All the courts came under the head of "regulars." They were sources of reportorial information which never failed. During the rest of the day we raked the town from end to end, gathering such material as we might, wherewith to fill our required column—and if there were no fires to report we started some.

At night we visited the six theaters, one after the other: seven nights a week, three hundred and sixty-five nights in the year. We remained in each of those places five minutes, got the merest passing glimpse of play and opera, and with that for a text we "wrote up" those plays and operas, as the phrase goes, torturing our souls every night from the beginning of the year to the end of it in the effort to find something to say about those performances which we had not said a couple of hundred times before. There has never been a time from that day to this, forty years, that I have been able to look at even the outside of a theater without a spasm of the dry gripes, as "Uncle Remus" calls it—and as for the inside, I know next to nothing about that, for in all this time I have seldom had a sight of it nor ever had a desire in that regard which couldn't have been overcome by argument.

After having been hard at work from nine or ten in the morning until eleven at night scraping material together, I took the pen and spread this muck out in words and phrases and made it cover as much acreage as I could. It was fearful drudgery, soulless drudgery, and almost destitute of interest. It was an awful slavery for a lazy man, and I was born lazy. I am no lazier now [1906] than I was forty years ago but that is because I reached the limit forty years ago. You can't go beyond possibility.

Finally there was an event. One Sunday afternoon I saw some hoodlums chasing and stoning a Chinaman who was heavily laden with the weekly wash of his Christian customers, and I noticed that a policeman was observing this performance with an amused interest—nothing more. He did not interfere. I wrote up the incident with considerable warmth and holy indignation. Usually I didn't want to read in the morning what I had written the night before; it had come from a torpid heart. But this item had come from a live one. There was fire in it and I believed there was literature—and so I sought for it in the paper next morning with eagerness. It wasn't there. It wasn't there the next morning, nor the next. I went up to the composing room and found it tucked away among condemned matter on the standing gallery. I asked about it. The foreman said Mr. Barnes had found it in a galley proof and ordered its extinction. And Mr. Barnes furnished his reasons—either to me or to the foreman, I don't remember which; but they were commercially sound. He said that the *Call* was like the New

York *Sun* of that day: it was the washerwoman's paper — that is, it was the paper of the poor; it was the only cheap paper. It gathered its livelihood from the poor and must respect their prejudices or perish. The Irish were the poor. They were the stay and support of the *Morning Call;* without them the *Morning Call* could not survive a month — and they hated the Chinamen. Such an assault as I had attempted could rouse the whole Irish hive and seriously damage the paper. The *Call* could not afford to publish articles criticizing the hoodlums for stoning Chinamen.

I was lofty in those days. I have survived it. I was unwise then. I am up-to-date now. . . .

But, as I was saying, I was loftier forty years ago than I am now and I felt a deep shame in being situated as I was — slave of such a journal as the *Morning Call.* If I had been still loftier I would have thrown up my berth and gone out and starved, like any other hero. But I had never had any experience. I had *dreamed* heroism, like everybody, but I had no practice and I didn't know how to begin. I couldn't bear to begin with starving. I had already come near to that once or twice in my life and got no real enjoyment out of remembering about it. I knew I couldn't get another berth if I resigned. I knew it perfectly well. Therefore I swallowed my humiliation and stayed where I was. But whereas there had been little enough interest attaching to my industries before, there was none at all now. I continued my work but I took not the least interest in it, and naturally there were results. I got to neglecting it. As I have said, there was too much of it for one man. The way I was conducting it now, there was apparently work enough in it for two or three. Even Barnes noticed that, and told me to get an assistant, on half wages.

There was a great hulking creature down in the counting room — good-natured, obliging, unintellectual — and he was getting little or nothing a week and boarding himself. A graceless boy of the counting-room force who had no reverence for anybody or anything was always making fun of this beach-comber, and he had a name for him which somehow seemed intensely apt and descriptive — I don't know why. He called him Smiggy McGlural. I offered the berth of assistant to Smiggy and he accepted it with alacrity and gratitude. He went at his work with ten times the energy that was left in me. He was not intellectual but mentality was not required or needed in a *Morning Call* reporter and so he conducted his office to perfection. I gradually got to leaving more and more of the work to McGlural. I grew lazier and lazier and within thirty days he was doing almost the whole of it. It was also plain that he could accomplish the whole of it and more all by himself and therefore had no real need of me.

It was at this crucial moment that that event happened which I mentioned a while ago. Mr. Barnes discharged me. It was the only time in my life that I have ever been discharged and it hurts yet— although I am in my grave. He did not discharge me rudely. It was not in his nature to do that. He was a large, handsome man, with a kindly face and courteous ways, and was faultless in his dress. He could not have said a rude, ungentle thing to anybody. He took me privately aside and advised me to resign. It was like a father advising a son for his good, and I obeyed.

I was on the world now, with nowhere to go. By my Presbyterian training I knew that the *Morning Call* had brought disaster upon itself. I knew the ways of Providence and I knew that this offense would have to be answered for. I could not foresee when the penalty would fall nor what shape it would take but I was as certain that it would come, sooner or later, as I was of my own existence. I could not tell whether it would fall upon Barnes or upon his newspaper. But Barnes was the guilty one and I knew by my training that the punishment always falls upon the innocent one, consequently I felt sure that it was the newspaper that at some future day would suffer for Barnes' crime.

Sure enough! Among the very first pictures that arrived in the fourth week of April [1906, just after the great San Francisco earth-quake]—there stood the *Morning Call* building towering out of the wrecked city like a Washington Monument; and the body of it was all gone and nothing was left but the iron bones! It was then that I said, "How wonderful are the ways of Providence!" I had known it would happen. I had known it for forty years. I had never lost confidence in Providence during all that time. It was put off longer than I was expecting but it was now comprehensive and satisfactory to make up for that. Some people would think it curious that Providence should destroy an entire city of four hundred thousand inhabitants to settle an account of forty years standing, between a mere discharged reporter and a newspaper, but to me there was nothing strange about that, because I was educated, I was trained, I was a Presbyterian and I knew how these things were done. I knew that in Biblical times if a man committed a sin the extermination of the whole surrounding nation — cattle and all — was likely to happen. I knew that Providence was not particular about the rest, so that He got somebody connected with the one He was after. . . .

DUE WARNING
[*Morning Call*, Sept. 18, 1864]

Some one carried away a costly and beautiful hat from the Occidental Hotel, (where it was doing duty as security for a board bill,) some ten days ago, to the great and increasing unhappiness of its owner. Its return to the place from whence it was ravished, or to this office, will be a kindness which we shall be only too glad to reciprocate if we ever get a precisely similar opportunity, and the victim shall insist upon it. The hat in question was of the "plug" species, and was made by Tiffany; upon its inner surface the name of "J. Smith" had once been inscribed, but could not easily be deciphered, latterly, on account of "Mark Twain" having been written over it. We do not know J. Smith personally, but we remember meeting him at a social party some time ago, and at that time a misfortune similar to the one of which we are now complaining happened to him. He had several virulent cutaneous diseases, poor fellow, and we have somehow acquired them, also. We do not consider that the hat had anything to do with the matter, but we mention the circumstance as being a curious coincidence. However, we do not desire to see the coincidence extend to the whole community, notwithstanding the fact that the contemplation of its progress could not do otherwise than excite a lively and entertaining solicitude on the part of the people, and therefore we hasten, after ten days' careful deliberation, to warn the public against the calamity by which they are threatened. And we will not disguise a selfish hope, at the same time, that these remarks may have the effect of weaning from our hat the spoiler's affections, and of inducing him to part with it with some degree of cheerfulness. We do not really want it, but it is a comfort to us in our sorrow to be able thus to make it (as a commodity of barter and sale to other parties,) something of a drug on the market, as it were.

SPIRIT OF THE LOCAL PRESS
[*Territorial Enterprise*, Dec. 1865]

San Francisco is a city of startling events. Happy is the man whose destiny it is to gather them up and record them in a daily newspaper! That sense of conferring benefit, profit and innocent pleasure upon one's fellow-creatures which is so cheering, so calmly blissful to the plodding pilgrim here below, is his, every day in the year. When he gets up in the morning he can do as old Franklin did, and say, "This day, and all days, shall be unselfishly devoted to the good of my fellow-creatures — to the amelioration of their condition — to the conferring of happiness upon them — to the storing of their minds with wisdom which shall fit them for their struggle with the hard world, here, and for the enjoyment of a glad eternity hereafter. And thus striving, so shall I be blessed!" And when he goes home at night, he can exult and say: "Through the labors of these hands and this brain, which God hath given me, blessed and wise are my fellow-creatures this day!

"I have told them of the wonder of the swindling of the friend of Bain, the unknown Bain from Petaluma Creek, by the obscure Catharine McCarthy, out of $300 — and told it with entertaining verbosity in half a column.

"I have told them that Christmas is coming, and people go strangely about, buying things — I have said it in forty lines.

"I related how a vile burglar entered a house to rob, and actually went away again when he found he was discovered. I told it briefly, in thirty-five lines.

"In forty lines I told how a man swindled a Chinaman out of a couple of shirts, and for fear the matter might seem trivial, I made a pretense of only having mentioned it in order to base upon it a criticism upon a grave defect in our laws.

"I fulminated again, in a covert way, the singular conceit that Christmas is at hand, and said people were going about in the most unaccountable way buying stuff to eat, in the markets — 52 lines.

"I glorified a fearful conflagration that came so near burning something, that I shudder even now to think of it. Three thousand dollars worth of goods destroyed by water — a man then went up and put out the fire with a bucket of water. I puffed our fine fire organization — 64 lines.

"I printed some other extraordinary occurrences — runaway horse — 28 lines; dog fight — 30 lines; Chinaman captured by officer

Rose for stealing chickens — 90 lines; unknown Chinaman dead on
Sacramento steamer — 5 lines; several 'Fourteener' [The Fourteenth
Regiment, stationed at the Presidio] items, concerning people frightened and boots stolen — 52 lines; case of soldier stealing a washboard
worth fifty cents — three-quarters of a column. Much other wisdom I
disseminated, and for these things let my reward come hereafter."

And his reward *will* come hereafter — and I am sorry enough to
think it. But such startling things do happen every day in this strange
city! — and how dangerously exciting must be the employment of writing them up for the daily papers!

—◆—

FROM **A LECTURE**
[*Ohio State Journal*, Jan. 6, 1872]

No other occupation brings a man into such familiar sociable relations
with all grades and classes of people. The last thing at night — midnight — he goes browsing around after items among police and jail-
birds, in the lock-up, questioning the prisoners, and making pleasant
and lasting friendships with some of the worst people in the world.
And the very next evening he gets himself up regardless of expenses,
puts on all the good clothes his friends have got — goes and takes dinner with the Governor, or the Commander-in-Chief of the District, the
United States Senator, and some more of the upper crust of society.
He is on good terms with all of them, and is present at every public
gathering, and has easy access to every variety of people. Why I break-
fasted almost every morning with the Governor, dined with the principal clergyman, and slept in the station house.

—◆—

FROM **MISSIONARIES WANTED FOR SAN FRANCISCO**
[*Morning Call*, June 28, 1864]

We do not like it, as far as we have got. We shall probably not fall so
deeply in love with reporting for a San Francisco paper as to make it
impossible ever to wean us from it. There is a powerful saving-clause
for us in the fact that the conservators of public information — the
persons whose positions afford them opportunities not enjoyed by
others to keep themselves posted concerning the important events of

the city's daily life—do not appear to know anything. At the offices and places of business we have visited in search of information, we have got it in just the same shape every time, with a promptness and uniformity which is startling, perhaps, but not gratifying. They all answer and say unto you, "I don't know." We do not mind that, so much, but we do object to a man's parading his ignorance with an air of overbearing egotism which shows you that he is proud of it. True merit is modest, and why should not true ignorance be?...

---

from STEAMER DEPARTURES
[*Territorial Enterprise*, Oct. 1896]

I feel savage this morning. And as usual, when one wants to growl, it is almost impossible to find things to growl about with any degree of satisfaction. I cannot find anything in the steamer departures to get mad at. Only, I wonder who "J. Schmeltzer" is?—and what does he have such an atrocious name for?—and what business has he got in the States?—who is there in the States who cares whether Schmeltzer comes or not? The conduct of this unknown Schmeltzer is exasperating to the last degree....

---

from THE KILLING OF JULIUS CAESAR LOCALIZED
[*The Californian*, Nov. 12, 1864]

Nothing in the world affords a newspaper reporter so much satisfaction as gathering up the details of a bloody and mysterious murder, and writing them up with aggravated circumstantiality. He takes a living delight in this labor of love—for such it is to him—especially if he knows that all the other papers have gone to press and his will be the only one that will contain the dreadful intelligence.

FROM A LETTER TO HIS BROTHER AND SISTER-IN-LAW

San F. — Oct. 19, 1865

My Dear Bro & Sister:

... I never had but two *powerful* ambitions in my life. One was to be a pilot, & the other a preacher of the gospel. I accomplished the one and failed in the other, *because* I could not supply myself with the necessary stock in trade — *i.e.* religion. I have given it up forever. I never had a "call" in that direction, anyhow, & my aspirations were the very ecstasy of presumption. But I *have* had a "call" to literature, of a low order — *i.e.* humorous. It is nothing to be proud of, but it is my strongest suit, & if I were to listen to that maxim of stern duty which says that to do right you *must* multiply the one or the two or the three talents which the Almighty entrusts to your keeping, I would long ago have ceased to meddle with things for which I was by nature unfitted & turned my attention to seriously scribbling to excite the *laughter* of God's creatures. Poor, pitiful business!

P.S. You had better shove this in the stove — for if we strike a bargain I don't want any absurd "literary remains" & "unpublished letters of Mark Twain" published after I am planted.

LAW & ORDER

———— ◆◆◆ ————

We have a criminal jury system
which is superior to any in the world;
and its efficiency is only marred
by the difficulty of finding twelve men
every day who don't know anything
and can't read.

———— ◆◆◆ ————

INTERESTING LITIGATION
[*Morning Call*, Sept. 15, 1864]

San Francisco beats the world for novelties; but the inventive faculties of her people are exercised on a specialty. We don't care much about creating things other countries can supply us with. We have on hand a vast quantity of a certain kind of material and we must work it up, and we do work it up often to an alarming pitch. Controversy is our forte. Californians can raise more legal questions and do the wager of combat in more ways than have been eliminated from the arcana of civil and military jurisprudence since Justinian wrote or Agamemnon fought. Suits—why we haven't names for half of them. A man has a spite at his neighbor—and what man or man's wife hasn't—and he forthwith prosecutes him in the Police Court, for having onions for breakfast, under some ordinance or statutory provision having about as much relation to the case as the title page of Webster's Dictionary. And then, there's an array of witnesses who are well posted in everything else except the matter in controversy. And indefatigable attorneys enlighten the Court by drawing from the witnesses the whole detailed history of the last century. And then again we are in doubt about some little matter of personal or public convenience, and slap goes somebody into Court under duress of a warrant. If we want to determine the age of a child who has grown out of our knowledge, we commence a prosecution at once against someone else with children, and elicit from witnesses enough chronological information to fill a whole encyclopedia, to prove that our child of a doubtful age was cotemporary with the children of defendant, and thus approximate to the period of nativity sought for. A settlement of mutual accounts is arrived at by a prosecution for obtaining goods or money under false pretences. Partnership affairs are elucidated in a prosecution for grand larceny. A burglary simply indicates that a creditor called at the house of his debtor the night before market morning, to collect a small bill. We have nothing but a civil code. A portion of our laws are criminal in name only. We have no law for crime. Cut, slosh around with pistols and dirk knives as you will, and the worst that comes of it is a petty charge of carrying concealed weapons; and murder is but an aggravated assault and battery. We go into litigation instinctively, like a young duck goes into the water. A man can't dig a shovel full of sand out of a drift that threatens to overwhelm his property, nor put a fence around his lot that some person has once driven a wagon across, but what he is dragged before some tribunal to answer to a misdemeanor. Personal revenge, or petty jealousies and animosities, or else the pursuit of information under difficulties, keep up a heavy calendar, and the Judge of the Court spends three-fourths of his time listening to old women's quarrels, and tales that ought, in many cases, to consign the witnesses themselves to the prison cell, and dismissing prosecutions that are brought without probable cause, nor the shadow of it. A prosecuting people we are, and we are getting no better every day. The census of the city can almost be taken now from the Police Court calendar; and a month's attendance on that institution will give one a familiar acquaintance with more than half of our domestic establishments.

THE KAHN OF TARTARY
[*Morning Call*, June 29, 1864]

Lena Kahn, otherwise known as Mother Kahn, or the Kahn of Tartary, who is famous in this community for her infatuated partiality for the Police Court as a place of recreation, was on hand there again yesterday morning. She was mixed up in a triangular row, the sides of the triangle being Mr. Oppenheim, Mrs. Oppenheim, and herself. It appeared from the evidence that she formed the base of the triangle — which is to say, she was at the bottom of the row, and struck the first blow. Moses Levi, being sworn, said he was in the neighborhood, and heard Mrs. Oppenheim scream; knew it was her by the vicious expression she always threw into her screams; saw the defendant (her husband) go into the Tartar's house and gobble up the partner of his bosom and his business, and rescue her from the jaws of destruction (meaning Mrs. Kahn,) and bring her forth to sport once more amid the ———. At this point the lawyer turned off Mr. Levi's gas, which seemed to be degenerating into poetry, and asked him what his occupation was? The Levite said he drove an express wagon. The lawyer—with that sensitiveness to the slightest infringement of the truth, which is so becoming to the profession—inquired severely if he did not sometimes drive the horse also! The wretched witness, thus detected before the multitude in his deep-laid and subtle prevarication, hung his head in silence. His evidence could no longer be respected, and he moved away from the stand with the consciousness written upon his countenance of how fearful a thing it is to trifle with the scruples of a lawyer. Mrs. Oppenheim next came forward and gave a portion of her testimony in damaged English, and the balance in dark and mysterious German. In the English glimpses of her story it was discernible that she had innocently trespassed upon the domain of the Kahn, and had been rudely seized upon in such a manner as to make her arm turn blue, (she turned up her sleeve and showed the Judge,) and the bruise had grown worse since that day, until at last it was tinged with a ghastly green, (she turned up her sleeve again for impartial judicial inspection,) and instantly after receiving this affront, so humiliating to one of gentle blood, she had been set upon without cause or provocation, and thrown upon the floor and "licked." This last expression possessed a charm for Mrs. Oppenheim, that no persuasion of Judge or lawyers could induce her to forego, even for the sake of bringing her wrongs into a stronger light, so long as those wrongs, in such an event, must be portrayed in language less pleasant to her ear. She said the Kahn had licked her, and she stuck to it and reiterated with unflinching firmness. Becoming confused by repeated assaults from the lawyers in the way of badgering questions, which her wavering senses could no longer comprehend, she relapsed at last into hopeless German again, and retired within the lines. Mr. Oppenheim then came forward and remained under fire for fifteen minutes, during which time he made it as plain as the disabled condition of his English would permit him to do, that he was not in anywise to blame, at any rate; that his wife went out after a warrant for the arrest of the Kahn; that she stopped to "make it up" with the Kahn, and the redoubtable Kahn tackled her; that he was dry-nursing the baby at the time, and when he heard his wife scream, he suspected, with a sagacity which did him credit, that she wouldn't have "hollered 'dout dere vas someding de matter;" therefore he piled the child up in a corner remote from danger, and moved upon the works of the Tartar; she had waltzed into the wife and finished her, and was already on picket duty, waiting for the husband, and when he came she smacked him over the head a couple of times with the deadly bludgeon she uses to elevate linen to the clothes-line with; and then, stimulated by this encouragement, he started to the Police Office to get out a warrant for the arrest of the victorious army, but the victorious army, always on the alert, was there ahead of him, and he now stood in the presence of the Court in the humiliating position of a man who had aspired to be plaintiff, but overcome by strategy, had sunk to the grade of defendant. At this point his mind wandered, his vivacious tongue grew thick with mushy German syllables, and the last of the Oppenheims sank to rest at the feet of justice. We had done less than our duty had we allowed this most important trial — freighted, as it was, with matters of the last importance to every member of this community, and every conscientious, law-abiding man and woman upon whom the sun of civilization shines today — to be given to the world in the columns, with no more elaboration than the customary "Benjamin Oppenheim, assault and battery, dismissed; Lena Oppenheim and Fredrika Kahn, held to answer." We thought, at first, of starting in that way, under the head of "Police Court," but a second glance at the case showed us that it was one of a most serious and extraordinary nature, and ought to be put in such a shape that the public could give to it that grave and deliberate consideration which its magnitude entitled it to.

PEEPING TOM OF COVENTRY
[*Morning Call*, Sept. 6, 1864]

An amorous old sinner, named John Fine, went to the North Beach bath-house on Sunday for a swim. Owing to the number of pounds he weighed, he was forced to wade — his weight being considerably over several stone he couldn't swim, for who ever heard of stones swimming. In order to make up the deficit of fun, he went to the partition that screens the ladies' department, and peeped through a crevice. Mr. Ills, the proprietor of the establishment, witnessed the untoward scrutiny, and ordered him away; but life's charms riveted Fine to the spot, and he heeded not the Ills, when his person suffered under the weight of another stone. The proprietor sent a projectile which struck him in the face, near the left eye. Astronomically speaking, Fine saw stars, but didn't think it a fine sight. He left at once and prosecuted Ills. Yesterday Mr. Ills was fined five dollars for assault and battery.

ADVICE TO WITNESSES
[*Morning Call*, Sept. 29, 1864]

Witnesses in the Police Court, who expect to be questioned on the part of the prosecution, should always come prepared to answer the following questions: "Was you there, at the time?" "Did you see it done, and if you did, how do you know?" "City and County of San Francisco?" "Is your mother living, and if so, is she well?" "You say the defendant struck the plaintiff with a stick. Please state to the Court what kind of a stick it was?" "Did it have the bark on, and if so, what kind of bark did it have on?" "Do you consider that such a stick would be just as good with the bark on, as with it off, or vicy versy?" "Why?" "I think you said it occurred in the City and County of San Francisco?" "You say your mother has been dead seventeen years—native of what place, and why?" "You don't know anything about this assault and battery, do you?" "Did you ever study astronomy?—hard, isn't it?" "You have seen this defendant before, haven't you?" "Did you ever slide on a cellar door when you were a boy?" "Well—that's all." "Stay: did this occur in the City and County of San Francisco?" The Prosecuting Attorney may mean well enough, but meaning well and doing well are two very different things. His abilities are of the mildest description, and do not fit him for a position like the one he holds, where energy, industry, tact, shrewdness, and some little smattering of law, are indispensable to the proper fulfilment of its duties. Criminals leak through his fingers every day like water through a sieve. He does not even afford a cheerful amount of competition in business to the sharp lawyers over whose heads he was elected to be set up as an ornamental effigy in the Police Court. He affords a great deal less than no assistance to the Judge, who could convict sometimes if the District

Attorney would remain silent, or if the law had not hired him at a salary of two hundred and fifty dollars a month to unearth the dark and ominous fact that the "offence was committed in the City and County of San Francisco." The man means well enough, but he don't know how; he makes of the proceedings in behalf of a sacred right and justice in the Police Court, a drivelling farce, and he ought to show his regard for the public welfare by resigning.

NUISANCE
[*Morning Call*, Sept. 27, 1864]

Mrs. Hall entered complaint against a groggery at the corner of Post and Taylor streets, as a nuisance, yesterday, in the Police Court. The case was dismissed. It might not have been, if she had gone to the expense of procuring more legal assistance to prosecute it. The Prosecuting Attorney is a powerful engine, in his way, but he is not infallible. If parties would start him in and let him worm out of the witnesses all the facts that have no bearing upon the case, and no connection with it, and whether the offence was committed "In the City'n County San Francisco" or not, and then have another talented lawyer to start in and find out all the facts that do bear upon the case and are really connected with it, what multitudes of rascals that now escape would suffer the just penalties of their transgressions. With his spectacles on, and his head tilted back at a proper angle, there is no question that the Prosecuting Attorney is an ornament to the Police Court; but whether he is particularly useful or not, or whether the Government could worry along without him or not, or whether it is necessary that a Prosecuting Attorney should give all his time, or bend all his energies, or throw all his soul into the one thing of being strictly ornamental, or not, are matters which do not concern us, and which we have never once thought about. Sometimes he has some of his witnesses there, and isn't that sufficient?

POLICE COURT TESTIMONY
[*Morning Call*, July 12, 1864]

If there is anything more absurd than the general average of Police Court testimony, we do not know what it is. Witnesses stand up here, every day, and swear to the most extravagant propositions with an easy indifference to consequences in the next world that is altogether refreshing. Yesterday—under oath—a witness said that while he was holding the prisoner at the bar so that he could not break loose, the prisoner "pushed my wife with his hand—so—*tried to push her over and kill her!*" There was no evidence to show that the prisoner had anything against the woman, or was bothering himself about anything but his scuffle with her husband. Yet the witness surmised that he had the purpose hidden away in his mind somewhere to take her life, and he stood right up to the rack and swore to it; and swore also that he tried to turn this noble Dutchwoman into a corpse, by the simple act of pushing her over. That same woman might be pushed over the Yo Semite Falls without being killed by it, although it stands to reason that if she struck fair and bounced, it would probably shake her up some.

ACCOMMODATING WITNESS
[*Morning Call*, Sept. 25, 1864]

A man was summoned to testify in the Police Court, yesterday, and simply because he said he would swear a jackass was a canary, if necessary, his services were declined. It was not generous to crush a liberal spirit like that.

FROM THE EVIDENCE IN THE CASE OF SMITH VS. JONES
[*Golden Era*, June 26, 1864]

REPORTED BY MARK TWAIN

I reported this trial simply for my own amusement, one idle day last week, and without expecting to publish any portion of it—but I have seen the facts in the case so distorted and misrepresented in the daily papers that I feel it my duty to come forward and do what I can to set the plaintiff and the defendant right before the public. This can best be done by submitting the plain, unembellished statements of the witnesses as given under oath before his Honor Judge Shepherd, in the Police Court, and leaving the people to form their own judgment of the matters involved, unbiased by argument or suggestion of any kind from me.

There is that nice sense of justice and that ability to discriminate between right and wrong, among the masses, which will enable them ... to decide without hesitation which is the innocent party and which the guilty in the remarkable case of Smith vs. Jones, and I have every confidence that before this paper shall have been out of the printing-press twenty-four hours, the high court of The People, from whose decision there is no appeal, will have swept from the innocent man all taint of blame or suspicion, and cast upon the guilty one a deathless infamy.

To such as are not used to visiting the Police Court, I will observe that there is nothing inviting about the place, there being no rich carpets, no mirrors, no pictures, no elegant sofa or arm-chairs to lounge in, no free lunch — and in fact, nothing to make a man who has been there once desire to go again — except in cases where his bail is heavier than his fine is likely to be, under which circumstances he naturally has a tendency in that direction again, of course, in order to recover the difference.

There is a pulpit at the head of the hall, occupied by a handsome gray-haired Judge, with a faculty of appearing pleasant and impartial to the disinterested spectator, and prejudiced and frosty to the last degree to the prisoner at the bar.

To the left of the pulpit is a long table for reporters; in front of the pulpit the clerks are stationed, and in the centre of the hall a nest of lawyers. On the left again are pine benches behind a railing, occupied by seedy white men, negroes, Chinamen, Kanakas — in a word, by the seedy and dejected of all nations — and in a corner is a box where more can be had when they are wanted.

On the right are more pine benches, for the use of prisoners, and their friends and witnesses.

An officer, in a gray uniform, and with a star upon his breast, guards the door.

A holy calm pervades the scene.

The case of Smith vs. Jones being called, each of these parties (stepping out from among the other seedy ones) gave the Court a particular and circumstantial account of how the whole thing occurred, and then sat down.

The two narratives differed from each other.

In reality, I was half persuaded that these men were talking about two separate and distinct affairs altogether, inasmuch as no single circumstance mentioned by one was even remotely hinted at by the other....

The testimony on the cross-examination went to show that during the fight, one of the parties drew a slung-shot and cocked it, but to the best of the witness' knowledge and belief, he did not fire; and at the same time, the other discharged a hand-grenade at his antagonist, which missed him and did no damage, except blowing up a bonnet store on the other side of the street, and creating a momentary diversion among the milliners. He could not say, however, which drew the slung-shot or which threw the grenade. (It was generally remarked by those in the court room, that the evidence of the witness was obscure and unsatisfactory.) Upon questioning him further, and confronting him with the parties to the case before the court, it transpired that the faces of Jones and Smith were unknown to him, and that he had been talking about an entirely different fight all the time.

Other witnesses were examined, some of whom swore that Smith was the aggressor, and others that Jones began the row; some said they fought with their fists, others that they fought with knives, others tomahawks, others revolvers, others clubs, others axes, others beer mugs and chairs, and others swore there had been no fight at all. However, fight or no fight, the testimony was straightforward and uniform on one point, at any rate, and that was, that the fuss was about two dollars and forty cents, which one party owed the other, but after all, it was impossible to find out which was the debtor and which the creditor.

After the witnesses had all been heard, his Honor, Judge Shepherd, observed that the evidence in this case resembled, in a great many points, the evidence before him in some thirty-five cases every day, on an average. He then said he would continue the case, to afford the parties an opportunity of procuring more testimony....

Now, with every confidence in the instinctive candor and fair dealing of my race, I submit the testimony in the case of Smith vs. Jones, to the People, without comment or argument, well satisfied that after a perusal of it, their judgment will be as righteous as it is final and impartial,and that whether Smith be cast out and Jones exalted, or Jones cast out and Smith exalted, the decision will be a holy and just one.

I leave the accused and the accuser before the bar of the world— let their fate be pronounced.

FROM ANOTHER OBSCENE PICTURE KNAVE CAPTURED —
HE SOLICITS THE CUSTOM OF SCHOOL GIRLS
[*Morning Call*, Aug. 6, 1864]

A scoundrel named George R. Powers has been detected in the obscene book trade and captured. He has been carrying on the trade after a fashion of his own. Over the signature of "Mrs. Amelia Barstow," he writes chatty, familiar letters to young girls in the California seminaries, soliciting patronage for his infamous books and pictures. He made a mistake, though, when he addressed the following epistle to a school girl of fourteen years of age, for her home teachings had not been of a character to enable her to appreciate it, and she sent it at once to her father. . . .

San Francisco July 21st, 1864

MISS ——:— I have just received from New York a large number of the *most delightful books* you can imagine. To refined young ladies of an amorous temperament, they are "just the thing." For five dollars sent to me through the Post Office, in two separate enclosures of two dollars and a half each, I will forward you two different volumes, each containing *five tinted engravings.* Accompanying the package will also be a beautiful *life photograph,* entitled "* * * * * * *." The strictest secrecy will be observed, which may be heightened by your transmitting a fictitious address, in case you reply to

MRS. AMELIA BARSTOW.

(We suppress the title of dear Amelia's "life photograph," as being somewhat too suggestive. —REPORTER.)

Officer Hess suggested the policy of writing an answer to Amelia's note, and getting it sent through the Post Office to her, as coming from the young girl she had addressed. He framed the following note, putting in punctuation marks with great liberality where they did not belong, and leaving them out where they did, and mimicking schoolgirl simplicity of phraseology, and proneness to tautology, with great ingenuity . . . :

* * * * *, July 27, 1864

MRS. AMELIA BARSTOW— Dear Madame:— I received your letter which you sent on the 21st of this month and I am glad, for I have been wishing for something nice to read for a long time. Father has not given me much money this month and I cannot send this time the amount you say; but if you will send me *one* book by sending two dollars and a half, please write and tell me so, and by return mail I will send it. A number of the girls in my class wants some books also, and if you will send one book for two dollars and a half some four or five others will send for some also. Please direct to Charles Harris for if directed to a Miss or Mrs. some of the teachers may get the letter.

Yours truly,

✿ ✿ ✿   ✿ ✿ ✿

... The decoy letter came back in due time, and was taken out by Mr. Powers while Mr. Hess was absent at lunch, but the clerk who officiates in the ladies' department at the Post Office took such a minute mental photograph of him, that the officer had no difficulty in following after and detecting his man in the street, from the description given of him. After walking around town for some time, Powers finally opened the letter, read it, and replaced it in his pocket. Hess entered into conversation with him, and in answer to certain questions, the fellow said he had no appointment to meet Mrs. Barstow at any particular place—expected to stumble on her in the street; said he had no particular occupation; was in the habit of taking her letters from the Post Office for her. It took him but a short time to discover that he was in the hands of an officer, and then his replies became decidedly non-committal. Hess asked him if he wrote the letter signed "Mrs. Amelia Barstow." Powers said, "If I were to say I did, what would be done with me? what could you make out of it?" When asked if Mrs. Barstow would come and clear him of suspicion if she knew he was about to suffer for an offence committed by her, he caught at the idea, and said she would; the thoughtless numskull even eagerly wrote her a note, which the officer was to deliver to her after accomplishing the hopeless task of finding her. That act furnished the officer all the information he lacked, and enabled him to "rest his case," but it ruined the unthinking Powers—for behold, the first words of the note, "Mrs. Amelia Barstow," were a perfect fac-simile of the name signed to the letter to the school-girl, and fully convicted him of being the writer of it. Powers will be tried this morning for offering to sell obscene pictures, and perhaps for opening other people's letters, and the chances are that he will be severely dealt with. He deserves it, for any one acquainted with the impressible nature of young girls, shut out from the world and doomed to irksome and monotonous school-life, knows the heightened charm and excitement they find in amusements that are contraband and have to be secured by risky evasions of the rules, and is also aware that a whole school might be corrupted by the circulation among them of a single volume of the lecherous trash dealt in by Mr. Powers.

—•—

A DARK TRANSACTION
[*Morning Call*, Aug. 24, 1864]

A gloom pervaded the Police Court, as the sable visages of Mary Wilkinson and Maria Brooks, with their cloud of witnesses, entered within its consecrated walls, each to prosecute and defend respectively in counter charges of assault and battery. The cases were consolidated, and crimination and recrimination ruled the hour. Mary said she was a meek-hearted Christian, who loved her enemies, including Maria, and had prayed for her on the very morning of the day when the latter threw a pail of water and a rock against her. Maria said she didn't throw; that she wasn't a Christian herself, and that Mary had the very devil in her. The case would always have remained in doubt, but Mrs. Hammond overshadowed the Court, and flashed defiance at counsel, from her eyes, while indignation and eloquence burst from her heaving bosom, like the long pent up fires of a volcano, whenever any one presumed to intimate that her statement might be improved in point of credibility, by a slight explanation. Even the gravity of the court was somewhat disturbed when three hundred weight of black majesty, hauteur, and conscious virtue, rolled on to the witness stand, like the fore quarter of a sunburnt whale, a living embodiment of Desdemona, Othello, Jupiter, Josh, and Jewhilikens. She appeared as counsel for Maria Brooks, and scornfully repudiated the relationship, when citizen Sam Platt, Esq., prefaced his interrogation with the endearing, "Aunty." "I'm not your Aunty," she roared. "I'm Mrs. Hammond," upon which the citizen S.P., Esq., repeated his assurances of distinguished regard, and caved a little. Mrs. Hammond rolled off the stand; and out of the Court room, like the fragment of a thunder cloud, leaving the "congregation," as she called it, in convulsions. Mary

Brooks and Maria Wilkinson were both convicted of assault and battery, and ordered to appear for sentence.

—◆◁◆—

PETTY POLICE COURT TRANSACTIONS
[*Morning Call*, June 15, 1864]

It is surprising to notice what trifling, picayune cases are frequently brought before the Police Judge by parties who conceive that their honor has been attacked, a gross outrage committed on their person or reputation, and they must have justice "though the heavens fall." *Distinguished* counsel are employed, witnesses are summoned and made to dance attendance to the successive steps of the complaints, and the patience of the Judge and Reporters is severely tested by the time occupied in their investigation which, after a close examination of witnesses, cross-questioning by the counsel, and perhaps some brilliant peroration at the close, with the especial injunction to the Court that it were better that ten guilty men should escape punishment rather than one innocent (one eye obliquely winking to their client) person should suffer; with a long breath of satisfaction that the agony is over about a hair-pulling case, a lost spoon or a broken window, the Judge dismisses the case, and, (if we must say it) the lawyers pocket their fees, and the client pockets his or her indignation that the defendant escaped the punishment which to their view was so richly deserved. Thus, yesterday, William Towerick, a deaf old man, complained that a woman struck him with a basket, on Mission street. The good looking German interpreter almost woke up the dead in his efforts to shout in the plaintiff's auricular appendage the respective questions propounded by counsel, but had eventually to give it up as a bad job and let the old lady the plaintiff's wife, try. Case dismissed. Then comes another complainant with a long chapter of grievances against one Rosa Bustamente, who didn't like her little poodle dog. Bad words from both parties and a flower pot thrown at somebody, bursting five panes of glass valued at twenty-five cents each. Court considered that plaintiff and defendant stood on nearly equal footing, and ordered the case dismissed.

—◆◁◆—

SHOP-LIFTING
[*Morning Call*, Aug. 7, 1864]

Lucy Adler was arrested and locked up in the city prison last night, for petty larceny—stealing shoes, ribbons, and small traps of all kinds exposed for sale in shops. She brought her weeping boy with her—a lad of nine years, perhaps—and they were followed by a large concourse of men and boys, whose curiosity was excited to the highest pitch to know "what was up with the old woman," as they expressed it. The officers, and also the merchants, say this woman will travel through a dozen small stores during the afternoon, and go home and "clean up" a perfect junk-shop as a result of her labors. She cabbages every light article of merchandise she can get her claws on. She always has her small boy with her, and if she is caught in a theft, the boy comes the sympathy dodge, and pumps tears and jerks sobs until the pity of the shopman is moved, and his parent released. The boy is always on hand, and if an officer snatches the woman she pulls the metaphorical string that turns on the boy's sympathetic shower-bath, and he is all tears and lamentations in a moment. At any rate, this is what they say of the cunning pair.

MRS. O'FARRELL
[*Morning Call*, July 30, 1864]

This faded relic of gentility—or, rather, this washed-out relic, for every tint of that description is gone—was brought to the station-house yesterday, in the arms of Officers Marsh and Ball, in a state of beastly intoxication. She cursed the Union and lauded the Confederacy for half an hour, and then she cast up part of her dinner; during the succeeding half hour, or perhaps it might have been three-quarters, she continued to curse the Federal Union and belch fuming and offensive blessings upon the Southern Confederacy, and then she cast up the balance of her dinner. She seemed much relieved. She so expressed herself. She observed to the prison-keeper, and casually to such as were standing around, although strangers to her, that she didn't care a d——n. She said it in that tone of quiet cheerfulness and contentment, which marks the troubled spirit at peace again after its stormy season of unrest. So they tackled her once more, and jammed her into the "dark cell," and locked her up. To such of her friends as gentle love for her may inspire with agonized suspense on her account, we would say: Banish your foreboding fears, for she's safe.

—◆—

BURGLAR ARRESTED
[*Morning Call*, June 7, 1864]

John Richardson, whose taste for a cigar must be inordinate, gratified it on Saturday night last by forcing his way into a tobacconist's on Broadway, near Kearny street, and helping himself to fourteen hundred "smokes." In his hurry, however, he did not select the best, as the stolen tobacco was only valued at fifty dollars. He was congratulating himself last evening in a saloon on Dupont street, in having secured weeds for himself and all his friends, when lo! a Rose [Detective George W. Rose] bloomed before his eyes, and he wilted. The scent of that flower of detectives was too strong even for the aroma of the stolen cigars. Richardson was conveyed to the station-house, where a kit of neat burglar's tools was found on his person. He is now reposing his limbs on an asphaltum floor—a bed hard as the ways of unrighteousness.

—◆—

ARRESTED FOR BIGAMY
[*Morning Call*, July 8, 1864]

Isaac Hingman has been bigamized. He was arrested for it yesterday, by Officer W. P. Brown, on a complaint sworn to by his most recent wife, that he has a much more former wife now living in another part of the State. The wife that makes the complaint, and who drew a blank, in the eye of the law, in the husband lottery, married the prisoner on the 24th of June, in this city. A man is not allowed to have a wife lying around loose in every county of California, as Isaac may possibly find to his cost before he gets through with this case. He might as well make up his mind to shed one of these women.

—◆—

THE BIGAMIST
[*Morning Call*, July 8, 1864]

We have mentioned elsewhere in our present issue the arrest of Isaac
Hingman, on a charge of bigamy. The woman he married last, went
to the station-house last night to see him. She says she worked for two
years in lager beer cellars here, and during that time, had saved six
hundred and fifty dollars. Hingman got this from her. He said he was
going down on the Colorado to open a saloon, and she was to go with
him. They were to leave today on a schooner, and he took her stove,
her beds and bedding, and all her clothing, and put them on board the
vessel. He told her he had been living with a woman at Auburn, and
he would have to send her some money in order to get rid of her and
her three children. The new wife gave him one hundred and thirty dollars for this purpose, and he went off and telegraphed his Auburn family to come down and go to the Colorado with him instead. The duped
beer-girl got the answering dispatch sent by the Auburn wife, in which
she acceded to the proposal, and said she would arrive by the boat last
night. Sergeant Evrard, of the Police, saw the dispatch. The woman
said Hingman told her, in the station-house, that the lucky Auburn
woman was his lawful wife. Officer Evrard sent a policeman, disguised,
to wait for the up-country wife at the Sheba Saloon, last night, and find
out what he could from her affecting the case. The story of the illegal
wife is plausible, and if it is true, Mr. Hingman ought to be severely
dealt with. But not too severely—we go in for moderation in all things,
and, considering all the circumstances of this case, it might be a questionable application of power to do more than hang him. To hang him
a little while—say thirty or forty minutes—ought to be about the fair
thing, though. He wants to marry too many people; and he needs
treatment that will tend to check this propensity.

THE BIGAMY CASE
[*Morning Call*, July 12, 1864]

The bigamy case came up in the Police Court yesterday morning, and
Judge Shepheard dismissed it, because the charge could not be substantiated, inasmuch as the only witnesses to be had were the two
alleged wives of the defendant—or rather, only one, the ephemeral

lager-beer wife, as the old original wife, the first location, or the discovery claim on the matrimonial lead, could not be compelled to testify against her husband, and thereby also knock the props from under her own good name and her eternal piece of mind. The injured and deserted relocation now proposes to have Hingman arrested again and tried on a charge of assault and battery. This unfortunate woman seems to have been very badly treated, and it is to be hoped she may get some little soothing satisfaction out of her assault and battery charge to reconcile her to her failure in the bigamy matter.

ASSAULT
[*Morning Call*, July 19, 1864]

Mrs. Catherine Moran was arraigned before Judge Cowles yesterday, on a charge of assault with an axe upon Mrs. Eliza Markee, with intent to do bodily injury. A physician testified that there were contused wounds on plaintiff's head, and also a cut through the scalp, which bled profusely. The fuss was all about a child, and that is the strangest part about it — as if, in a city so crowded with them as San Francisco, it were worthwhile to be particular as to the fate of a child or two. However, mothers appear to go more by instinct than political economy in matters of this kind. Mrs. Markee testified that she heard war going on among the children, and she rushed down into the yard and found her Johnny sitting on the stoop, building a toy wagon, and Mrs. Moran standing over him with an axe, threatening to split his head open. She asked the defendant not to split her Johnny. The defendant at once turned upon her, threatening to kill her, and struck her two or three times with the axe, when she, the plaintiff, grabbed the defendant by the arms and prevented her from scalping her entirely. Blood was flowing profusely. Mr. Killdig described the fight pretty much as the plaintiff had done, and said he parted, or tried to part the combatants, and that he called upon Mr. Moran to assist him, but that neutral power said the women had been sour a good while — let them fight it out. Another witness substantiated the main features of the foregoing testimony, and said the warriors were all covered with blood, and the children of both, to the number of many dozens, had fled in disorder and taken refuge under the house, crying, and saying their mothers were killing each other. Mrs. Murphy, for the defence, testified as follows: "I was coomun along, an' Misses Moran says to me, says she, this is the redwood stick she tried to take me life wid, or wan o' thim other sticks, Missis Murphy, dear, an' says I, Missis Moran, dairlin',"—Here she was shut off, merely because the Court did not care about knowing what Mrs. Moran told her about the fight, and consequently we have nothing further of this important witness's testimony to offer. The case was continued. Seriously, instead of a mere ordinary she-fight, this is a fuss of some consequence, and should not be lightly dealt with. It was an earnest attempt at man-slaughter—or woman-slaughter, at any rate, which is nearly as bad.

———

DISGRACEFUL PERSECUTION OF A BOY
[*The Galaxy*, May 1870]

In San Francisco, the other day, "A well-dressed boy, on his way to Sunday-School, was arrested and thrown into the city prison for stoning Chinamen."

What a commentary is this upon human justice! What sad prominence it gives to our human disposition to tyrannize over the weak! San Francisco has little right to take credit to herself for her treatment of this poor boy. What had the child's education been? How should he suppose it was wrong to stone a Chinaman? Before we side against him, along with outraged San Francisco, let us give him a chance—let us hear the testimony for the defense.

He was a "well-dressed" boy, and a Sunday-school scholar, and therefore the chances are that his parents were intelligent, well-to-do people, with just enough natural villainy in their composition to make them yearn after the daily papers, and enjoy them; and so this boy had opportunities to learn all through the week how to do right, as well as on Sunday.

It was in this way that he found out that the great commonwealth of California imposes an unlawful mining-tax upon John the foreigner, and allows Patrick the foreigner to dig gold for nothing—probably because the degraded Mongol is at no expense for whisky, and the refined Celt cannot exist without it.

It was in this way that he found out that a respectable number of the tax-gatherers—it would be unkind to say all of them—collect the tax twice, instead of once; and that, inasmuch as they do it solely to discourage Chinese immigration into the mines, it is a thing that is much applauded, and likewise regarded as being singularly facetious.

It was in this way that he found out that when a white man robs a sluice-box (by the term white man is meant Spaniards, Mexicans, Portuguese, Irish, Hondurans, Peruvians, Chileans, etc., etc.), they make him leave the camp; and when a Chinaman does that thing, they hang him.

It was in this way that he found out that in many districts of the vast Pacific coast, so strong is the wild, free love of justice in the hearts of the people, that whenever any secret and mysterious crime is committed, they say, "Let justice be done, though the heavens fall," and go straightaway and swing a Chinaman.

It was in this way that he found out that by studying one half of each day's "local items," it would appear that the police of San Francisco were either asleep or dead, and by studying the other half it would seem that the reporters were gone mad with admiration of the energy, the virtue, the high effectiveness, and the dare-devil intrepidity of that very police—making exultant mention of how "the Argus-eyed officer So-and-so" captured a wretched knave of a Chinaman who was stealing chickens, and brought him gloriously to the city prison; and how "the gallant officer Such-and-such-a-one" quietly kept an eye on the movements of an "unsuspecting, almond-eyed son of Confucius" (your reporter is nothing if not facetious), following him around with that far-off look of vacancy and unconsciousness always so finely affected by that inscrutable being, the forty-dollar policeman, during a waking interval, and captured him at last in the very act of placing his hands in a suspicious manner upon a paper of tacks, left by the owner in an exposed situation; and how one officer performed this prodigious thing, and another officer that, and another the other—and pretty much every one of these performances having for a dazzling central incident a Chinaman guilty of a shilling's worth of crime, an unfortunate, whose misdemeanor must be hurrahed into something enormous in order to keep the public from noticing how many really important rascals went uncaptured in the meantime, and how overrated those glorified policemen actually are.

It was in this way that the boy found out that the legislature, being aware that the Constitution has made America an asylum for the poor and the oppressed of all nations, and that, therefore, the poor and oppressed who fly to our shelter must not be charged a disabling admission fee, made a law that every Chinaman, upon landing, must be *vaccinated* upon the wharf, and pay to the state's appointed officer *ten dollars* for the service, when there are plenty of doctors in San Francisco who would be glad enough to do it for him for fifty cents.

It was in this way that the boy found out that a Chinaman had no rights that any man was bound to respect; that he had no sorrows that any man was bound to pity; that neither his life nor his liberty was worth the purchase of a penny when a white man needed a scape-goat; that nobody loved Chinamen, nobody befriended them, nobody spared them suffering when it was convenient to inflict it; everybody, individuals, communities, the majesty of the state itself, joined in hating, abusing, and persecuting these humble strangers.

And, therefore, what *could* have been more natural than for this sunny-hearted boy, tripping along to Sunday-school, with his mind teeming with freshly learned incentives to high and virtuous action, to say to himself:

"Ah, there goes a Chinaman! God will not love me if I do not stone him."

And for this he was arrested and put in the city jail.

Everything conspired to teach him that it was a high and holy thing to stone a Chinaman, and yet he no sooner attempts to do his duty than he is punished for it — he, poor chap, who has been aware all his life that one of the principal recreations of the police, out toward the Gold Refinery, is to look on with tranquil enjoyment while the butchers of Brannan Street set their dogs on unoffending Chinamen, and make them "flee for their lives."*

Keeping in mind the tuition in the humanities which the entire "Pacific coast" gives its youth, there is a very sublimity of incongruity in the virtuous flourish with which the good city fathers of San Francisco proclaim (as they have lately done) that "The police are positively ordered to arrest all boys, of every description and wherever found, who engage in assaulting Chinamen."

---

*I have many such memories in my mind, but am thinking just at present of one particular one, where the Brannan Street butchers set their dogs on a Chinaman who was quietly passing with a basket of clothes on his head; and while the dogs mutilated his flesh, a butcher increased the hilarity of the occasion by knocking some of the Chinaman's teeth down his throat with half a brick. This incident sticks in my memory with a more malevolent tenacity, perhaps, on account of the fact that I was in the employ of a San Francisco journal at the time, and was not allowed to publish it because it might offend some of the peculiar element that subscribed for the paper. — M.T.

Still, let us be truly glad they have made the order, notwithstanding its inconsistency; and let us rest perfectly confident the police are glad, too. Because there is no personal peril in arresting boys, provided they be of the small kind, and the reporters will have to laud their performances just as loyally as ever, or go without items.

The new form for local items in San Francisco will now be: "The ever-vigilant and efficient officer So-and-so succeeded, yesterday afternoon, in arresting Master Tommy Jones, after a determined resistance," etc., etc., followed by the customary statistics and final hurrah, with its unconscious sarcasm: "We are happy in being able to state that this is the forty-seventh boy arrested by this gallant officer since the new ordinance went into effect. The most extraordinary activity prevails in the police department. Nothing like it has been seen since we can remember."

from POLICE COURT
[*Morning Call*, July 20, 1864]

Stephen Storer, for assault and battery, was sentenced to imprisonment for ten days, or to pay a fine of twenty-five dollars. Catherine Moran, whom we spoke of yesterday as having attempted to segregate Mrs. Markee with an axe, was sentenced to forty days' imprisonment, or to pay a fine of one hundred and fifty dollars — and served her right. Mr. Swartz was arraigned on some charge or other — petty larceny, perhaps — in trying to steal a kiss from the widow Ellen Niemeyer, while she was locked up in the City Prison — a delicate attention, which, considering the extremely mild stagger she makes of beauty, she ought to have regarded as a most reckless and desperate compliment, rather than as a crime. We did not remain to hear the result of the trial. . . .

MONEY & POVERTY

 **California is a noble old State.
The echoes of the cry of distress
jingle with the ring of dollars.**

FROM **DANIEL IN THE LION'S DEN—AND OUT AGAIN ALL RIGHT**
[*The Californian*, Nov. 5, 1864]

Some people are not particular about what sort of company they keep.
I am one of that kind. Now for several days I have been visiting the
Board of Brokers, and associating with brokers, and drinking with
them, and swapping lies with them, and being as familiar and sociable with them as I would with the most respectable people in the
world. I do this because I consider that a broker goes according to the
instincts that are in him, and means no harm, and fulfils his mission
according to his lights, and has a right to live, and be happy in a general way, and be protected by the law to some extent, just the same as
a better man. I consider that brokers come into the world with souls—
I am satisfied they do; and if they wear them out in the course of a long
career of stock-jobbing, have they not a right to come in at the
eleventh hour and get themselves half-soled, like old boots, and be
saved at last? Certainly—the father of the tribe did that, and do we
say anything against Barabbas for it today? No! we concede his right
to do it; we admire his mature judgment in selling out of a worked-
out mine of iniquity and investing in righteousness, and no man denies,
or even doubts, the validity of the transaction. Other people may think
as they please, and I suppose I am entitled to the same privilege; therefore, notwithstanding what others may believe, I am of the opinion that
a broker can be saved. Mind, I do not say that a broker *will* be saved,
or even that it is uncommon likely that such a thing will happen—I

only say that Lazarus was raised from the dead, the five thousand were fed with twelve loaves of bread, the water was turned into wine, the Israelites crossed the Red Sea dry-shod, and a broker *can* be saved. True, the angel that accomplishes the task may require all eternity to rest himself in, but has that got anything to do with the establishment of the proposition? Does it invalidate it? does it detract from it? I think not. I am aware that this enthusiastic and maybe highly-colored vindication of the brokers may lay me open to suspicion of bribery, but I care not; I am a native of Washoe, and I will stand by anybody that stands by Washoe.

The place where stocks are daily bought and sold is called by interested parties the Hall of the San Francisco Board of Brokers, but by the impartial and disinterested the Den of the Forty Thieves; the latter name is regarded as the most poetic, but the former is considered the most polite. The large room is well stocked with small desks, arranged in semi-circular ranks like the seats of an amphitheatre, and behind these sit the th— the brokers. The portly President, with his gavel of office in his hand, an abundance of whiskers and moustaches on his face, spectacles on nose, an expression of energy and decision on his countenance and an open plaza on his head, sits, with his three clerks, in a pulpit at the head of the hall. . . .

The session of the Board being duly opened, the roll is rapidly called, the members present responding, and the absentees being noted by the clerks for fines:

"Ackerman, (Here!) Adams, Atchison, (Here!) Babcock, Bocock, (Here!) Badger, Blitzen, Bulger, Buncombe, (Here!) Caxton, (Here!) Cobbler, Crowder, Clutterback, (Here!) Dashaway, Dilson, Dodson, Dummy (Here!)"—and so on, the place becoming lively and animated, and the members sharpening their pencils, disposing their printed stock-lists before them, and getting ready for a sowing of unrighteousness and a harvest of sin.

In a few moments the roll-call was finished, the pencils all sharpened, and the brokers prepared for business—some with a leg thrown negligently over the arms of their chairs, some tilted back comfortably with their knees against their desks, some sitting half upright and glaring at the President, hungry for the contention to begin—but not a rascal of them tapping his teeth with his pencil—only dreamy, absent-minded people do that.

Then the President called "Ophir [Mine]!" and after some bid-

ding and counter-bidding, "Gould and Curry!" and a Babel arose—
an infernal din and clatter of all kinds and tones of voices, inextrica-
bly jumbled together like original chaos, and above it all the following
observation by the President pealed out clearly and distinctly, and with
a rapidity of enunciation that was amazing:

"Fift'naitassfrwahn fift'nseftfive bifferwahn fift'naitfive botherty!"

I said I believed I would go home. My broker friend who had procured my admission to the Board asked why I wanted to go so soon,
and I was obliged to acknowledge to him that I was very unfamiliar
with the Kanaka language, and could not understand it at all unless a
man spoke it exceedingly slow and deliberately.

"Oh," said he, "sit still; that isn't Kanaka; it's English, but he talks
fast and runs one word into another; it is easy SOLD! to understand
when you GIVE FIFTEEN-NINETY BUYER TEN NO DEPOSIT! come to get
used to it. He always talks so, and sometimes he says THAT'S MINE! JIG-
GERS SOLD ON SLADERTY'S BID! his words so fast that even some of
the members cannot comprehend them readily. Now what he said
then was NO SIR! I DIDN'T SAY BUYER THIRTY, I SAID REGULAR WAY!
'Fifteen-eighty, (meaning fifteen hundred and eighty dollars,) asked
for one, (one foot,) fifteen-seventy-five bid for one, fifteen-eighty-five
buyer thirty, (thirty days' time on the payment,)' 'TWASN'T MY BID, IT
WAS SWIGGINS TO BABCOCK! and he was repeating the bids and offers
of the members after them as fast as they were made. I'LL TAKE IT,
CASH!"

I felt relieved, but not enlightened. My broker's explanation had
got so many strange and incomprehensible interpolations sandwiched
into it that I began to look around for a suitable person to translate that
for me also, when it occurred to me that those interpolations were
bids, offers, etc., which he had been throwing out to the assembled
brokers while he was talking to me. It was all clear, then, so I have put
his side-remarks in small capitals so that they may be clear to the
reader likewise, and show that they have no connection with the subject matter of my friend's discourse.

And all this time, the clatter of voices had been going on. And
while the storm of ejaculations hurtled about their heads, these brokers sat calmly in their several easy attitudes, but when a sale was
made—when, in answer to some particularly liberal bid, somebody
sung out "SOLD" down came legs from the arms of chairs, down came
knees propped against desks, forward shot the heads of the whole

tribe with one accord, and away went the long ranks of pencils dancing over the paper! The sale duly recorded by all, the heads, the legs and the knees came up again, and the negligent attitudes were resumed once more....

Sometimes on the "second call" of stocks — that is, after the list has been gone through with in regular order, and the members are privileged to call up any stock they please — strategy is driven to the utmost limit by the friends of some pet wildcat or other, to effect sales of it to disinterested parties. The seller "offers" at a high figure, and the "bidder" responds with a low one; then the former comes warily down a dollar at a time, and the latter approaches him from below at about the same rate; they come nearer and nearer, skirmish a little in close proximity, get to a point where another bid or another offer would commit the parties to a sale, and then in the imminence of the impending event, the seller hesitates a second and is silent. But behold! as has been said of Woman, "The Broker who hesitates is lost!" The nervous and impatient President can brook no silence, no delay, and calls out: "Awstock?" (Any other stock?) Somebody yells "Burning Moscow!" and the tender wildcat, almost born, miscarries. Or perhaps the skirmishers fight shyly up to each other, counter and cross-counter, feint and parry, back and fill, and finally clinch a sale in the centre — the bidder is bitten, a smile flits from face to face, down come the legs, forward the ranks of heads, the pencils charge on the stock-lists, and the neat transaction is recorded with a rare gusto.

But twelve pages of foolscap are warning me to cut this thrilling sketch short, notwithstanding it is only half finished. However, I cannot leave the subject without saying I was agreeably disappointed in those brokers; I expected to see a set of villains with the signs of total depravity hung out all over them, but now I am satisfied there is some good in them; that they are not entirely and irredeemably bad; and I have been told by a friend, whose judgment I respect, that they are not any more unprincipled than they look. This was said by a man who would scorn to stoop to flattery. At the same time, though, as I scanned the faces assembled in that hall, I could not help imagining I could see old St. Peter admitting that band of Bulls and Bears into Paradise — see him standing by the half-open gate with his ponderous key pressed thoughtfully against his nose, and his head canted critically to one side, as he looks after them tramping down the gold-paved avenue, and mutters to himself: "Well, *you're* a nice lot, any way! Humph! I think you'll find it sort of lonesome in heaven, for if my judgment is sound, you'll not find a good many of *your* stripe in there!"

FROM **ROUGHING IT**

For two months [in late 1864] my sole occupation was avoiding acquaintances; for during that time I did not earn a penny, or buy an article of any kind, or pay my board. I became a very adept at "slinking." I slunk from back street to back street, I slunk away from approaching faces that looked familiar, I slunk to my meals, ate them humbly and with a mute apology for every mouthful I robbed my generous landlady of, and at midnight, after wanderings that were but slinkings away from cheerfulness and light, I slunk to my bed. I felt meaner, and lowlier and more despicable than the worms. During all this time I had but one piece of money — a silver ten-cent piece — and I held to it and would not spend it on any account, lest the consciousness coming strong upon me that I was *entirely* penniless, might suggest suicide. I had pawned everything but the clothes I had on; so I clung to my dime desperately, till it was smooth with handling....

Misery loves company. Now and then at night, in out-of-the-way, dimly lighted places, I found myself happening on another child of misfortune. He looked so seedy and forlorn, so homeless and friendless and forsaken, that I yearned toward him as a brother. I wanted to claim kinship with him and go about and enjoy our wretchedness together. The drawing toward each other must have been mutual; at any rate we got to falling together oftener, though still seemingly by accident; and although we did not speak or evince any recognition, I think the dull anxiety passed out of both of us when we saw each other, and then for several hours we would idle along contentedly, wide apart, and glancing furtively in at home lights and fireside gatherings, out of the night shadows, and very much enjoying our dumb companionship.

A GRACEFUL COMPLIMENT
[*Territorial Enterprise*, Dec. 1865]

One would hardly expect to receive a neat, voluntary compliment from so grave an institution as the United States Revenue Office, but such has been my good fortune. I have not been so agreeably surprised in many a day. The Revenue officers, in a communication addressed to me, fondle the faltering fiction that I am a man of means, and have got "goods, chattels and effects"—and even "real estate!" Gentlemen, you couldn't have paid such a compliment as that to any man who would appreciate it higher, or be more grateful for it than myself. We will drink together, if you object not.

I am taxed on my income! This is perfectly gorgeous! I never felt so important in my life before. To be treated in this splendid way, just like another William B. Astor! Gentlemen, we must drink.

Yes, I am taxed on my income. And the printed page which bears this compliment—all slathered over with fierce-looking written figures—looks as grand as a steamboat's manifest. It reads thus:

"COLLECTOR'S OFFICE,
U. S. INTERNAL REVENUE, FIRST DIS'T. CAL.

Name	M. Twain
Residence	At Large
List and amount of tax	$31 25
Penalty	3 12
Warrant	2 45
Total amount	$36 82
Date	November 20, 1865.

C. ST GG,
Deputy Collector
Please present this at the Collector's office."

Now I consider that really handsome. I have got it framed beautifully, and I take more pride in it than any of my other furniture. I trust it will become an heirloom and serve to show many generations of my posterity that I was a man of consequence in the land—that I was also the recipient of compliments of the most extraordinary nature from high officers of the national government.

On the other side of this complimentary document I find some happy blank verse headed "Warrant," and signed by the poet "Frank Soulé, Collector of Internal Revenue." Some of the flights of fancy in this Ode are really sublime, and show with what facility the poetic fire can render beautiful the most unpromising subject. For instance: "You are hereby commanded to distrain upon so much of the goods, chattels and effects of the within named person, *if any such can be found, etc.*" However, that is not so much a flight of fancy as a flight of humor. It is a fine flight, though, anyway. But this one is equal to anything in Shakspeare: "But in case sufficient goods, chattels and effects cannot be found, then you are hereby commanded to seize so much of the real estate of said person as may be necessary to satisfy the tax." There's poetry for you! They are going to commence on my real estate. This is very rough. But then the officer is expressly instructed to find it first. That is the saving clause for me. I will get them to take it all out in real estate. And then I will give them all the time they want to find it in.

But I can tell them of a way whereby they can ultimately enrich the Government of the United States by a judicious manipulation of this little bill against me — a way in which even the enormous national debt may be eventually paid off! Think of it! Imperishable fame will be the reward of the man who finds a way to pay off the national debt without impoverishing the land; I offer to furnish that method and crown these gentlemen with that fadeless glory. It is so simple and plain that a child may understand it. It is thus: I perceive that by neglecting to pay my income tax within ten days after it was due, I have brought upon myself a "penalty" of three dollars and twelve cents extra tax for that ten days. Don't you see?—let her run! Every ten days, $3 12; every month of 31 days, $10; every year, $120; every century, $12,000; at the end of a hundred thousand years, $1,200,000,000 will be the interest that has accumulated. . . .

RELIGION & MORALITY

Immorality is not decreasing in San Francisco.

FROM **IMPORTANT CORRESPONDENCE**
[*The Californian*, May 6, 1865]

BETWEEN MR. MARK TWAIN OF SAN FRANCISCO,
AND REV. BISHOP HAWKS, D.D., OF NEW YORK,
REV. PHILLIPS BROOKS OF PHILADELPHIA, AND
REV. DR. CUMMINS OF CHICAGO, CONCERNING
THE OCCUPANCY OF GRACE CATHEDRAL

For a long time I have taken a deep interest in the efforts being made to induce the above-named distinguished clergymen—or, rather, some one of the them—to come out here and occupy the pulpit of the noble edifice known as Grace Cathedral. And when I saw that the vestry were uniformly unsuccessful, although doing all that they possibly could to attain their object, I felt it my duty to come forward and throw the weight of my influence—such as it might be—in favor of the laudable undertaking. That by so doing I was not seeking to curry favor with the vestry—and that my actions were prompted by no selfish motive of any kind whatever—is sufficiently evidenced by the fact that I am not a member of Grace Church, and never had any conversation with the vestry upon the subject in hand, and never even hinted to them that I was going to write the clergymen. What I have done in the matter I did of my own free will and accord, without any solicitation from anybody, and my actions were dictated solely by a spirit of enlarged charity and good feeling toward the congregation of Grace Cathedral. I seek no reward for my services; I desire none but the approval of my own conscience and the satisfaction of knowing I have done that which I conceived to be my duty, to the best of my ability. M.T.

The correspondence which passed between myself and the Rev. Dr. Hawks was as follows:

LETTER FROM MYSELF TO BISHOP HAWKS.

SAN FRANCISCO, March, 1865

Rev. Dr. Hawks—*Dear Doctor.*—Since I heard that you have telegraphed the vestry of Grace Cathedral here, that you cannot come out to San Francisco and carry on a church at the terms offered you, viz: $7,000 a year, I have concluded to write you on the subject myself. A word in your ear: say nothing to anybody—keep dark—but just pack up your traps and come along out here—I will see that it is all right. That $7,000 dodge was only a *bid*—nothing more. They never expected you to clinch a bargain like that. I will go to work and get up a little competition among the cloth, and the result of it will be that you will make more money in six months here than you would in New York in a year. I can do it. I have a great deal of influence with the clergy here, and especially with the Rev. Dr. Wadsworth and the Rev. Mr. Stebbins—I write their sermons for them. (This latter fact is not generally known, however, and maybe you had as well not mention it.) I can get them to strike for higher wages any time.

You would like this berth. It has a greater number of attractive features than any I know of. It is such a magnificent field, for one thing,—why, sinners are so thick that you can't throw out your line without hooking several of them; you'd be surprised—the flattest old sermon a man can grind out is bound to corral half a dozen. You see, you can do such a land-office business on such a small capital. Why, I wrote the most rambling, incomprehensible harangue of a sermon you ever heard in your life for one of the Episcopalian ministers here, and he landed seventeen with it at the first dash; then I trimmed it up to suit Methodist doctrine, and the Rev. Mr. Thomas got eleven more; I tinkered the doctrinal points again, and Stebbins made a lot of Unitarian converts with it; I worked it over once more, and Dr. Wadsworth did almost as well with it as he usually does with my ablest compositions. It was passed around, after that, from church to church, undergoing changes of dress as before, to suit the vicissitudes of doctrinal climate, until it went the entire rounds. During its career we took in, altogether, a hundred and eighteen of the most abject reprobates that ever traveled on the broad road to destruction.

You would find this a remarkably easy berth—one man to give out the hymns, another to do the praying, another to read the chapter from the Testament—you would have nothing in the world to do but read the litany and preach—no, not read the litany, but sing it. They sing the litany here, in the Pontifical Grand Mass style, which is pleasanter and more attractive than to read it. You need not mind that, though; the tune is not difficult, and requires no more musical taste or education than is required to sell "Twenty-four—self-sealing—envelopes—for f-o-u-r cents," in your city. I like to hear the litany sung. Perhaps there is hardly enough variety in the music, but still the effect is very fine. Bishop Kip never could sing worth a cent, though. However, he has gone to Europe now to learn. Yes, as I said before, you would have nothing in the world to do but preach and sing that litany; and, between you and me, Doc, as regards the music, if you could manage to ring in a few of the popular and familiar old tunes that the people love so well you would be almost certain to create a sensation. I think I can safely promise you that. I am satisfied that you could do many a thing that would attract less attention than would result from adding a spirited variety to the music of the litany.

Your preaching will be easy. Bring along a barrel of your old obsolete sermons; the people here will never know the difference.

Drop me a line, Hawks; I don't know you, except by reputation, but I like you all the same. And don't you fret about the salary. I'll make *that* all right, you know. You need not mention to the vestry of Grace Cathedral, though, that I have been communicating with you on this subject. You see, I do not belong to their church, and they might think I was taking too much trouble on their account—though I assure you, upon my honor, it is no trouble in the world to me; I don't mind it; I am not busy now, and I would rather do it than not. All I want is to have a sure thing that you get your rights. You can depend upon me. I'll see you through this business as straight as a shingle; I haven't been drifting around all my life for nothing. I know a good deal more than a boiled carrot, though I may not appear to.

And although I am not of the elect, so to speak, I take a strong interest in these things, nevertheless, and I am not going to stand by and see them come any seven-thousand-dollar arrangement over you. I have sent them word in your name that you won't take less than $18,000, and that you can get $25,000 in greenbacks at home. I also intimated that I was going to write your sermons — I thought it might have a good effect, and every little helps, you know. So you can just pack up and come along — it will be all right — I am satisfied of that. You needn't bring any shirts, I have got enough for us both. You will find there is nothing mean about *me* — I'll wear your clothes, and you can wear mine, just the same as so many twin brothers. When I like a man, I *like* him, and I go my death for him. My friends will all be fond of you, and will take to you as naturally as if they had known you a century. I will introduce you, and you will be all right. You can always depend on them. If you were to point out a man and say you did not like him, they would carve him in a minute.

Hurry along, Bishop. I shall be on the lookout for you, and will take you right to my house and you can stay there as long as you like, and it shan't cost you a cent.

Very truly yours,
MARK TWAIN.

... I suppose I shall come in under the head of "sinners at large"—but I don't mind that; I am no better than any other sinner and I am not entitled to especial consideration. They pray for the congregation first, you know—and with considerable vim; then they pray mildly for other denominations; then for the near relations of the congregation; then for their distant relatives; then for the surrounding community; then for the State; then for the Government officers; then for the United States; then for North America; then for the whole Continent; then for England, Ireland and Scotland; France, Germany and Italy; Russia, Prussia and Austria; then for the inhabitants of Norway, Sweden and Timbuctoo; and those of Saturn, Jupiter and New Jersey; and then they give the niggers a lift, and the Hindoos a lift, and the Turks a lift, and the Chinese a lift; and then, after they have got the fountain of mercy baled out as dry as an ash-hopper, they bespeak the sediment left in the bottom of it for us poor "sinners at large."

It ain't just exactly fair, *is* it? Sometimes, (being a sort of a Presbyterian in a general way, and a brevet member of one of the principal churches of that denomination,) I stand up in devout attitude, with downcast eyes, and hands clasped upon the back of the pew before me, and listen attentively and expectantly for awhile; and then rest upon one foot for a season; and then upon the other; and then insert my hands under my coat-tails and stand erect and look solemn; and then fold my arms and droop forward and look dejected; and then cast my eye furtively at the minister; and then at the congregation; and then grow absent-minded, and catch myself counting the lace bonnets; and marking the drowsy members; and noting the wide-awake ones; and averaging the bald heads; and afterwards descend to indolent conjectures as to whether the buzzing fly that keeps stumbling up the window-pane and sliding down backwards again will ever accomplish his object to his satisfaction; and, finally, I give up and relapse into a dreary reverie — and about this time the minister reaches my department, and brings me back to hope and consciousness with a kind word for the poor "sinners at large."

Sometimes we are even forgotten altogether and left out in the cold — and then I call to mind the vulgar little boy who was fond of hot biscuits, and whose mother promised him that he should have all that were left if he would stay away and keep quiet and be a good little boy while the strange guest ate his breakfast; and who watched that voracious guest till the growing apprehension in his young bosom gave place to demonstrated ruin, and then sung out: "There! I know'd how it was goin' to be — I know'd how it was goin' to be, from the start! Blamed if he hain't gobbled the last biscuit!"

I do not complain, though, because it is very seldom that the Hindoos and the Turks and the Chinese get all the atoning biscuits and leave us sinners at large to go hungry. They *do* remain at the board a long time, though, and we often get a little tired waiting for our turn. How would it do to be less diffuse? How would it do to ask a blessing upon the specialities — I mean the congregation and the immediate community — and then include the whole broad universe in one glowing, fervent appeal? How would it answer to adopt the simplicity and the beauty and the brevity and the comprehensiveness of the Lord's Prayer as a model? But perhaps I am wandering out of my jurisdiction.

The letters I wrote to the Rev. Phillips Brooks of Philadelphia, and the Rev. Dr. Cummins of Chicago, urging them to come here and take charge of Grace Cathedral, and offering them my countenance and support, will be published next week, together with their replies to the same.

A TERRIBLE WEAPON
[*Morning Call*, Sept. 21, 1864]

A charge of assault with a deadly weapon, preferred in the Police Court yesterday, against Jacob Friedberg, was dismissed, at the request of all parties concerned, because of the scandal it would occasion to the Jewish Church to let the trial proceed, both the assaulted man and the man committing the assault being consecrated servants of that Church. The weapon used was a butcher-knife, with a blade more than two feet long, and as keen as a razor. The men were butchers, appointed by dignitaries of the Jewish Church to slaughter and inspect all beef intended for sale to their brethren, and in a dispute some time ago, one of them partly split the other's head open, from the top of the forehead to the end of his nose, with the sacred knife, and also slashed one of his hands. From these wounds the sufferer has only just recovered. The Jewish butcher is not appointed to his office in this country, but is chosen abroad by a college of Rabbis and sent hither. He kills beeves designed for consumption by Israelites, (or any one else, if they choose to buy,) and after careful examination, if he finds that the animal is in any way diseased, it is condemned and discarded; if the contrary, the seal of the Church is placed upon it, and it is permitted to be sent into the market — a custom that might be adopted with profit by all sects and creeds. It is said that the official butcher always assures himself that the sacred knife is perfectly sharp and without a wire edge, before he cuts a bullock's throat; he then draws it with a single lightning stroke (and at any rate not more than two strokes are admissible,) and if the knife is still without a wire edge after the killing, the job has been properly done; but if the contrary is the case, it is adjudged that a bone has been touched and pain inflicted upon the animal, and consequently the meat cannot receive the seal of approval and must be thrown aside. It is a quaint custom of an ancient Church, and sounds strangely enough to modern ears. Considering that the dignity of the Church was in some sense involved in the misconduct of its two servants, the dismissal of the case without a hearing was asked and granted.

REFLECTIONS ON THE SABBATH
[*Golden Era*, March 18, 1866]

The day of rest comes but once a week, and sorry I am that it does not come oftener. Man is so constituted that he can stand more rest than this. I often think regretfully that it would have been so easy to have two Sundays in a week, and yet it was not so ordained. The omnipotent Creator could have made the world in three days just as easily as he made it in six, and this would have doubled the Sundays. Still it is not our place to criticise the wisdom of the Creator. When we feel a depraved inclination to question the judgment of Providence in stacking up double eagles in the coffers of Michael Reese and leaving better men to dig for a livelihood, we ought to stop and consider that we are not expected to help order things, and so drop the subject. If all-powerful Providence grew weary after six days' labor, such worms as we are might reasonably expect to break down in three, and so require two Sundays — but as I said before, it ill becomes us to hunt up flaws in matters which are so far out of our jurisdiction. I hold that no man can meddle with the exclusive affairs of Providence and offer suggestions for their improvement, without making himself in a manner conspicuous. Let us take things as we find them — though, I am free to confess, it goes against the grain to do it, sometimes.

What put me into this religious train of mind, was attending church at Dr. Wadsworth's this morning. I had not been to church before for many months, because I never could get a pew, and therefore had to sit in the gallery among the sinners. I stopped that because my proper place was down among the elect, inasmuch as I was brought up a Presbyterian, and consider myself a brevet member of Dr. Wadsworth's church. I always was a brevet. I was sprinkled in infancy, and look upon that as conferring the rank of Brevet Presbyterian. It affords none of the emoluments of the Regular Church — simply confers honorable rank upon the recipient and the right to be punished as a Presbyterian hereafter; that is, the substantial Presbyterian punishment of fire and brimstone instead of this heterodox hell of remorse of conscience of these blamed wildcat religions. The heaven and hell of the wildcat religions are vague and ill defined but there is nothing mixed about the Presbyterian heaven and hell. The Presbyterian hell is all misery; the heaven all happiness — nothing to do. But when a man dies on a wildcat basis, he will never rightly know hereafter which department he is in — but he will think he is in hell anyhow, no matter which place he goes to; because in the good place they pro-gress, pro-gress, pro-gress — study, study, study, all the time — and if this isn't hell I don't know what is; and in the bad place he will be worried by remorse of conscience. Their bad place is preferable, though, because eternity is long, and before a man got half through it he would forget what it was he had been so sorry about. Naturally he would then become cheerful again; but the party who went to heaven would go on progressing and progressing, and studying and studying until he would finally get discouraged and wish he were in hell, where he wouldn't require such a splendid education.

Dr. Wadsworth never fails to preach an able sermon; but every now and then, with an admirable assumption of not being aware of it, he will get off a firstrate joke and then frown severely at any one who is surprised into smiling at it. This is not fair. It is like throwing a bone to a dog and then arresting him with a look just as he is going to seize it. Several people there on Sunday suddenly laughed and as suddenly stopped again, when he gravely gave the Sunday school books a blast and spoke of "the good little boys in them who always went to Heaven, and the bad little boys who infallibly got drowned on Sunday," and then swept a savage frown around the house and blighted every smile in the congregation.

LETTER TO THE CALIFORNIAN, AUG. 25, 1866

Farallones, August 20, 1866

Publishers *Californian:*

Gentlemen:—You had better hire me to fill the vacant editorship of the Californian. What you want is a good Moral tone to the paper. If I have got a strong suit, that is it. If I am a wild enthusiast on any subject, that is the one. I am peculiarly fitted for such a position. I have been a missionary to the Sandwich Islands, and I have got the hang of all that sort of thing to a fraction. I gave such excellent satisfaction in Hawaii nei that they let me off when my time was up. I was justly considered to be the high chief of that Serious Family down there. I mention here—and I mention it modestly—I mention it with that fatal modesty which has always kept me down—that the missionaries always spoke of me as the Moral Phenomenon when I was down there. They were amazed to behold to what a dizzy altitude human morality may be hoisted up, as exemplified in me. I am honestly proud of the title they have conferred upon me, and shall always wear it in remembrance of my brief but gratifying missionary labors in the Islands.

What you want is Morality. You have run too much poetry; you have slathered—so to speak–(missionary term,)—you have slathered too many frivolous sentimental tales into your paper; too much wicked wit and too much demoralizing humor; too much harmful elevating literature. What the people are suffering for, is Morality. Turn them over to me. Give me room according to my strength. I can fetch them!

Let me hear from you. You could not do better than hire me. I can bring your paper right up. You ought to know, yourself, that when I play my hand in the high moral line, I take a trick every time.

Yours,
"Mark Twain"
Surnamed THE MORAL PHENOMENON

IN THE HOUSE OF
THE SPIRITS

> *What would you think of a ghost that came to your bedside at dead of night and had kittens?*

MARK TWAIN AMONG THE SPIRITS
[*Golden Era*, Feb. 4, 1866]

There was an audience of about 400 ladies and gentlemen present, and plenty of newspaper people—neuters. I saw a good-looking, earnest-faced, pale-red-haired, neatly dressed, young woman standing on a little stage behind a small deal table with slender legs and no draw-ers—the table, understand me; I am writing in a hurry, but I do not desire to confound my description of the table with my description of the lady. The lady was Mrs. Foye.

As I was coming up town with the *Examiner* reporter, in the early part of the evening, he said he had seen a gambler named Gus Gra-ham shot down in a town in Illinois years ago, by a mob, and as prob-ably he was the only person in San Francisco who knew of the circumstance, he thought he would "give the spirits Graham to chaw on awhile." (N.B. This young creature is a Democrat, and speaks with the native strength and inelegance of his tribe.) In the course of the show he wrote his old pal's name on a slip of paper and folded it up tightly and put [it] in a hat which was passed around, and which already had about five hundred similar documents in it. The pile was dumped on the table and the medium began to take them up one by one and lay them aside, asking: "Is this spirit present?—or this?—or this?" About one in fifty would rap, and the person who sent up the name would rise in his place and question the defunct. At last a spirit seized the medium's hand and wrote "Gus Graham" backwards. Then the medium went skirmishing through the papers for the corresponding name. And that old sport knew his card by the back! When the medium came to it, after picking up fifty others, he rapped! A committee-man unfolded the paper and it was the right one. I sent for it and got it. It was all right. However, I suppose "all them Democrats" are on sociable terms with the devil. The young man got up and asked:

"Did you die in '51? —'52? —'53? —'54? —"

Ghost—"Rap, rap, rap."

"Did you die of cholera?—diarrhea?—dysentery?—dog-bite?—small-pox?—violent death? —"

"Rap, rap, rap."

"Were you hanged?—drowned?—stabbed?—shot? —"

"Rap, rap, rap."

"Did you die in Mississippi?—Kentucky?—New York?—Sandwich Islands?—Texas?—Illinois? —"

"Rap, rap, rap."

"In Adams county?—Madison?—Randolph? —"

"Rap, rap, rap."

It was no use trying to catch the departed gambler. He knew his hand and played it like a Major.

I was surprised. I had a very dear friend, who, I had heard, had gone to the spirit land, or perdition, or some of those places, and I desired to know something concerning him. There were something concerning him. There was something so awful, though, about talking with living, sinful lips to the ghostly dead, that I could hardly bring myself to rise and speak. But at last I got tremblingly up and said with low and reverent voice:

"Is the spirit of John Smith present?"

"Whack! whack! whack! whack!"

God bless me. I believe all the dead and damned John Smiths between hell and San Francisco tackled that poor little table at once! I was considerably set back—stunned, I may say. The audience urged me to go on, however, and I said:

"What did you die of?"

The Smiths answered to every disease and casualty that man can die of.

"Where did you die!"

They answered yes to every locality I could name while my geography held out.

"Are you happy where you are?"

There was a vigorous and unanimous "No!" from the late Smiths.

"Is it warm there?"

An educated Smith seized the medium's hand and wrote:

"It's no name for it."

"Did you leave any Smiths in that place when you came away?"

"Dead loads of them."

I fancied, I heard the shadowy Smiths chuckle at this feeble joke—the rare joke that there could be live loads of Smiths were all are dead.

"How many Smiths are present?"

"Eighteen millions—the procession now reaches from here to the other side of China."

"Then there are many Smiths in the kingdom of the lost?"

"The Prince Apollyon calls all newcomers Smith on general principles; and continues to do so until he is corrected, if he chances to be mistaken."

"What do lost spirits call their dread abode?"

"They call it the Smithsonian Institute."

I got hold of the right Smith at last—the particular Smith I was after—my dear, lost, lamented friend—and learned that he died a violent death. I feared as much. He said his wife talked him to death. Poor wretch!

But without any nonsense, Mrs. Foye's seance was a very astonishing affair to me—and a very entertaining one. The *Examiner* man's "old pard," the gambler, was too many for me. He answered every question exactly right; and his disembodied spirit, invisible to mortal eyes, must have been prowling around that hall last night. That is, unless this pretended spiritualism is only that other black art called clairvoyance, after all. And yet, the clairvoyant can only tell what is in your mind—but once or twice last night the spirits brought facts to the minds of their questioners which the latter had forgotten before. Well, I cannot make anything out of it. I asked the *Examiner* man what he thought of it, and he said, in the Democratic dialect: "Well, I don't know—I don't know—but it's d—d funny." He did not mean that it was laughable—he only meant that it was perplexing. But such is the language of Democracy.

———•———

MARK TWAIN ON THE NEW WILD CAT RELIGION
[*Golden Era*, March 4, 1866]

Another spiritual investigator—G. C. De-Merrit—passed his examination to-day, after a faithful attendance on the *seances* of the Friends of Progress, and was shipped, a raving maniac, to the insane asylum at Stockton—an institution which is getting to be quite a College of Progress.

People grow exasperated over these frequently occurring announcements of madness occasioned by fighting the tiger of spiritualism, and I think it is not fair. They abuse the spiritualists unsparingly, but I can remember when Methodist camp meetings and Campbellite revivals used to stock the asylums with religious lunatics, and yet the public kept their temper and said never a word. We don't cut up when madmen are bred by the old legitimate regular stock religions, but we can't allow wildcat religions to indulge in such disastrous experiments. I do not really own in the old regular stock, but I lean strongly toward it, and I naturally feel some little prejudice against all wildcat religions—still, I protest that it is not fair to excuse the one and abuse the other for the self-same rascality. I do not love the wildcat, but at the same time I do not like to see the wildcat imposed on merely because it is friendless. I know a great many spiritualists—good and worthy persons who sincerely and devotedly love their wildcat religion, (but not regarding it as wildcat themselves, though, of course,)—and I know them to be persons in every way worthy of respect. They are men of business habits and good sense.

Now when I see such men as these, quietly but boldly come forward and consent to be pointed at as supporters of a wildcat religion, I almost feel as if it were presumptuous in some of us to assert without qualification that spiritualism *is* wildcat. And when I see these same persons cherishing, and taking to their honest bosoms and fondling this wildcat, with genuine affection and confidence, I feel like saying, "Well, if this is a wildcat religion, it pans out wonderfully like the old regular, after all." No—it goes against the grain; but still, loyalty to my Presbyterian bringing-up compels me to stick to the Presbyterian decision that spiritualism is neither more nor less than wildcat.

I do not take any credit to my better-balanced head because I never went crazy on Presbyterianism. We go too slow for that. You never see us ranting and shouting and tearing up the ground. You never heard of a Presbyterian going crazy on religion. Notice us, and you will see how we do. We get up of a Sunday morning and put on the best harness we have got and trip cheerfully down town; we subside into solemnity and enter the church; we stand up and duck our heads and bear down on a hymn book propped on the pew in front when the minister prays; we stand up again while our hired choir are singing, and look in the hymn book and check off the verses to see that they don't shirk any of the stanzas; we sit silent and grave while the minister is preaching, and count the waterfalls and bonnets furtively, and catch flies; we grab our hats and bonnets when the benediction is begun; when it is finished, we shove, so to speak. No frenzy—no fanaticism—no skirmishing; everything perfectly serene. You never see any of us Presbyterians getting in a sweat about religion and trying to massacre the neighbors. Let us all be content with the tried and safe old regular religions, and take no chances on wildcat.

---

from **MORE SPIRITUAL INVESTIGATIONS**
[*Golden Era*, March 11, 1866]

I shall have this matter of spiritualism "down to a spot," yet, if I do not go crazy in the meantime. I stumbled upon a private fireside seance a night or two ago, where two old gentlemen and a middle-aged gentleman and his wife were communicating (as they firmly believed) with the ghosts of the departed. They have met for this purpose every week for years. They do not "investigate"—they have long since become strong believers, and further investigations are not needed by them. I knew some of these parties well enough to know that whatever deviltry was exhibited would be honest, at least, and that if there were any humbugging done they themselves would be as badly humbugged as any spectator. We kept the investigations going for three hours, and it was rare fun. . . .

The first ghost that announced his presence spelled this on the dial: "My name is Thomas Tilson; I was a preacher. I have been dead many years. I know this man Mark Twain well!"

I involuntarily exclaimed: "The very devil you do?" That old dead parson took me by surprise when he spelled my name, and I felt the cold chills creep over me. Then the ghost and I continued the conversation:

"Did you know me on earth?"

"No. But I read what you write, every day, almost. I like your writings."

"Thank you. But how do you read it?—do they take the *Territorial Enterprise* in h— or rather, heaven, I beg your pardon?"

"No. I read it through my affinity."

"Who is your affinity?"

"Mac Crellish of the *Alta*!"

This excited some laughter, of course—and I will remark here that both ghosts and mediums indulge in jokes, conundrums, doggerel rhymes, and laughter—when the ghost says a good thing he wags the minute hand gaily to and fro to signify laughter.

"Did Mac Crellish ever know you?"

"No. He didn't know me, and doesn't suspect that he is my affinity—but he is, nevertheless. I impress him and influence him every day. If he starts to do what I think he ought not to do, I change his mind."

This ghost then proceeded to go into certain revelations in this connection which need not be printed.

William Thompson's ghost came up. Said he knew me; loved me like a brother; never knew me on earth, though. Said he had been a school teacher in Mott street, New York; was an assistant teacher when he was only fifteen years old, and appeared to take a good deal of pride in the fact. Said he was with me constantly.

"Well," I said, "you get into some mighty bad company sometimes, Bill, if you travel with me." He said it couldn't hurt him.

One of the irrepressible Smiths took the stand, now. He told his name, and said, "I am here!"

"Staunch and true!" said I.

"Colors blue! and liberty forever!" quoth the poetical Smith.

The medium said, "Mr. Smith, Mr. Twain here has been abusing the Smith family—can't you give him a brush?"

And Smith spelled out, "If I only had a brush!" and wagged the minute hand in a furious burst of laughter. Smith thought that was a gorgeous joke. And it might be so regarded in perdition, where Smith lives, but will not excite much admiration here.

Then Smith asked, "Why don't you have some whiskey here?" He was informed that the decanter had just been emptied, Mr. Smith said: "I'll go and fetch some." In about a minute he came back and said: "Don't get impatient—just sit where you are and wait till you see me coming with that whiskey!" and then shook a boisterous laugh on the dial and cleared out. And I supose this old Smarty from h—is going around in the other world yet, bragging about this cheap joke.

A Mr. Wentworth, a very intelligent person for a dead man, came and spelled out a "lecture" of two foolscap pages, on the subject of "Space," but I haven't got space to print it here. It was very beautifully written; the style was smooth, and flowing, the language was well chosen, and the metaphors and similes were apt and very poetical. The only fault I could find about the late Mr. Wentworth's lecture on "Space" was, that there was nothing in it about space. The essayist seemed to be only trying to reconcile people to the loss of friends, by showing that the lost friends were unquestionably in luck in being lost, and therefore should not be grieved for—and the essayist did the thing gracefully and well but devil a word did he say about "Space."

Very well; the *Bulletin* may abuse spiritualism as much as it pleases, but whenever I can get a chance to take a dead and damned Smith by the hand and pass a joke or swap a lie with him, I am going to do it. I am not afraid of such pleasant corpses as these ever running me crazy. I find them better company than a good many live people.

MARK TWAIN A COMMITTEE MAN
[*Golden Era*, Feb. 11, 1866]

[I attended the *seance* last night.] After the house was crowded with ladies and gentlemen, Mrs. Foye stepped out upon the stage and said it was usual to elect a committee of two gentlemen to sit up there and see that everything was conducted with perfect honesty and fairness. She said she wished the audience to name gentlemen whose integrity, whose conscientiousness—in a word whose high moral character, in every respect, was notorious in the community. The majority of the audience arose with one impulse and called my name. This handsome compliment was as grateful as it was graceful, and I felt the tears spring to my eyes. I trust I shall never do anything to forfeit the generous

confidence San Francisco has thus shown in me. This touching compliment is none the less grateful to me when I reflect that it took me
two days to get it up. I "put up" that hand myself. I got all my friends
to promise to go there and vote for me to be on that committee—and
having reported a good deal in Legislatures, I knew how to do it right.
I had a two-thirds vote secured—I wanted enough to elect me over
the medium's veto, you know. I was elected, and I was glad of it. I
thought I would feel a good deal better satisfied if I could have a
chance to examine into this mystery myself, without being obliged to
take somebody else's word for its fairness, and I did not go on that
stand to find fault or make fun of the affair—a thing which would not
speak well for my modesty when I reflect that so many men so much
older and wiser than I am see nothing in Spiritualism to scoff at, but
firmly believe in it as a religion.

Mr. Whiting was chosen as the other committeeman, and we sat
down at a little table on the stage with the medium, and proceeded to
business. We wrote the names of various departed persons. Mr. W.
wrote a good many, but I found that I did not know many dead people; however, I put in the names of two or three whom I had known
well, and then filled out the list with names of citizens of San Francisco
who had been distinguished in life, so that most persons in the audience could tell whether facts stated by such spirits concerning themselves were correct or not. I will remark here that not a solitary spirit
summoned by me paid the least attention to the invitation. I never got
a word out of any of them. One of Mr. Whiting's spirits came up and
stated some things about itself which were correct. Then some five
hundred closely folded slips of paper containing names, were dumped
in a pile on the table, and the lady began to lay them aside one by one.
Finally a rap was heard. I took the folded paper; the spirit, so-called,
seized the lady's hand and wrote "J. M. Cooke" backwards and upside
down on a sheet of paper. I opened the slip I held, and, as Captain Cut-
tle would say, "J. M. Cooke" was the "dientical" name in it. A gentleman in the audience said he sent up the name. He asked a question
or so, and then the spirit wrote "Would like to communicate with you
alone." The privacy of this ghost was respected, and he was permitted to go to thunder again unmolested. "William Nelson" reported
himself from the other world, and in answer to questions asked by a
former friend of his in the audience, said he was aged 24 when he
died; died by violence; died in a battle; was a soldier; had fought both

in the infantry and cavalry; fell at Chickamauga; had been a Catholic on earth—was not one now. Then in answer to a pelting volley of questions, the shadowy warrior wrote: "I don't want to answer any more about it." Exit Nelson.

About this time it was suggested that a couple of Germans be added to the committee, and it was done. Mr. Wallenstein, an elderly man, came forward, and also Mr. Ollendorf, a spry young fellow, cocked and primed for a sensation. They wrote some names. Then young Ollendorf said something which sounded like:

"Ist ein geist hierans?" (bursts of laughter from the audience).

Three raps—signifying that there was a geist hierans.

"Vollen sie schriehen?" (more laughter). Three raps.

"Finzig stollen, linsowftterowlickter-hairowfterfrowleineruback-folderol?" (Oh, this is too rough, you know. I can't keep the run of this sort of thing.) Incredible as it may seem, the spirit cheerfully answered yes to that astonishing proposition.

Young Ollendorf sprang to his feet in a state of consuming excitement. He exclaimed:

"Laties and shentlemen! I write de name for a man vot lifs! Speerit rabbing dells me he ties in yahr eighteen hoondert und dwelf, but he yoos as live und helty as —"

The Medium—"Sit down, sir!"

Mr. O.—"But de speerit cheat!—dere is no such speerit—" (All this time applause and laughter by turns from the audience.)

Medium—"Take your seat, sir, and I will explain this matter."

And she explained. And in that explanation she let off a blast which was so terrific that I half expected to see young Ollendorf shoot up through the roof. She said he had come up there with fraud and deceit and cheating in his heart, and a kindred spirit had come from the land of shadows to commune with him! She was terribly bitter. She said in substance, though not in words, that perdition was full of just such fellows as Ollendorf, and they were ready on the slightest pretext to rush in and assume anybody's name, and rap, and write, and lie, and swindle with a perfect looseness whenever they could rope in a living affinity like poor Ollendorf to communicate with! (Great applause and laughter.)

Ollendorf stood his ground with good pluck, and was going to open his batteries again, when a storm of cries arose all over the house. "Get down! Go on! Clear out! Speak on—we'll hear you! Climb down from that platform! Stay where you are—Vamose! Stick to your post—say your say!"

The medium rose up and said if Ollendorf remained, she would not. She recognized no one's right to come there and insult her by practicing a deception upon her and attempting to bring ridicule upon so solemn a thing as her religious belief.

The audience then became quiet, and the subjugated Ollendorf retired from the platform.

The other German raised a spirit, questioned it at some length in his own language, and said the answers were correct. The medium claims to be entirely unacquainted with the German language.

A spirit seized the medium's hand and wrote "G. L. Smith" very distinctly. She hunted through the mass of papers, and finally the spirit rapped. She handed me the folded paper she had just picked up. It had "T. J. Smith" in it. (You can never depend on these Smiths; you call for one and the whole tribe will come clattering out of hell to answer you.) Upon further inquiry it was discovered that both these Smiths were present. We chose "T. J." A gentleman in the audience said that was his Smith. So he questioned him, and Smith said he died by violence; he had been a teacher; not a school-teacher, but (after some hesitation) a teacher of religion, and was a sort of cross between a Universalist and a Unitarian; has got straightened out and changed his opinion since he left here; said he was perfectly happy. Mr. George Purnell, having been added to the committee, proceeded in connection with myself, Mrs. Foye and a number of persons in the audience, to question this talkative and frolicksome old parson. Among spirits, I judge he is the gayest of the gay. He said he had no tangible body; a bullet could pass through him and never make a hole; rain could pass through him as through vapor, and not discommode him in the least (wherefore I suppose he don't know enough to come in when it rains—or don't care enough); says heaven and hell are simply mental conditions—spirits in the former have happy and contented minds; and those in the latter are torn by remorse of conscience; says as far as he is concerned, he is all right—he is happy; would not say whether he was a very good or a very bad man on earth (the shrewd old water-proof nonentity!—I asked the question so that I might average my own chances for his luck in the other world, but he saw my drift); says he has an occupation there—puts in his time teaching and being taught; says there are spheres—grades of perfection—he is making pretty good progress—has been promoted a sphere or so since his matriculation; (I said mentally: "Go slow, old man, go slow—you have got all eternity before you"—and he replied not); he don't know how many spheres there are (but I suppose there must be millions, because if a man goes galloping through them at the rate this old Universalist is doing, he will get through an infinitude of them by the time he has been there as long as old Sesostris and those ancient mummies; and there is no estimating how high he will get in even the infancy of eternity—I am afraid the old man is scouring along rather too fast for the style of his surroundings, and the length of time he has got on his hands); says spirits cannot feel heat or cold (which militates somewhat against all my notions of orthodox damnation—fire and brimstone); says spirits commune with each other by thought—they have no language; says the distinctions of the sex are preserved there—and so forth and so on.

The old parson wrote and talked for an hour, and showed by his quick, shrewd, intelligent replies, that he had not been sitting up nights in the other world for nothing, he had been prying into everything worth knowing, and finding out everything he possibly could—as he said himself, when he did not understand a thing he hunted up a spirit who could explain it; consequently he is pretty thoroughly posted; and for his accommodating conduct and its uniform courtesy to me, I sincerely hope he will continue to progress at his present velocity until he lands on the very roof of the highest sphere of all, and thus achieves perfection.

I have made a report of those proceedings which every person present will say is correct in every particular. But I do not know any more about the queer mystery than I did before. I could not even tell where the knocks were made, though they were not two feet from me. Sometimes they seemed to be on the corner of the table, sometimes under the center of it, and sometimes they seemed to proceed from the medium's knee joints. I could not locate them at all, though; they only had a general seeming of being in any one spot; sometimes they even seemed to be in the air. As to where that remarkable intelligence emanates from which directs those strangely accurate replies, that is beyond my reason. I cannot any more account for that than I could explain those wonderful miracles performed by Hindoo jugglers. I cannot tell whether the power is supernatural in either case or not, and I never expect to know as long as I live. It is necessarily impossible to know—and it is mighty hard to fully believe what you don't know.

But I am going to see it through, now, if I do not go crazy— an eccentricity that seems singularly apt to follow investigations of spiritualism.

OBSERVATIONS, OPINIONS, & ADVICE

———◆———

> I am a suffering victim of my infernal disposition to be always trying to oblige somebody without being asked to do it.

———◆———

from **ANSWERS TO CORRESPONDENTS**
[*The Californian*, June 10, 1865]

ARITHMETICUS, *Virginia, Nevada.*—"If it would take a cannon-ball $3\frac{1}{3}$ seconds to travel four miles, and $3\frac{3}{8}$ seconds to travel the next four, and $3\frac{5}{8}$ seconds to travel the next four, and if its rate of progress continued to diminish in the same ratio, how long would it take to go fifteen hundred millions of miles?"

I don't know.

[*The Californian*, June 24, 1865]

ARITHMETICUS, *Virginia, Nevada.*—"I am an enthusiastic student of mathematics, and it is so vexatious to me to find my progress constantly impeded by these mysterious arithmetical technicalities. Now do tell me what the difference is between Geometry and Conchology?"

Here *you* come again, with your diabolical arithmetical conundrums, when I am suffering death with a cold in the head. If you could have seen the expression of ineffable scorn that darkened my countenance a moment ago and was instantly split from the centre in every direction like a fractured looking-glass by my last sneeze, you never would have written that disgraceful question. Conchology is a science which has nothing to do with mathematics; it relates only to shells. At the same time, however, a man who opens oysters for a hotel, or shells a fortified town, or sucks eggs, is not, strictly speaking, a conchologist—a fine stroke of sarcasm, that, but it will be lost on such an intellectual clam as you. Now compare conchology and geometry together, and you will see what the difference is, and your question will be answered. But don't torture me with any more of your ghastly arithmetical horrors (for I do detest figures anyhow,) until you know I am rid of my cold. I feel the bitterest animosity toward you at this moment—bothering me in this way, when I can do nothing but sneeze and quote poetry and snort pocket-handkerchiefs to atoms. If I had you in range of my nose, now, I would blow your brains out.

——◆——

from **HOW, FOR INSTANCE?**
[*Territorial Enterprise*, Aug. 1866]

Coming down from Sacramento on the *Capital* the other night, I found on a center table, a pamphlet advertisement of an Accident Insurance Company. It interested me a good deal with its General Accidents and its Hazardous tables, and Extra Hazardous furniture of the same description, and I would like to know something more about it. It is a new thing to me. I want to invest if I come to like it. I want to ask merely a few questions of the man who carries on this Accident shop, if you think you can spare so much space to a far-distant stranger. I am an Orphan.

He publishes this list as accidents he is willing to insure people against:

GENERAL ACCIDENTS

Include the Traveling Risk, and also all forms of Dislocations, Broken Bones, Ruptured Tendons, Sprains, Concussions, Crushings, Bruising, Cuts, Stabs, Gunshot Wounds, Poisoned Wounds, Burns and Scalds, Freezing, Bites, Unprovoked Assaults by Burglars, Robbers or Murderers, the action of Lightning or Sunstroke, the Effects of Explosions, Chemicals, Floods and Earthquakes, Suffocation by Drowning or Choking—where such accidental injury totally disables the person insured from following his usual avocation or causes death within three months from the time of the happening of the injury.

I want to address this party as follows:

Now, Smith—I suppose likely your name is Smith—you don't

184

know me and I don't know you, but I am willing to be friendly. I am acquainted with a good many of your family — I know John as well as I know any man — and I think we can come to an understanding about your little game without any hard feelings. For instance:

Do you allow the same money on a dog-bite that you do on an earthquake?

Do you take special risks for special accidents? — that is to say, could I, by getting a policy for dog-bites alone, get it cheaper than if I took a chance in your whole lottery? And if so, and supposing I got insured against earthquakes, would you charge any more for San Francisco earthquakes than for those that prevail in places that are better anchored down?

And if I had a policy on earthquakes alone, I couldn't collect on a dog-bite, may be, could I?

If a man had such a policy and an earthquake shook him up and loosened his joints a good deal, but not enough to incapacitate him from engaging in pursuits which did not require him to be tight, wouldn't you pay him some of his pension?

. . . Why do you discriminate between Provoked and Unprovoked Assaults by Burglars? If a burglar entered my house at dead of night, and I, in the excitement natural to such an occasion, should forget myself and say something that provoked him, and he should cripple me, wouldn't I get anything?

But if I provoked him by pure accident, I would have you there I judge? — because you would have to pay for the Accident part of it anyhow, seeing that insuring against accident is just your strong suit, you know. . . .

You say you have "issued over sixty thousand policies, forty-five of which have proved fatal and been paid for." Now, do you know, Smith, that that looks just a little shaky to me, in a measure? You appear to have it pretty much all your own way, you see. It is all very well for the lucky forty-five that have died "and been paid for," but how about the other fifty-nine thousand nine hundred and fifty-five? You have got their money, haven't you? but somehow the lightning don't seem to strike and they don't get any chance at you. Won't their families get fatigued waiting for their dividends? Don't your customers drop off rather slow, so to speak?

You will ruin yourself publishing such damaging statements as that, Smith. I tell you as a friend. If you had said that the fifty-nine thousand nine hundred and fifty-five died and that forty-five lived, you would have issued about four tons of policies the next week. But people are not going to get insured, when you take so much pains to prove that there is such precious little use in it. Good-bye, Smith.

Yours,
Mark Twain

ORIGIN OF ILLUSTRIOUS MEN
[*The Californian*, Sept. 29, 1866]

You have done fair enough about Franklin and Shakespeare, and several parties not so well known — parties some of us never heard of, in fact — but you have shirked the fellows named below. Why this mean partiality?

JOHN SMITH was the son of his father. He formerly resided in New York and other places, but he has moved to San Francisco, now.

WM. SMITH was the son of his mother. This party's grandmother is deceased. She was a brick.

JOHN BROWN was the son of old Brown. The body of the latter lies mould'ring in the grave.

EDWARD BROWN was the son of old Brown by a particular friend.

HENRY JONES was a son of a sea-cook.

WM. JONES was a son of a gun.

JOHN JONES was a Son of Temperance.

In early life GABRIEL JONES was actually a shoemaker. He is a shoemaker yet.

Previous to the age of 85, CALEB JONES had never given any evidence of extraordinary ability. He has never given any since.

PATRICK MURPHY is said to have been of Irish extraction.

JAMES PETERSON was the son of a common weaver, who was so miraculously poor that his friends were encouraged to believe that in case the Scriptures were strictly carried out he would "inherit the earth." He never got his property.

JOHN DAVIS' father was a soap-boiler, and not a very good soap-boiler at that. John never arrived at maturity — died in childbirth, he and his mother.

JOHN JOHNSON was a blacksmith. He died. It was published in the papers, with a head over it, "DEATHS." It was therefore thought he died to gain notoriety. He has got an aunt living somewhere.

Up to the age of 34, HOSEA WILKERSON never had any home but Home, Sweet Home, and even when he had that he had to sing it himself. At one time it was believed that he would have been famous if he had become celebrated. He died. He was greatly esteemed for his many virtues. There was not a dry eye in the crowd when they planted him.

<hr />

FROM A COMPLAINT ABOUT CORRESPONDENTS
[*The Californian*, March 24, 1866]

What do you take us for, on this side of the continent? I am addressing myself personally, and with asperity, to every man, woman and child east of the Rocky Mountains. How do you suppose our minds are constituted, that you will write us such execrable letters—such poor, bald, uninteresting trash? You complain that, by the time a man has been on the Pacific Coast six months, he seems to lose all concern about matters and things and people in the distant East, and ceases to answer the letters of his friends and even his relatives. It is your own fault. You need a lecture on the subject—a lecture which ought to read about as follows:

There is only one brief, solitary law for letter-writing, and yet you either do not know that law, or else you are so stupid that you never think of it. It is very easy and simple: Write only about things and people your correspondent takes a living interest in.

Cannot you remember that law, hereafter, and abide by it? If you are an old friend of the person you are writing to, you know a number of his acquaintances, and you can rest satisfied that even the most trivial things you can write about them will be read with avidity out here on the edge of sunset.

Yet how *do* you write?—how do the most of you write? Why, you drivel and drivel, and drivel along, in your wooden-headed way, about people one never heard of before, and things which one knows nothing at all about and cares less. There is no sense in that. Let me show up your style with a specimen or so. Here is a paragraph from my Aunt Nancy's last letter—received four years ago, and not answered immediately—not at all, I may say.

St. Louis, 1862.

"Dear Mark: We spent the evening very pleasantly at home, yesterday. The Rev. Mr. Macklin and wife, from Peoria, were here. He is an humble laborer in the vineyard and takes his coffee strong. He is also subject to neuralgia — neuralgia in the head — and is so unassuming and prayerful. There are few such men. We had soup for dinner likewise. Although I am not fond of it. Oh, Mark, why *don't* you try to lead a better life? Read II. Kings, from chap. 2 to chap. 24 inclusive. It would be so gratifying to me if you would experience a change of heart. Poor Mrs. Gabrick is dead. You did not know her. She had fits, poor soul. On the 14th the entire army took up the line of march from————"

I always stopped there, because I knew what was coming — the war news, in minute and dry detail — for I could never drive it into those numsculls that the overland telegraph enabled me to know here in San Francisco every day all that transpired in the United States the day before, and that the pony express brought me exhaustive details of all matters pertaining to the war, at least two weeks before their letters could possibly reach me. So I naturally skipped their stale war reports, even at the cost of also skipping the inevitable suggestions to read this, that, and the other batch of chapters in the Scriptures, with which they were interlarded at intervals like snares wherewith to trap the unwary sinner. . . .

My venerable mother is a tolerably good correspondent — she is above the average, at any rate. She puts on her spectacles and takes her scissors and wades into a pile of newspapers and slashes out column after column — editorials, hotel arrivals, poetry, telegraph news, advertisements, novellettes, old jokes, recipes for making pies, cures for "biles" — anything that comes handy; it don't matter to her; she is entirely impartial; she slashes out a column, and runs her eye down it over her spectacles (she looks over them because she can't see through them, but she prefers them to her more serviceable ones because they have got gold rims to them) — runs her eye down the column and says, "Well, it's from a St. Louis paper, anyway," and jams it into the envelope along with her letter. She writes about everybody I ever knew or ever heard of, but unhappily she forgets that when she tells me that "J. B. is dead; and that W. L. is going to marry T. D."; and that "B. K. and R. M. and L. P. J. have all gone to New Orleans to live," it is more than likely that years of absence may have so dulled my recollection of once familiar names that their unexplained initials will be as unintelligible as Hebrew unto me. She never writes a name in full, and so I never know who she is talking about. Therefore I have to guess—and this was how it came that I mourned the death of Bill Kribben when I should have rejoiced over the dissolution of Ben Kenfuron. I failed to cipher the initials out correctly.

The most useful and interesting letters we get here from home are from children seven or eight years old. This is the petrified truth. Happily they have got nothing to talk about but home, and neighbors, and family—things their betters think unworthy of transmission thousands of miles. They write simply and naturally, and without straining for effect. They tell all they know, and then stop. They seldom deal in abstractions or moral homilies. Consequently their epistles are brief; but, treating as they do of familiar scenes and persons, always entertaining. Now therefore, if you would learn the art of letter-writing, let a little child teach you. I have preserved a letter from a small girl eight years of age—preserved it as a curiosity, because it was the only letter I ever got from the States that had any information in it. It runs thus:

St. Louis, 1865.

"Uncle Mark, if you was here I could tell you about Moses in the Bulrushers again. I know it better, now. Mr. Sowerby has got his leg broke off a horse. He was riding it on Sunday. Margaret, that's the maid, Margaret has took all the spittoons, and slop-buckets, and old jugs out of your room, because she says she don't think you're ever coming back any more, you been gone so long. Sissy McElroy's mother has got another little baby. She has them all the time. It has got little blue eyes, like Mr. Swimley that boards there, and looks just like him. I have got a new doll, but Johnny Anderson pulled one of its legs out. Miss Doosenberry was here to day; I give her your picture, but she said she didn't want it. My cat has got more kittens, O, you can't think—twice as many as Lottie Belden's. And there's one such a sweet little buff one with a short tail, and I named it for you. All of them's got names, now—General Grant, and Halleck, and Moses, and Margaret, and Deuteronomy, and Captain Semmes, and Exodus, and Leviticus, and Horace Greeley—all named but one, and I am saving it because the one that I named for You's been sick all the time since, and I reckon it'll die. (It appears to have been mighty rough on the short-tailed kitten, naming it for me—I wonder how the reserved victim will stand it.) Uncle Mark, I do believe Hattie Caldwell likes you, and I know she thinks you are pretty, because I heard her say nothing couldn't hurt your good looks—nothing at all—she said even if you was to have the small-pox ever so bad you would be just as good-looking as you was before. And my ma says she's ever so smart. [Very.] So no more this time, because General Grant and Moses is fighting.

Annie"

This child treads on my toes, in every other sentence, with a perfect looseness, but in the simplicity of her time of life she doesn't know it.

I consider that a model letter—an eminently readable and entertaining letter—and, as I said before, it contains more matter of interest and more real information than any letter I ever received from the East. I had rather hear about the cats at home and their truly remarkable names, than listen to a lot of stuff about people I am not acquainted with, or read "The Evil Effects of the Intoxicating Bowl," illustrated on the back with a picture of a ragged scalliwag pelting away right and left, in the midst of his family circle, with a junk bottle.

TRAVELS IN CALIFORNIA

> Those rotten, lop-eared, whopper-jawed, jack-legged ... Californians ... How I _hate_ everything that looks, or tastes, or smells like California!
>
> I fell in love with the most cordial and sociable city in the union.... San Francisco was Paradise to me.

OVER THE MOUNTAINS.
[*Territorial Enterprise*, Sept. 13, 1863]

The trip from Virginia to Carson [City] by Messrs. Carpenter & Hoog's stage is a pleasant one, and from thence over the mountains by the Pioneer would be another, if there were less of it. But you naturally want an outside seat in the day time, and you feel a good deal like riding inside when the cold night winds begin to blow; yet if you commence your journey on the outside, you will find that you will be allowed to enjoy the desire I speak of unmolested from twilight to sunrise. An outside seat is preferable, though, day or night. All you want to do is prepare for it thoroughly. You should sleep forty-eight hours in succession before starting so that you may not have to do anything of that kind on the box. You should also take a heavy overcoat with you. I did neither. I left Carson feeling very miserable for want of sleep, and the voyage from there to Sacramento did not refresh me perceptibly. I took no overcoat, and I almost shivered the shirt off myself during that long night ride from Strawberry Valley to Folsom. Our driver was a very companionable man, though, and this was a happy circumstance for me, because, being drowsy and worn out, I would have gone to sleep and fallen overboard if he had not enlivened the dreary hours with his conversation. Whenever I stopped coughing, and went to nodding, he always watched me out of the corner of his eye until I got to pitching in his direction, and then he would stir me up and inquire if I were asleep. If I said "No," (and I was apt to do that,) he always said "it was a bully good thing for me that I warn't, you know," and then went on to relate cheerful anecdotes of people who had got to nodding by his side when he wasn't noticing, and had fallen off and broken their necks. He said he could see those fellows before him now, all jammed and bloody and quivering in death's agony—"G'lang! d—n that horse, he knows there's a parson and an old maid inside, and that's what makes him cut up so; I've saw him act jes' so more'n a thousand times!" The driver always lent an additional charm to his conversation by mixing his horrors and his general information together in this way. "Now," said he, after urging his team at a furious speed down the grade for a while, plunging into deep bends in the road brimming with a thick darkness almost palpable to the touch, and darting out again and again on the verge of what instinct told me was a precipice, "Now, I seen a poor cuss—but you're asleep again, you know, and you've rammed your head agin' my side-pocket and busted a bottle of nasty rotten medicine that I'm taking to the folks at the Thirty-five Mile House; do you notice that flavor? ain't it a ghastly old stench? The man that takes it down there don't live on anything else—it's vittles and drink to him; anybody that ain't used to him can't go a-near him; he'd stun 'em—he'd suffocate 'em; his breath smells like a graveyard after an earthquake—you Bob! I allow to skelp that ornery horse, yet, if he keeps on this way; you see he's been on the overland till about two weeks ago, and every stump he sees he cal'lates it's an Injun." I was awake by this time, holding on with both hands and bouncing up and down just as I do when I ride a horseback. The driver took up the thread of his discourse and proceeded to soothe me again: "As I was saying, I see a poor cuss tumble off along here one night—he was monstrous drowsy, and went to sleep when I'd took my eye off of him for a moment—and he fetched up agin a boulder, and in a second there wasn't anything left of him but a promiscus pile of hash! It was moonlight, and when I got down and looked at him he was quivering like jelly, and sorter moaning to himself, like, and the bones of his legs was sticking out through his pantaloons every which way, like that." (Here the driver mixed his fingers up after the manner of a stack of muskets, and illuminated them with the ghostly light of his cigar.) "He warn't in misery long though. In a minute and a half he was deader'n a smelt—Bob! I say I'll cut that horse's throat if he stays on this route another week." In this way the genial driver caused the long hours to pass sleeplessly away, and if he drew upon his imagination for his fearful histories, I shall be the last to blame him for it, because if they had taken a milder form I might have yielded to the dullness that oppressed me, and got my own bones smashed out of my hide in such a way as to render me useless forever after—unless, perhaps, some one chose to turn me to account as an uncommon sort of hat-rack.

from ROUGHING IT

We rumbled over the plains and valleys, climbed the Sierras to the clouds, and looked down upon summer-clad California. And I will remark here, in passing, that all scenery in California requires *distance* to give it its highest charm. The mountains are imposing in their sublimity and their majesty of form and altitude, from any point of view—but one must have distance to soften their ruggedness and enrich their tintings; a Californian forest is best at a little distance, for there is a sad poverty of variety in species, the trees being chiefly of one monotonous family—redwood, pine, spruce, fir—and so, at a near view there is a wearisome sameness of attitude in their rigid arms, stretched downward and outward in one continued and reiterated appeal to all men to "Sh!—don't say a word!—you might disturb somebody!" Close at hand, too, there is a reliefless and relentless smell of pitch and turpentine; there is a ceaseless melancholy in their sighing and complaining foliage; one walks over a soundless carpet of beaten yellow bark and dead spines of the foliage till he feels like a wandering spirit bereft of a footfall; he tires of the endless tufts of needles and yearns for substantial, shapely leaves; he looks for moss and grass to loll upon, and finds none, for where there is no bark there is naked clay and dirt, enemies to pensive musing and clean apparel. Often a grassy plain in California, is what it should be, but often, too, it is best contemplated at a distance, because although its grass blades are tall, they stand up vindictively straight and self-sufficient, and are unsociably wide apart, with uncomely spots of barren sand between.

One of the queerest things I know of, is to hear tourists from "the States" go into ecstasies over the loveliness of "ever-blooming California." And they always do go into that sort of ecstasies. But perhaps they would modify them if they knew how old Californians, with the memory full upon them of the dust-covered and questionable summer greens of Californian "verdure," stand astonished, and filled with worshiping admiration, in the presence of the lavish richness, the brilliant green, the infinite freshness, the spendthrift variety of form and species and foliage that make an Eastern landscape a vision of Paradise itself. The idea of a man falling into raptures over grave and sombre California, when that man has seen New England's meadow-expanses and her maples, oaks and cathedral-windowed elms decked in summer attire, or the opaline splendors of autumn descending upon her forests, comes very near being funny—would be, in fact, but that it is so pathetic. No land with an unvarying climate can be very beautiful. The tropics are not, for all the sentiment that is wasted on them. They seem beautiful at first, but sameness impairs the charm by and by. *Change* is the handmaiden Nature requires to do her miracles with. The land that has four well-defined seasons, cannot lack beauty, or pall with monotony. Each season brings a world of enjoyment and interest in the watching of its unfolding, its gradual, harmonious development, its culminating graces—and just as one begins to tire of it, it passes away and a radical change comes, with new witcheries and new glories in its train. And I think that to one in sympathy with nature, each season, in its turn, seems the loveliest.

FROM AN UNBIASED CRITICISM
[*The Californian*, March 18, 1865]

I had a very comfortable time in Calaveras county, in spite of the rain, and if I had my way I would go back there, and argue the sewing machine question around Coon's bar-room stove again with the boys on rainy evenings. Calaveras possesses some of the grandest natural features that have ever fallen under the contemplation of the human mind—such as the Big Trees, the famous Morgan gold mine which is the richest in the world at the present time, perhaps, and "straight" whisky that will throw a man a double somerset and limber him up like boiled maccaroni before he can set his glass down. Marvelous and incomprehensible is the straight whisky of Angels' Camp!

Carson City, Oct. 25, 1861

I have already laid a timber claim on the borders of a Lake (Bigler) [Tahoe] which throws Como in the shade. . . . I had better stop about "the Lake," though—for whenever I think of it I want to go there and *die*, the place is so beautiful. I'll build a country seat there one of these days that will make the Devil's mouth water if he ever visits the earth. . . .

FROM THE CALIFORNIAN
[*Morning Call*, Sept. 4, 1864]

Mr. Webb will now go and rest a while on the shores of Lake Tahoe. He has chosen to rest himself by fishing, and he is wise; for the fish in Lake Tahoe are not troublesome; they will let a man rest there till he rots, and never inflict upon him the fatigue of putting on a fresh bait.

FROM THE AUTOBIOGRAPHY OF MARK TWAIN

Yreka . . . acquired its curious name—when in its first days it much needed a name—through an accident. There was a bakeshop with a canvas sign which had not yet been put up but had been painted and stretched to dry in such a way that the word BAKERY, all but the B, showed through and was reversed. A stranger read it wrong end first, YREKA, and supposed that that was the name of the camp. The campers were satisfied with it and adopted it.

FROM ROUGHING IT

I have elsewhere spoken of the endless winter of Mono, California, and but this moment of the eternal spring of San Francisco. Now if we travel a hundred miles in a straight line, we come to the eternal summer of Sacramento. One never sees summer clothing or mosquitoes in San Francisco—but they can be found in Sacramento. Not always and unvaryingly, but about one hundred and forty-three months out of twelve years, perhaps. Flowers bloom there, always, the reader can easily believe—people suffer and sweat, and swear, morning, noon and night, and wear out their stanchest energies fanning themselves. It gets hot there, but if you go down to Fort Yuma you will find it hotter. Fort Yuma is probably the hottest place on earth. The thermometer stays at one hundred and twenty in the shade there all the time — except when it varies and goes higher. It is a U. S. military post, and its occupants get so used to the terrific heat that they suffer without it. There is a tradition (attributed to John Phenix*) that a very, very wicked soldier died there, once, and of course, went straight to the hottest corner of perdition,—and the next day he *telegraphed back for his blankets*. There is no doubt about the truth of this statement— there can be no doubt about it. I have seen the place where that soldier used to board. In Sacramento it is fiery summer always, and you can gather roses, and eat strawberries and ice-cream, and wear white linen clothes, and pant and perspire, at eight or nine o'clock in the morning, and then take the cars, and at noon put on your furs and your skates, and go skimming over frozen Donner Lake, seven thousand feet above the valley, among snow banks fifteen feet deep, and in the shadow of grand mountain peaks that lift their frosty crags ten thousand feet above the level of the sea. There is a transition for you! Where will you find another like it in the Western hemisphere? And some of us have swept around snow-walled curves of the Pacific Railroad in that vicinity, six thousand feet above the sea, and looked down as the birds do, upon the deathless summer of the Sacramento Valley, with its fruitful fields, its feathery foliage, its silver streams, all slumbering in the mellow haze of its enchanted atmosphere, and all infinitely softened and spiritualized by distance—a dreamy, exquisite glimpse of fairyland, made all the more charming and striking that it was caught through a forbidden gateway of ice and snow, and savage crags and precipices.

---

*It has been purloined by fifty different scribblers who were too poor to invent a fancy but not ashamed to steal one. —M. T.

from **A LETTER FROM SACRAMENTO**
[*Territorial Enterprise*, Feb. 25, 1866]

I arrived in the City of Saloons this morning at 3 o'clock, in company with several other disreputable characters, on board the good steamer *Antelope,* Captain Poole, commander. I know I am departing from usage in calling Sacramento the City of Saloons instead of the City of the Plains, but I have my justification — I have not found any plains, here, yet, but I have been in most of the saloons, and there are a good many of them. You can shut your eyes and march into the first door you come to and call for a drink, and the chances are that you will get it. And in a good many instances, after you have assuaged your thirst, you can lay down a twenty and remark that you "copper the ace," and you will find that facilities for coppering the ace are right there in the back room. In addition to the saloons, there are quite a number of mercantile houses and private dwellings. They have already got one capitol here, and will have another when they get it done. They will have fine dedicatory ceremonies when they get it done, but you will have time to prepare for that — you needn't rush down here right away by express. You can come as slow freight and arrive in time to get a good seat.

THE "HIGH GRADE" IMPROVEMENT

The houses in the principal thoroughfares here are set down about eight feet below the street level. This system has its advantages. First — It is unique. Secondly — It secures to the citizen a firm, dry street in high water, whereon to run his errands and do her shopping, and thus does away with the expensive and perilous canoe. Thirdly — It makes the first floor shady, very shady, and this is a great thing in a warm climate. Fourthly — It enables the inquiring stranger to rest his elbows on the second story window sill and look in and criticize the bedroom arrangements of the citizens. Fifthly — It benefits the plebeian second floor boarders at the expense of the bloated aristocracy of the first — that is to say, it brings the plebeians down to the first floor and degrades the aristocrats to the cellar. Lastly — Some persons call it a priceless blessing because children who fall out of second story windows now, cannot break their necks as they formerly did — but that this can strictly be regarded in the light of a blessing, is, of course, open to grave argument.

But joking aside, the energy and the enterprise the Sacramentans have shown in making this expensive grade improvement and raising their houses up to its level is in every way creditable to them, and is a sufficient refutation of the slander so often leveled at them that they are discouraged by the floods, lack confidence in their ability to make their town a success, and are without energy. A lazy and hopeless population would hardly enter upon such costly experiments as these when there is so much high ground in the State which they could fly to if they chose.

BRIEF CLIMATE PARAGRAPH

This is the mildest, balmiest, pleasantest climate one can imagine. The evenings are especially delightful—neither too warm nor too cold. I wonder if it is always so?

THE LULLABY OF THE RAIN

I got more sleep this morning than I needed. When I got tired, very tired, walking around, and went to bed in room No. 121, Orleans Hotel, about sunrise, I asked the clerk to have me called at a quarter past 9 o'clock. The request was complied with, punctually. As I was about to roll out of bed I heard it raining. I said to myself, I cannot knock around town in this kind of weather, and so I may as well lie here and enjoy the rain. I am like everybody else in that I love to lie abed and listen to the soothing sound of pattering rain-drops, and muse upon old times and old scenes of by-gone days. While I was a happy, careless schoolboy again, (in imagination,) I dropped off to sleep. After a while I woke up. Still raining. I said to myself, it will stop directly— I will dream again—there is time enough. Just as (in memory) I was caught by my mother clandestinely putting up some quince preserves in a rag to take to my little sweetheart at school, I dropped off to sleep again, to the soft music of the pattering rain. I woke up again, after a while. Still raining! I said. This will never do. I shall be so late that I shall get nothing done. I could dream no more; I was getting too impatient for that. I lay there and fidgeted for an hour and a half, listening with nervous anxiety to detect the least evidence of a disposition to "let up" on the part of the rain. But it was of no use. It rained on steadily, just the same. So, finally, I said: I can't stand this; I will go to the window and see if the clouds are breaking, at any rate. I looked up, and the sun was blazing overhead. I looked down—and then I "gritted my teeth" and said: "Oh, d—n a d——d landlord that would keep a d——d fountain in his back yard!"

After mature and unimpassioned deliberation, I am still of the opinion that that profanity was justifiable under the circumstances.

I Try to Out "Sass" the Landlord — and Fail

I got down stairs at ten minutes past 12, and went up to the landlord, who is a large, fine-looking man, with a chest on him which must have made him a most powerful man before it slid down, and said, "Is breakfast ready?"

"Is breakfast *ready*?" said he.

"Yes — is breakfast READY?"

"Not quite," he says, with the utmost urbanity, "not quite; you have arisen too early, my son, by a matter of eighteen hours as near as I can come at it."

Humph! I said to myself, these people go slow up here; it is a wonder to me that they ever get up at all.

"Ah well," said I, "it don't matter — it don't matter. But, ah — perhaps you design to have lunch this week, some time?"

"Yes," he says, "I have designed all along to have lunch this week, and by a most happy coincidence you have arrived on the very day. Walk into the dining room."

As I walked forward I cast a glance of chagrin over my shoulder and observed, "Old Smarty from Mud Springs, I apprehend."

And he murmured, "Young Lunar Caustic from San Francisco, no doubt."

Well, let it pass. If I didn't make anything off that old man in the way of "sass," I cleaned out his lunch table, anyhow. I calculated to get ahead of him some way. And yet I don't know but the old scallawag came out pretty fair, after all. Because I only staid in his hotel twenty-four hours and ate one meal, and he charged me five dollars for it. If I were not just ready to start back to the bay, now, I believe I would go and tackle him once more. If I only had a fair chance, that old man is not any smarter than I am. (I will risk something that it makes him squirm every time I call him "that old man," in this letter. People who voted for General Washington don't like to be reminded that they are old.) But I like the old man, and I like his hotel too, barring the d——barring the fountain I should say.

from MARK TWAIN ON BOOT-BLACKS
[*Golden Era*, March 11, 1866]

The boot-blacking facilities of Sacramento are unsurpassed by those of any city in the world I should judge. There is a boot-blacking stand in front of every saloon—which is to say, there are boot-blacking stands all along. All these prominent localities which, in other cities, are usually sacred to the peanut interest, are here seized upon and held by the boot-black. These mute facts tell the stranger that Sacramento, which is now so irreproachably cleanly, has long and fearful attacks of alternate mud and dust. In further evidence of this, I remarked that out of the one hundred and eight-four gentlemen who lounged about the front of the Orleans Hotel when I came down and asked for breakfast at ten minutes past 12 o'clock today and didn't get any, a hundred and seventy had their boots blacked. The other fourteen were undergoing the boot-blacking operation in chairs backed up against the neighboring walls. Now there was not a particle of dust in the air, and no mud under foot; and nothing but inveterate habit could have made these people all go and get their boots blacked with such singular unanimity when there was no real necessity for it. I never saw a place before where everybody, without exception, had their boot blacked. Every time I noticed, today, that my boots were attracting attention, I went and got them blacked....

from MARK TWAIN'S INTERIOR NOTES
[*San Francisco Bulletin*, Nov. 30, 1866]

This is the most generally well built town in California—nothing in it, hardly, but fine, substantial brick houses. I found there many a man who had made his fortune in Washoe, and didn't have the shrewdness to hold on to it, and so had wandered back to his old Marysville home. It is a pity to see such a town as this go down, but the citizens say the railroads are sapping its trade and killing it. They are a sociable, cheerful-spirited community, and if the town should die, they would hardly die with it.

FROM MARK TWAIN'S INTERIOR NOTES
[*San Francisco Bulletin*, Nov. 30, 1866]

[Grass Valley] reminded me somewhat of Virginia in her palmy days. There are a great many old time Washoe miners there, and some are doing remarkably well. There are ten dividend-paying mines in the camp (some of them very heavy concerns in this respect,) and a dozen more that are in a fair way to come under the same head. The bullion shipments are large and gradually increasing. Grass Valley is an old quartz mining camp—one of the oldest in the State—and it has always been the wise policy of her thoughtful business men to preserve the prosperity of the place from the injurious effects of exaggerated newspaper reports and mining excitements, and the plan has worked well as a general thing. Still, business promises to be overdone there, notwithstanding. The place can very comfortably support its present population, but additions are being made to it every day, and there is a disposition to open two stores and two shops where one would suffice for the present. Miners, also, go there from various parts of this State and Nevada, to apply for work, and they are not likely to get it, because none but men like those Cornishmen, who are used to working in extremely hard rock, are of much account there.

FROM A LETTER TO HIS MOTHER AND SISTER

Been down to San José (generally pronounced Sannozay—emphasis on last syllable)—today—50 miles from here, by Railroad. Town of 6,000 inhabitants, buried in flowers & shrubbery.

INEXPLICABLE NEWS FROM SAN JOSÉ
[*Morning Call*, Aug. 23, 1864]

We have before us a letter from an intelligent correspondent, dated "Sarrozay, (San José?) Last Sunday;" we had previously ordered this correspondent to drop us a line, in case anything unusual should happen in San José during the period of his sojourn there. Now that we have got his chatty letter, however, we prefer, for reasons of our own, to make extracts from it, instead of publishing it in full. Considering the expense we were at in sending a special correspondent so far, we are sorry to be obliged to entertain such a preference. The very first paragraph in this blurred and scrawling letter pictured our friend's condition, and filled us with humiliation. It was abhorrent to us to think that we, who had so well earned and so proudly borne the appellation of "M. T., The Moral Phenomenon," should live to have such a letter addressed to us. It begins thus:

"MR. MARK TWAIN — Sir: Sarrozay's beauriful place. Flowers — or maybe it's me — smells delishs — like sp-sp-sp(ic!)irits turpentine. Hiccups again. Don' mind them — had 'em three days."

As we remarked before, it is very humiliating. So is the next paragraph:

"Full of newspaper men — re porters. One from Alta, one from Flag, one from Bulletin, two from MORRING CALL, one from Sacramento Union, one from Carson Independent. And all drunk — all drunk but me. By Georshe! I'm 'stonished."

The next paragraph is still worse:

"Been out to Leland of the Occidental, and Livingston in the Warrum Springs, and Steve, with four buggies and a horse, which is a sp-splennid place — splennid place."

Here follow compliments to Nolan, Conductor of the morning train, for his kindness in allowing the writer to ride on the engine, where he could have "room to enjoy himself strong, you know," and to the Engineer for his generosity in stopping at nearly every station to give people a "chance to come on board, you understand." Then his wandering thoughts turn again affectionately to "Sarrozay" and its wonders:

"Sarrozay's lovely place. Shade trees all down both sides street, and in the middle and elsewhere, and gardens — second street back of Connental Hotel. With a new church in a tall scaffolding — I watched her an hour, but can't understand it. I don' see how they got her in — I don' see how they goin' to get her out. Corralled for good, praps. Hic! Them hiccups again. Comes from s-sociating with drunken beasts."

Our special next indulges in some maudlin felicity over the prospect of riding back to the city in the night on the back of the fire-breathing locomotive, and this suggests to his mind a song which he remembers to have heard somewhere. That is all he remembers about it, though, for the finer details of its language appear to have caved into a sort of general chaos among his recollections.

> "The bawr stood on the burring dock,
> Whence all but him had f-flowed — f-floored — f-fled —
> The f'flumes that lit the rattle's back
> Sh-shone round him o'er the shed —"

"I dono what's the marrer withat song. It don't appear to have any sense in it, somehow — but she used to be abou the fines' f-fusion —"

Soothing slumber overtook the worn and weary pilgrim at this point, doubtless, and the world may never know what beautiful thought it met upon the threshold and drove back within the portals of his brain, to perish in forgetfulness. After this effort, we trust the public will bear with us if we allow our special correspondent to rest from his exhausting labors for a season — a long season — say a year or two.

---

from ROUGHING IT

We held a council and decided to make the best of our misfortune and enjoy a week's holiday on the borders of the curious Lake. Mono, it is sometimes called, and sometimes the "Dead Sea of California." It is one of the strangest freaks of Nature to be found in any land, but it is hardly ever mentioned in print and very seldom visited, because it lies away off the usual routes of travel and besides is so difficult to get at that only men content to endure the roughest life will consent to take upon themselves the discomforts of such a trip. On the morning of our second day, we traveled around to a remote and particularly wild spot on the borders of the Lake, where a stream of fresh, ice-cold water entered it from the mountain side, and then we went regularly into camp. We hired a large boat and two shot-guns from a lonely ranchman who lived some ten miles further on, and made ready for comfort and recreation. We so on got thoroughly acquainted with the Lake and all it peculiarities.

Mono Lake lies in a lifeless, treeless, hideous desert, eight thousand feet above the level of the sea, and is guarded by mountains two thousand feet higher, whose summits are always clothed in clouds.

This solemn, silent, sailless sea—this lonely tenant of the loneliest spot on earth—is little graced with the picturesque. It is an unpretending expanse of grayish water, about a hundred miles in circumference, with two islands in its centre, mere upheavals of rent and scorched and blistered lava, snowed over with gray banks and drifts of pumice stone and ashes, the winding sheet of the dead volcano, whose vast crater the lake has seized upon and occupied.

The lake is two hundred feet deep, and its sluggish waters are so strong with alkali that if you only dip the most hopelessly soiled garment into them once or twice, and wring it out, it will be found as clean as if it had been through the ablest of washer-women's hands. While we camped there our laundry work was easy. We tied the week's washing astern of our boat, and sailed a quarter of a mile, and the job was complete, all to the wringing out. If we threw the water on our heads and gave them a rub or so, the white lather would pile up three inches high. This water is not good for bruised places and abrasions of the skin. We had a valuable dog. He had raw places on him. He had more raw places on him than sound ones. He was the rawest dog I almost ever saw. He jumped overboard one day to get away from the flies. But it was bad judgment. In his condition, it would have been just as comfortable to jump into the fire. The alkali water nipped him in all the raw places simultaneously, and he struck out for the shore with considerable interest. He yelped and barked and howled as he went—and by the time he got to the shore there was no bark to him—for he had barked the bark all out of his inside, and the alkali water had cleaned the bark all off his outside, and he probably wished he had never embarked in any such enterprise. He ran round and round in a circle, and pawed the earth and clawed the air, and threw double summersets, sometimes backwards and sometimes forwards, in the most extraordinary manner. He was not a demonstrative dog, as a general thing, but rather of a grave and serious turn of mind, and I never saw him take so much interest in anything before. He finally struck out over the mountains, at a gait which we estimated at about two hundred and fifty miles an hour, and he is going yet. That was about nine years ago. We look for what is left of him along here every day.

A white man cannot drink the water of Mono Lake, for it is nearly pure lye. It is said that the Indians in the vicinity drink it sometimes, though. It is not improbable, for they are among the purest liars I ever saw. (There will be no additional charge for this joke, except to parties requiring an explanation of it. This joke has received high commendation from some of the ablest minds of the age.)

There are no fish in Mono Lake — no frogs, no snakes, no polliwogs — nothing, in fact, that goes to make life desirable. Millions of wild ducks and sea-gulls swim about the surface, but no living thing exists *under* the surface, except a white feathery sort of worm, one half an inch long, which looks like a bit of white thread frayed out at the sides. If you dip up a gallon of water, you will get about fifteen thousand of these. They give to the water a sort of grayish-white appearance. Then there is a fly, which looks something like our house fly. These settle on the beach to eat the worms that wash ashore — and any time, you can see there a belt of flies an inch deep and six feet wide, and this belt extends clear around the lake — a belt of flies one hundred miles long. If you throw a stone among them, they swarm up so thick that they look dense, like a cloud. You can hold them under water as long as you please — they do not mind it — they are only proud of it. When you let them go, they pop up to the surface as dry as a patent office report, and walk off as unconcernedly as if they had been educated especially with a view to affording instructive entertainment to man in that particular way. Providence leaves nothing to go by chance. All things have their uses and their part and proper place in Nature's economy: the ducks eat the flies — the flies eat the worms — the Indians eat all three — the wild cats eat the Indians — the white folks eat the wild cats — and thus all things are lovely.

Mono Lake is a hundred miles in a straight line from the ocean — and between it and the ocean are one or two ranges of mountains — yet thousands of sea-gulls go there every season to lay their eggs and rear their young. One would as soon expect to find sea-gulls in Kansas. And in this connection let us observe another instance of Nature's wisdom. The islands in the lake being merely huge masses of lava, coated over with ashes and pumice stone, and utterly innocent of vegetation or anything that would burn; and sea-gulls' eggs being entirely useless to anybody unless they be cooked, Nature has provided an unfailing spring of boiling water on the largest island, and you can put your eggs in there, and in four minutes you can boil them as hard as any statement I have made during the past fifteen years. Within ten feet of the boiling spring is a spring of pure cold water, sweet and wholesome. So, in that island you get your board and washing free of charge — and if nature had gone further and furnished a nice American hotel clerk who was crusty and disobliging, and didn't know anything about the time tables, or the railroad routes—or—anything—and was proud of it—I would not wish for a more desirable boarding house.

Half a dozen little mountain brooks flow into Mono Lake, but *not a stream of any kind flows out of it.* It neither rises nor falls, apparently, and what it does with its surplus water is a dark and bloody mystery.

There are only two seasons in the region round about Mono Lake—and these are, the breaking up of one winter and the beginning of the next. More than once (in Esmeralda) I have seen a perfectly blistering morning open up with the thermometer at ninety degrees at eight o'clock, and seen the snow fall fourteen inches deep and that same identical thermometer go down to forty-four degrees under shelter, before nine o'clock at night. Under favorable circumstances it snows at least once in every single month in the year, in the little town of Mono. So uncertain is the climate in summer that a lady who goes out visiting cannot hope to be prepared for all emergencies unless she takes her fan under one arm and her snow shoes under the other. When they have a Fourth of July procession it generally snows on them, and they do say that as a general thing when a man calls for a brandy toddy there, the bar-keeper chops it off with a hatchet and wraps it up in a paper, like maple sugar. And it is further reported that the old soakers haven't any teeth—wore them out eating gin cocktails and brandy punches. I do not endorse that statement—I simply give it for what it is worth—and it is worth—well, I should say, millions, to any man who can believe it without straining himself. But I do endorse the snow on the Fourth of July—because I know that to be true.

Our wanderings were wide and in many directions; and now I could give the reader a vivid description of the Big Trees and the marvels of the Yo Semite—but what has this reader done to me that I should persecute him? I will deliver him into the hands of less conscientious tourists and take his blessing. Let me be charitable, though I fail in all virtues else.

SELECTED BIBLIOGRAPHY

Benson, Ivan. *Mark Twain's Western Years.* Stanford University Press, 1938.

Clemens, Samuel L. *The Autobiography of Mark Twain.* Charles Neider, ed. Harper & Row, 1959.

Clemens, Samuel L. *Clemens of the "Call," Mark Twain in San Francisco.* Edgar M.Branch, ed. University of California Press, 1969.

Clemens, Samuel L. *Early Tales & Sketches,* Vols. I & II. Edgar M. Branch and Robert H. Hirst, with Harriet Elinor Smith, eds. University of California Press, 1980, 1981.

Clemens, Samuel L. *Mark Twain of the Enterprise: Newspaper Articles & Other Documents 1862–1864.* Henry Nash Smith and Frederick Anderson, eds. University of California Press, 1957.

Clemens, Samuel L. *Mark Twain Speaking.* Paul Fatout, ed. Indiana University Press, 1960.

Clemens, Samuel L. *Mark Twain's Letter to the California Pioneers.* DeWitt and Snelling, 1911.

Clemens, Samuel L. *Mark Twain's Letters, Vol. I: 1853–1866.* Edgar Marquess Branch, Michael B. Frank, and Kenneth M. Sanderson, eds. University of California Press, 1988.

Clemens, Samuel L. *Mark Twain's Notebooks & Journals, Vol. I (1855–1873).* Frederick Anderson, Michael B. Frank, and Kenneth Sanderson, eds. University of California Press, 1975.

Clemens, Samuel L. *Mark Twain's San Francisco.* Bernard Taper, ed. McGraw-Hill, 1963.

Clemens, Samuel L. *Roughing It.* Franklin R. Rogers and Paul Baender, eds. University of California Press, 1972.

Clemens, Samuel L. *Sketches New and Old.* Harper & Brothers, 1907.

Clemens, Samuel L. *Sketches of the Sixties by Bret Harte and Mark Twain.* John Howell, ed. John Howell, 1926.

Clemens, Samuel L. *The Washoe Giant in San Francisco: Heretofore Uncollected Sketches by Mark Twain.* Franklin Walker, ed. George Fields, 1938.

Kaplan, Justin. *Mark Twain and His World.* Simon & Schuster, 1974.

Kaplan, Justin. *Mr. Clemens and Mark Twain.* Simon & Schuster, 1966.

Lennon, Nigey. *Mark Twain in California.* Chronicle Books, 1982.

Paine, Albert Bigelow. *Mark Twain, A Biography.* 4 vols. Harper & Brothers, 1912.

Sanborn, Margaret. *Mark Twain: The Bachelor Years.* Doubleday, 1990.

Stegner, Wallace, ed. *Selected American Prose, 1841–1900: The Realistic Movement.* Holt, Rinehart and Winston, 1958.

A NOTE ON THE TEXT

Note on excerpts, spelling, and grammar: This edition reproduces the original texts, including misspellings and grammatical errors, as written by Mark Twain, except that the excerpts from *The Autobiography of Mark Twain* may have been edited by Charles Neider. Brackets have been used in this edition to indicate explanatory material added by the publisher. Ellipses indicate that a passage has been omitted from the text. The orignal title of an article, essay, or book appears in bold type at the beginning of each piece; the piece is complete unless the word "from" appears before the title, in which case the piece has been excerpted. *Roughing It* was originally published in 1872.

Note on newspapers: The place and date of original publication of articles appear in brackets below the title. The full names of newspapers frequently cited as sources are: San Francisco *Golden Era,* San Francisco *Dramatic Chronicle,* San Francisco *Examiner,* San Francisco *Evening Bulletin,* San Francisco *Morning Call,* and Virginia City (Nevada) *Territorial Enterprise.*